Praise for the Cedar Cove novels by #1 *New York Times* bestselling author

DEBBIE MACOMBER

"Readers new to Macomber's considerable narrative charms will have no problem picking up the story, while loyal fans are in for a treat."
—*Booklist* on *6 Rainier Drive*

"Those who enjoy good-spirited, gossipy writing will be hooked."
—*Publishers Weekly* on *6 Rainier Drive*

"Debbie Macomber is a skilled storyteller."
—*Publishers Weekly* on *50 Harbor Street*

"The books in Macomber's contemporary Cedar Cove series are irresistibly delicious and addictive."
—*Publishers Weekly* on *44 Cranberry Point*

"Readers will return to Macomber's Cedar Cove with the ease of fitting back in at the family reunion."
—*BookPage* on *44 Cranberry Point*

"Excellent characterization will keep readers anticipating the next visit to Cedar Cove."
—*Booklist* on *311 Pelican Court*

"As always, Debbie Macomber has scored a perfect '10.'"
—*RT Book Reviews* on *311 Pelican Court*

"Macomber's endearing characters offer courage and support to one another and find hope and love in the most unexpected places."
—*Booklist* on *204 Rosewood Lane*

"Macomber is known for her honest portrayals of ordinary women in small-town America, and this tale cements her position as an icon of the genre."
—*Publishers Weekly* on *16 Lighthouse Road*

Dear Friends,

It's time for another visit to Cedar Cove. (And if this is your first visit, let me reassure you that it won't take long to catch up.) Come and spend a few hours with Grace, Olivia and their families, plus Rachel (and Nate and Bruce) and Bobby and Teri Polgar and…a cast of hundreds. Well, maybe not hundreds, although it sometimes feels that way.

I created Cedar Cove because of the popularity of my earlier series, particularly MIDNIGHT SONS and HEART OF TEXAS. Every day I received reader mail that asked what happened to such and such a character. It occurred to me that I should write an ongoing series, one without a predetermined end. Each book would be an update on the characters, with multiple plotlines. The fact that you've stuck with me into the seventh book validates what all those early reader letters told me. You wanted to go back, or in this case forward.

In addition to the Cedar Cove books, there's the Blossom Street series and my annual Christmas romantic comedy. As well, I occasionally do other kinds of projects (like *The Wyoming Kid*, my Harlequin American Romance novel, which was reissued in *Wyoming Brides*). And I "refresh" some of my older books when they're released again.

Because Cedar Cove is based on the very real town of Port Orchard, Washington, some of you have come to visit us here. Welcome! A number of the businesses and streets are loosely based on those in Port Orchard, and I've put together a Cedar Cove map. You can either download it from my Web site at www.DebbieMacomber.com or stop by our Chamber of Commerce for a free copy. If you aren't online just send me a SASE at P.O. Box 1458, Port Orchard, WA 98366 and I'll be happy to mail you one.

By the way, I also love to hear from readers. You can reach me via my Web site or at the address mentioned above.

I hope you enjoy *74 Seaside Avenue*. Look carefully at the house on the cover. It's the very one in which my husband, Wayne, and I have lived for the past twelve years.

Debbie Macomber

DEBBIE MACOMBER

74 SEASIDE AVENUE

ISBN-13: 978-0-7783-2969-5

74 SEASIDE AVENUE

For questions and comments about the quality of this book please contact us at CustomerService@Harlequin.com.

www.Harlequin.com

Printed in U.S.A.

To
Susan Plunkett, Krysteen Seelen,
Linda Nichols
and
Lois Dyer
All gifted authors
All treasured friends

Some of the Residents of Cedar Cove, Washington

Olivia Lockhart Griffin: Family court judge in Cedar Cove. Mother of **Justine** and **James.** Married to **Jack Griffin,** editor of the *Cedar Cove Chronicle.* They live at 16 Lighthouse Road.

Charlotte Jefferson Rhodes: Mother of **Olivia** and of **Will Jefferson.** Now married to widower **Ben Rhodes,** who has sons **David** and **Steven,** neither of whom lives in Cedar Cove.

Justine (Lockhart) Gunderson: Daughter of Olivia. Mother of **Leif.** Married to **Seth Gunderson.** The Gundersons owned The Lighthouse restaurant, recently destroyed by fire. They live at 6 Rainier Drive.

James Lockhart: Olivia's son and Justine's younger brother. In the Navy. Lives in San Diego with his wife, Selina, daughter, Isabella, and son, Adam.

Stanley Lockhart: Olivia's ex-husband; father of James and Justine. Lives in Seattle.

Will Jefferson: Olivia's brother, Charlotte's son. Formerly of Atlanta. Now divorced, retired and moving back to Cedar Cove.

Grace Sherman Harding: Olivia's best friend. Librarian. Widow of **Dan Sherman.** Mother of **Maryellen Bowman** and **Kelly Jordan.** Married to **Cliff Harding,** a retired engineer who is now a horse breeder living in Olalla, near Cedar Cove. Grace's previous address: 204 Rosewood Lane (now a rental property).

Cal Washburn: Horse trainer, employed by **Cliff Harding.**

Vicki Newman: Local veterinarian, romantically involved with Cal.

Maryellen Bowman: Oldest daughter of Grace and Dan Sherman. Mother of **Katie and Drake.** Married to **Jon Bowman,** photographer.

Joseph and Ellen Bowman: father and stepmother of Jon, grandparents of Katie and Drake. They live in Oregon.

Zachary Cox: Accountant, married to **Rosie.** Father of **Allison** and **Eddie Cox.** The family lives at 311 Pelican Court. **Allison** is attending university in Seattle, while her boyfriend, **Anson Butler,** has joined the military.

Cecilia Randall: Navy wife. Married to **Ian Randall.** Parents of **Aaron.** Lived in Cedar Cove until recently. Now transferred to San Diego.

Rachel Pendergast: Works at the Get Nailed salon. Friends with widower **Bruce Peyton** and his daughter, **Jolene.** Romantically involved with sailor **Nate Olsen.**

Bob and Peggy Beldon: Retired. Own the Thyme and Tide B & B at 44 Cranberry Point.

Roy McAfee: Private investigator, retired from Seattle police force. Two adult children, **Mack** and **Linnette.** Married to **Corrie,** who works as his office manager. The McAfees live at 50 Harbor Street.

Linnette McAfee: Daughter of Roy and Corrie. Lived in Cedar Cove and worked as a physician assistant in the new medical clinic. Leaving for North Dakota. Her brother, **Mack,** a fireman in training, is moving to Cedar Cove.

Gloria Ashton: Sheriff's deputy in Cedar Cove. Biological daughter of Roy and Corrie McAfee.

Troy Davis: Cedar Cove sheriff. Married to **Sandy.** Father of **Megan.**

Faith Beckwith: Troy Davis's high school girlfriend, now a widow.

Bobby Polgar and Teri Miller Polgar: He is an international chess champion; she's a hair stylist at Get Nailed. Their home is at 74 Seaside Avenue.

Pastor Dave Flemming: Local Methodist minister.

One

Late Thursday afternoon, Teri Polgar went to the grocery store. Roaming the air-conditioned aisles, she decided to make her specialty—a macaroni-and-cheese casserole—for dinner that night. Some might consider it more of a winter meal, not really suitable for the middle of July, but Teri liked it any time of year. And Bobby—well, Bobby was hardly aware of *what* season it was, or for that matter, what time of day.

When she got home, she found her husband in front of a chessboard, deep in concentration. That in itself wasn't unusual. But the board was set up on the kitchen table *and* her younger brother was sitting across from him. Two out-of-the-ordinary occurrences.

Johnny grinned sheepishly when she walked in with her bag of groceries. "I came by for a quick visit and Bobby insisted on teaching me," he explained.

Bobby mumbled something, probably an acknowledgment of her presence. He often muttered to himself, lost in his own world of chess moves and strategies. To say her husband was a bit unconventional would be an understatement. Bobby Polgar was an international chess sensation, one of the top-ranked players in the world.

"How's it going?" Teri asked as she set the groceries on the counter.

Johnny answered with a good-natured shrug. "Haven't got a clue. Ask Bobby."

"Hi, sweetheart," she said, moving to her husband's side of the table. Slipping her arms around his neck, she kissed his cheek.

Bobby's hand squeezed hers and he looked across at Johnny. "Always protect your queen," he advised her brother, who nodded patiently.

"Can you stay for dinner?" she asked Johnny. A visit from him, especially on a weekday, was a pleasant surprise. Teri was proud of Johnny, but she also felt protective of him. That was only natural, she supposed, because she'd practically raised him herself. Her family—like Bobby, was unconventional—but in a completely different way. At last count, her mother had been married six times. Or was it seven? Teri had lost count.

Her sister was more like her mother than Teri had ever been, but at least Christie was smart enough not to marry the losers who walked in and out of her life. Not that Teri was exempt from some of life's painful lessons herself. Particularly those that fell into the category of men-who-use-and-abuse.

Teri still had a hard time believing Bobby Polgar could love her. She worked in a hair and nail salon and considered herself the farthest thing from an intellectual. Bobby always said she had a real-world intelligence, practical and intuitive rather than cerebral, like his. She loved him for saying that and was even starting to believe it. In fact, she loved everything about him. The happiness she felt was still new to her and it actually frightened her a little.

She had reasons to be concerned, real-world reasons, she thought wryly, although she made light of them. Recently two men had approached her, bodyguard-types who looked like they belonged in an episode of *The Sopranos.* They had gangster written all over them. They hadn't really done anything, though, other than scare her for a few minutes.

Teri wasn't sure what that was all about. Apparently these goons had been sent as a warning to Bobby. The message seemed to be that their boss, whoever he was, could get to her at any time. Fat chance of that! Teri was street-smart and she'd learned how to take care of herself, although she had to admit those two had given her pause.

If Bobby knew who was responsible for the threat against her, he wasn't saying. But she'd noticed that her husband hadn't played in a single tournament since she'd been approached by those men.

"I gotta get back," Johnny said in answer to her question about dinner.

"Just stay for another couple of hours," she wheedled. "I'm making my special macaroni-and-cheese casserole." That would entice her brother like nothing else. It was his favorite dish.

"Checkmate," Bobby said triumphantly, apparently unaware of the conversation around him.

"Is there a way out of this?" Johnny asked, returning his attention to the chessboard.

Bobby shook his head. "Nope. You're in the Black Hole."

"The what?" Teri and Johnny said simultaneously.

"The Black Hole," Bobby told them. "Once a player finds him or herself in this set of circumstances, it's impossible to win."

Johnny shrugged. "Then there's nothing left to do but concede." He laid down his king and sighed. "Really, there was never any doubt as to the outcome of this game."

"You play well for a beginner," Bobby told him.

Teri ruffled her younger brother's hair, despite knowing how much he hated it. "Consider that a compliment."

Johnny smiled. "I will." He pushed back his chair and looked at Teri. "Ter, don't you think it's time you introduced Bobby to Mom and Christie?"

Bobby turned from Johnny to Teri and innocently said, "I *would* like to meet your family."

"No, you wouldn't." She immediately busied herself unpacking the groceries. She set the cottage cheese—an essential ingredient in her macaroni recipe—on the counter, along with a box of Velveeta cheese.

"Mom asked me about you and Bobby," her brother informed her.

"Is she still with Donald?" This was the latest husband. Teri had purposely avoided any discussion of her family with Bobby. They hadn't been married long and she hated to disillusion him so soon. Once he met the family, he might well have serious doubts about *her,* and the truth was, she wouldn't blame him.

"Things are shaky." Johnny glanced over at Bobby. "Donald has sort of a drinking problem."

"Donald!" Teri cried. "What about Mom?"

"She's cutting back." Johnny had always been quick to defend their mother.

Donald had showed promise in the beginning. Apparently he and her mother had met at an Alcoholics Anonymous meeting. Unfortunately, they'd quickly gone from supporting each other in sobriety to becoming drinking buddies. Neither of them could hold a job for long. How they survived financially, Teri didn't know. She had no intention of assisting them the way she did Johnny. It went without saying that any money she gave them would immediately go toward another bottle of booze or another night at their local bar.

Crossing her arms, Teri leaned against the kitchen counter. "Mom's cutting back? Yeah, right."

"Even so, you should have Christie over to meet Bobby." He turned toward him. "Christie's our sister."

"Why didn't you tell me you have a sister?" Bobby asked. He seemed perplexed that Teri had never mentioned Christie. He knew about her, of course, because he'd had Teri's background checked—a fact he'd revealed in his usual dispassionate way.

She had her reasons for not mentioning her younger sister and Johnny knew it. She pointed an accusatory finger at him. "Don't talk to me about Christie, okay?"

"What is it with you and her?" Johnny grumbled.

"You're too young to understand all the details," she said, brushing aside his question. She and Christie were, for all intents and purposes, estranged, although Teri maintained a superficial civility on public occasions.

"Come on, Ter, you and Bobby are *married.* He should meet the family."

"I don't think so."

"You don't want me to meet your family?" Bobby gazed up at her with a hurt expression. He didn't realize that this conversation had nothing to do with him and everything to do with her mother and sister.

"Yes, I do…someday." She gently patted Bobby's arm. "I thought we'd get settled in the house before I invited them."

"We are settled." Bobby gestured around him at the gleaming appliances and polished oak floors.

"Not *that* settled. We'll have them over in a while." She was thinking four or five years—longer if she could get away with it.

"Mom and Christie would really like to meet Bobby," Johnny said again.

Now Teri understood why her younger brother had shown up at the house unannounced. He'd been sent as an emissary by their mother and Christie. His mission was to pave the way for an introduction to the rich and famous Bobby Polgar, who'd been foolish enough to marry *her.*

"They'll have to meet him sooner or later," Johnny said with perfect logic. "You can't avoid it forever, you know."

"I know." Teri released a slow sigh.

"Might as well be now."

Teri could see that she wasn't going to escape the dreaded family gathering, so she'd simply take Johnny's advice. "Okay, okay, I'll have everyone over for dinner."

"Great." Johnny gave her a wide grin.

"I'll regret it afterward," she muttered under her breath.

"Why?" Bobby asked, obviously still perplexed by her reaction.

She hardly knew how to explain.

"Are your mother and sister like you?"

"No way!" Teri had done everything possible to make

choices that didn't resemble theirs—with only partial success. While it was true that she never drank to excess, she'd made more than one mistake in the relationship department. Until she met Bobby…

"I'll like them, won't I?" Bobby asked next, smiling at her with childlike faith.

She responded with a noncommital shrug. Her mother and sister were similar to each other in their behavior and their loser attitudes, although Teri didn't think Christie had a drinking problem so much as a man problem. Put a man in front of her, any man, and she couldn't resist.

"Is Christie still with…" For the life of her, she couldn't remember the last man her sister had been living with.

"Charlie," Johnny supplied.

"I thought it was Toby."

"He's the one before Charlie," her brother said. "And no, Charlie dumped her last month."

Oh, great. That meant her sister was on the prowl. This scenario couldn't get much worse.

"Christie will make a play for Bobby," she said.

Johnny shook his head firmly. "No, she won't. You two are married."

"Why would that stop her? It hasn't before. Trust me, she'll make a play—"

"Christie likes chess?" Bobby interrupted excitedly.

Clearly he didn't grasp the exchange going on between Teri and her brother. "No, Bobby. But my sister will think you're the most brilliant, handsomest man in the world."

Bobby grinned. "Like you do."

Despite her agitation, Teri nodded. "Only more so," she said grimly.

"You're jealous," Johnny accused her.

"Not Teri," Bobby said, getting up from the table. "She knows I love her."

Teri wrapped her arms around Bobby and hugged him close. "Thank you," she whispered.

"For what?"

"For loving me."

"That's easy," Bobby assured her.

"Listen, you two lovebirds, I wish I could stay but I've got to get back. I have a research paper that's due tomorrow." With Teri's encouragement, Johnny was taking a summer course to get a head start on the next school year. He pushed back his chair and stood. "So you'll get in touch with Mom?"

"I suppose." Teri sighed, already resigned to the inevitable.

"Christie, too," her brother insisted. "She *is* our sister."

"Mark my words. Bobby won't be safe with her around." *And neither will my marriage,* she thought darkly.

Teri hated to disparage their sister. But experience told her exactly what to expect. Sure as anything, Christie would throw herself at Bobby. The fact that he was married wouldn't matter. Not to Christie. Every boyfriend Teri'd ever had, her sister had attempted to seduce. Bobby wouldn't be the exception, and because he was her husband, Christie would probably consider him an especially worthwhile challenge.

Poor Bobby. He had no idea. He'd certainly never encountered a family like hers.

"Next weekend?" Johnny asked hopefully.

"No," Teri said. She needed time to prepare herself for

this. "Give me a week to get organized. Two weeks from Saturday."

If Johnny was disappointed by the delay, it didn't show. "See you then," he said and kissed her cheek on his way out the door.

Bobby slid his arm around her shoulders. Teri reminded herself yet again that she loved her husband and he loved her. Despite that, she couldn't entirely quell her fears.

While Bobby Polgar was unlike any man she'd ever known, he was still a man. He'd be just as susceptible to Christie's beauty and her undeniable charm as every other boyfriend she'd had.

"I'm happy to be meeting your family," Bobby said after Johnny had left.

Smiling proved difficult. Poor Bobby, she thought again. He didn't know what he was letting himself in for.

Two

Troy Davis had been the duly elected sheriff of Cedar Cove for nearly seventeen years. He'd been raised in this town, graduating from the local high school. Afterward, like many of his friends, he'd enlisted in the army, where he'd served as an MP. He'd trained at the Presidio in San Francisco, and just before shipping out to a base in Germany, he'd spent a three-day leave touring the city. That was where, on a foggy June morning in 1965, he'd met Sandy Wilcox.

After spending the day together, they'd exchanged addresses and corresponded during his tour of duty. When he was discharged, Troy had asked Sandy to marry him. By then she was in college and he'd joined her at SFU in San Francisco. In 1970, they were married and settled in his hometown of Cedar Cove, where Troy had accepted a job in law enforcement. He'd worked as a deputy until he ran for sheriff and won. Life had been good to him, to both of them. And then Sandy had gotten sick….

"Dad?"

Troy looked up from where he was seated in the living

room, staring down at the carpeted floor. "Pastor Flemming's here," Megan said quietly. She'd come over to help him organize Sandy's things—figure out what should go where.

Deep in thought, Troy hadn't even heard the doorbell. He stood as the other man walked into the room.

"I came to see how you're doing," the pastor from Cedar Cove Methodist church said. He was a soft-spoken, caring man who'd officiated at Sandy's funeral services with compassion and sincerity. Many an afternoon, Troy had found Dave Flemming sitting with his wife, reading from the Bible or praying with her or sometimes just chatting. He'd been touched by the sympathy the pastor had extended, first to Sandy and now to Megan and him.

Troy wasn't sure how to respond to the pastor's concern. "We're coping as well as we can," Troy said.

No death was easy and although Troy had felt he was prepared to lose Sandy, he wasn't. As sheriff, he'd certainly seen his share of death, and it wasn't something he'd ever get used to. But this one struck at the very foundations of his life. Nobody was ever truly ready to lose a wife or mother, he supposed, and Sandy's death had hit both him and Megan hard.

"If you need anything, just say the word."

"I will." Troy gestured toward the sofa. "Would you care to sit down?" he asked.

"I've made a fresh pot of coffee," his daughter added. "Will you have some?"

Troy was proud of what a good hostess Megan had become. Ever since Sandy's multiple sclerosis had become so much worse, his daughter often filled that role for him, something she'd continued to do after her marriage. Troy appreciated the way she'd willingly stepped in for her mother. She'd accompanied him to various functions in Sandy's place, and occasionally held dinners for family friends. They'd grown especially close since Sandy had gone into the nursing home two years before.

"Thank you, no," Dave told them. "I can't stay. But I'd like to help in any way I can. If it's too painful for you to sort through Sandy's things, for instance, I'd be happy to ask some of the ladies at church to lend a hand."

"No, no, we're fine," Troy assured him.

"Everything's under control," Megan said. She'd already begun packing up her mother's clothes and personal effects.

"I'll leave you two, then," Dave said and after shaking Troy's hand, the pastor let himself out.

"We're going to be all right, aren't we, Dad?" his daughter asked him in a tentative voice that reminded him of how she'd sounded as a child.

Draping his arm around her thin shoulders, Troy nodded. He usually managed to hide his pain. And for Megan's sake he even tried to smile. She had enough grief of her own to carry.

"Of course we're going to be fine." With his daughter at his side he walked into the bedroom he'd shared with his wife for more than thirty years. Boxes crammed with Sandy's clothes were scattered across the carpet. Half the closet was spread on the queen-size bed—dresses, sweaters, skirts and blouses, most of which had hung there for years without being touched.

Sandy had been in the nursing home for two years. He'd understood, when they settled her into the care facility, that she wouldn't be coming home again. Still, he'd had difficulty reconciling himself to the knowledge that MS would eventually take her life.

It didn't. Not exactly. As with most people suffering from this disease, her immune system was so compromised that she died of pneumonia. Although it could've been almost any virus or infection…

For her sake, Troy had made the pretense of believing she'd move home one day, but in reality he'd always known. He brought her whatever she asked for. As the months dragged on, Sandy stopped asking. She had everything she needed at the nursing home. Her large-print Bible, a few precious photographs and a lap robe Charlotte Jefferson had knit before she married Ben Rhodes. Sandy's needs were simple and her demands few. As the weeks and months passed, she needed less and less.

Troy had left everything in the house exactly the way it was the day he'd taken her to the nursing home. In the beginning that seemed important to Sandy. It was to him, too. It helped perpetuate the pretense that she'd recover. She'd needed to believe it, until she no longer could, and he'd wanted to hold on to the slightest shred of hope.

"I'm not sure what to do with all of Mom's clothes." Megan stood in the middle of the bedroom, her arms hanging limply at her sides. Sandy's half of the walk-in closet was bare.

"I had no idea Mom had so many clothes," Megan said helplessly. "Should we donate them to charity?"

Troy wished now that he'd asked Pastor Flemming about that. Perhaps the church had a program that collected items for the poor.

"We should." Still, if it was up to him, he wouldn't change a thing. Or at least not for a while… He didn't understand why Megan thought it was important to pack up the remnants of her mother's life so soon. When she'd arrived with the cardboard boxes, Troy hadn't argued, but frankly, he didn't see the necessity of rushing into this.

"Most of them are outdated now." Megan held up a pink sweater, one Sandy had always loved.

"Leave everything here for now," he suggested.

"No." The vehemence with which his daughter responded surprised Troy.

"Megan, let's not do something we might regret later."

"No," she said again, shaking her head. "Mom's gone. She'll never hold her grandchildren. She'll never go shopping with me again. She'll never share a recipe with me. She'll…she'll…" Tears rained down her pale cheeks.

Troy felt utterly incapable of easing her grief. He'd never been good at dealing with emotions and was at an even greater loss now. Megan was an only child and she'd been close to her mother. Both Sandy and Troy had wanted more children. For years, they'd tried for a second child, until after the third miscarriage, when Troy had said *enough.* They should be grateful they had a beautiful daughter, he'd told her, instead of yearning for a larger family.

"It's only been two months," he reminded Megan as gently as possible.

"No, Dad," she said. "It's been a lot longer than that."

Troy understood this far better than Megan seemed to realize. In the end, Sandy barely resembled the woman he'd married. Her death, while tragic, was a release from the physical nightmare that had become her reality. Sandy had lived with MS for at least thirty years. Not until after she miscarried the third pregnancy had she been tested.

Then, and only then, were the physicians able to put a name to the seemingly random symptoms she'd been experiencing for years. Multiple sclerosis.

"Let's not donate anything just yet," Troy said.

"Mom's *gone,*" Megan repeated in the same emotionally charged tone. "We both have to accept it."

Troy didn't have any choice but to accept the fact that his wife was dead. He wanted to tell Megan that he was well aware Sandy was gone. He was the one who walked into an empty house every night, the one who slept alone in a big bed.

Ninety per cent of his free time had been spent at the nursing home with Sandy. Now he was bereft and at loose ends. He knew he'd never be the same. Like him, Megan was hurting and she needed to vent her grief, so he said nothing.

"I'll help you pack everything up and I'll put the boxes in the basement," he murmured. "When you're ready… when we both are, I'll bring them upstairs again. Then, and only then, should we think about donating your mother's things to charity. If we decide to do it, I'll ask Pastor Flemming to suggest an agency. There might even be one at the church." If not, he'd go to St. Vincent de Paul or the Salvation Army, both organizations Sandy had supported.

For a moment it looked as if Megan wanted to argue with him.

"Agreed?" he pressed.

His daughter reluctantly nodded. Glancing at her watch, she gnawed on her lower lip. That told him how close she was to breaking down. "Craig will be home any minute. I should leave."

"Go." He gestured toward the door.

His daughter hesitated. "But the bedroom's a mess."

"I'll take care of it."

She shook her head. "That's unfair, Dad. I…I didn't mean for you to have to deal with all this."

"All I'm going to do is fold everything, put it inside these boxes and haul them downstairs."

"You're sure?" she asked uncertainly.

He nodded. The truth was, Troy would rather be alone right now.

She edged her way into the living room and toward the front door. "I hate leaving you with this…."

"Don't worry about it." He was more than capable of packing away a few boxes of clothes.

Megan reached slowly for her purse. "You've thought about dinner?"

So far he hadn't. "I'll open a can of chili."

"Promise?"

"Of course." Not that skipping dinner would do him any harm. Troy figured he could easily afford to lose twenty pounds. Most of that extra weight had snuck up on him after he'd moved Sandy to the nursing home. Meals became haphazard after that. He'd fallen victim to the fast-food chains; there weren't many in Cedar Cove, but the few that had opened in town he knew well. Because of his job and its demands on his time, he often missed breakfast and sometimes even lunch. Then he'd arrive home ravenous late in the evening and he'd eat whatever was quick and easy, which usually meant high-calorie processed food. He couldn't remember the last time he'd actually made a green salad or eaten fresh fruit.

With Sandy gone, he'd lost his emotional balance. Troy

felt a sense of emptiness, a gap where his love for Sandy used to be. He still *loved* her, of course, but the duties and responsibilities attached to that love had disappeared. They'd represented a big part of his life in the last few years.

Sandy dead at fifty-seven—it wasn't supposed to happen like this. He should've been the one to die first; he was the one in a dangerous profession. Practically every day someone in law enforcement was killed in the line of duty. He should've died before his wife did. That was what all the statistics predicted. Then Sandy would've been able to live comfortably on his pension for another ten or twenty years. Instead, his wife was gone and he was floundering.

"I'll give you a call later," his daughter said as she walked to the front door.

"Okay." Troy stood on the porch and watched her pull out of the driveway. He felt so drained, it took an inordinate amount of energy to step back and close the door.

The house had never seemed quieter. Standing by the threshold, he was astonished by the total lack of sound. Silence reverberated around him. Generally he turned on the radio for company, or if he was desperate, the television. But tonight, even that seemed to require more ambition than he could muster.

As he went back into the bedroom with Sandy's clothes strewn about, Grace Sherman drifted into his mind. Grace Harding now, since she'd married Cliff.

Funny that he'd think about one of his high-school friends at a time like this. And yet, it made sense. What came to mind was an incident shortly after Dan's disappearance. Hard to believe that had been six years ago. Dan Sherman was found dead a year later.

Troy never knew exactly what had driven the other man into his own private hell. He wasn't sure he wanted to know either, although he suspected it had something to do with Dan's experience in Vietnam. The war had left Dan permanently damaged in some way. Not in body but in mind, in spirit. He'd become reclusive, unfriendly, refusing to share his memories and fears even with other Vietnam vets like Bob Beldon.

When Dan disappeared, Troy had taken the missing-persons report. Several months later, he'd been called by a neighbor, who was concerned about Grace. In her pain and anger, she'd tossed Dan's clothing onto the front yard of their home on Rosewood Lane.

Now, standing in his own room surrounded by Sandy's things, Troy remembered the sight of Dan's clothes scattered on the grass—and he understood the powerful emotions that had led Grace to explode in such an uncharacteristic display. A part of him didn't want to deal with the residual effects of Sandy's life. Just limping from one day to the next was painful enough.

His gaze fell on the pink sweater Megan had so recently shown him. He picked it up and buried his nose in the soft wool. There was still a hint of his wife's favorite perfume and he breathed it in, deeply, greedily. She'd worn this sweater at Easter last year. Troy had pushed her wheelchair to the open-air church services overlooking the cove. Sandy had always been a morning person, even toward the end. He used to tease her that she'd been born with a happy gene.

Her smile was one of the things he'd loved most about her. No matter how much he growled or muttered in the mornings, she'd respond cheerfully, often making him laugh. He closed his eyes as the pain cut through him. Never again would he see Sandy's smile or hear her joyful voice.

With a heavy heart, he carefully folded the pink sweater and placed it inside the box. He wasn't ready to see someone else wearing his wife's clothes. Since they lived in a small town, it was bound to happen sooner or later. Most likely when he was least expecting it or least prepared to deal with it. Troy would turn a corner and run into another woman wearing Sandy's favorite dress. He didn't know how he'd react to that. The mere thought twisted his gut.

The phone rang in the distance, and for half a second he was tempted just to let the caller leave a message—or not. But too many years as a cop had made it impossible to ignore a ringing phone.

To Troy's surprise it was his daughter.

"Dad," she said, "you're right. Keep Mom's things for now. Keep everything."

Troy could tell Megan had been crying.

"Okay," he said. "Okay, Meggie."

"If you want, I'll come back tomorrow and finish packing it all up."

"I'll do it," he said. Hard as that would be, he was better able to deal with this one last task than his daughter. Megan's composure had shattered, while he moved through his days in a state of numbness that masked the pain.

Three

Barbecued chicken, a green salad, garlic bread—a perfect dinner for a perfect summer day. With mixed berries and ice cream for dessert. Justine Gunderson enjoyed making her leisurely preparations for tonight's meal.

She pulled the covered bowl of chicken breasts out of the refrigerator. She flipped them in their soy-and-honey marinade, then set the container back inside. Like many of her favorite recipes, this one had come from her grandmother, Charlotte Jefferson Rhodes.

Leif, her almost-five-year-old son, was playing in the backyard with his dog. Penny, a cocker spaniel–poodle mix, chased after the boy, barking excitedly. The pure joy of the moment made Justine smile as she stepped through the patio doors. Seth would be home soon and he'd barbecue the chicken while she put the finishing touches on the salad. Leif would start setting the outdoor table, since he loved arranging the napkins and colorful place mats.

As this little domestic scene played out in her mind, she

felt a sense of tranquility. Even now, all these months after the fire that had destroyed their restaurant, Justine was unaccustomed to the three of them having an uninterrupted evening together.

So much of her life—*their* lives—had been consumed by The Lighthouse. The restaurant had completely absorbed their time and energy. Until the fire, Justine and Seth rarely saw each other. Everything was always done in a rush as they divided the duties involved in running the restaurant, taking care of the house and, most important of all, raising their son. Thankfully, they'd reached a compromise concerning the new restaurant they planned to open.

"Mommy, look!" Leif shouted, throwing a stick for Penny.

The dog instantly leaped forward, racing after the stick. She picked it up, then crouched a few feet away, tail wagging frantically, and challenged the boy to grab the stick.

"Penny, bring it to Leif," Justine called out.

"She's as stubborn as every other female in this house," Seth said from behind Justine. "Well, the *only* other female." He slid his arms around her waist and kissed the side of her neck. Leaning into her husband, Justine tucked her hands around his and closed her eyes, reveling in the moment.

"I didn't hear you come in," she said.

"Daddy, Daddy!" Leif shouted, dashing across the freshly cut lawn.

Seth scooped his son into his arms and lifted him high over his head. "I see you're training Penny to play catch."

"She won't give me the stick."

"She'll learn," Seth told him. "Come on, we'll both work with her."

While Seth and Leif played with Penny, Justine went into the house to pour her husband a cold drink. The doorbell rang; abandoning the glass of iced tea, Justine hurried to answer it.

Her grandmother stood there, clutching the huge purse Leif called her "granny bag." Among other things, it contained her current knitting project, a roll of mints, a comb and a notebook—but no cellphone or credit cards. Delighted to see her, Justine threw both arms around Charlotte in a tight hug.

"I hope you don't mind me coming by like this," Charlotte said as Justine led her into the house. "I was in the neighborhood—well, relatively speaking. Olivia said you wanted to talk to me."

"Grandma, you're welcome anytime, you know that!"

"Well, normally I wouldn't stop in without warning, but I was chatting with your mother this afternoon and she said you wanted to ask me about recipes."

"I do." Justine slipped her hand in Charlotte's and they moved into the kitchen.

"I was just getting Seth a glass of iced tea," Justine said. "Can I get one for you, too?"

"Please." Charlotte set her large bag on an empty chair and sat down. These days, it was unusual to find her without Ben, her husband of three years.

As if reading her thoughts, Charlotte explained. "An old friend of Ben's is visiting from out of town. I stayed long enough to meet Ralph, then made my excuses. All that talk about navy life is too much for me." She pulled her knitting out of the bag and resumed the sweater she was working on. Her grandmother didn't believe in idle hands.

Justine brought two glasses of tea and sat across from her.

"Now, what can I do for you?" Charlotte asked. "You need recipes for the tearoom?"

"Yes." Justine rested both elbows on the table. "I've been doing a lot of thinking about it," she said. Although the building process hadn't yet begun, she had a clear vision of the kind of restaurant she wanted. The menu had to be exactly right, and Justine couldn't think of anyone better to consult than her own grandmother.

"It's a good idea to plan ahead." Charlotte paused in her knitting to look at Justine. "Olivia told me you're going to serve breakfast, lunch and a high tea, then close in the evenings."

Justine nodded. "Seth and I decided we'd rather have our evenings together. Leif's flourished in the last few months with both of us home." The arson that had destroyed The Lighthouse had eventually—and unexpectedly—turned out to be a blessing in a very nasty disguise. She was grateful no one had been hurt or worse. And grateful that this crime had changed their lives in a positive way.

"You're wise to put your family first."

Justine suspected her marriage wouldn't have survived another year at the rate they'd been going. She glanced out at the yard, where Seth frolicked with their son and Penny.

"You said you talked to Mom. Were you at the courthouse today?" Her grandmother liked to watch Justine's mother at work. Charlotte sat proudly in Olivia's courtroom and knitted away, although her visits had become less frequent now that she'd married Ben.

"Actually I ran into her this morning while I was in town. She was on her way to a doctor's appointment."

Justine tensed. She didn't remember her mother mentioning that, and they spoke nearly every day. "Oh."

"It's nothing serious," Charlotte said quickly. "Just a routine visit, she told me. For her mammogram."

"Oh, good." Justine relaxed in her chair, crossed her legs and picked up her own glass of iced tea. "I'd like some of your recipes, Grandma," she began.

"Any in particular?" Charlotte's fingers manipulated the needles and yarn with familiar ease.

"I was hoping to get the recipe you have for scones." They were a long-time family favorite and Charlotte baked them for nearly every family function.

Charlotte seemed pleased. "The herb-and-cheese scones are the ones I like best."

"Me, too."

Her grandmother paused reflectively. "My mother used to make those scones, so that recipe actually came from her. I have a couple of other scone recipes I'll write out for you, as well," she added. "Clyde's favorite was a walnut-and-butter scone. Ben prefers the herb-and-cheese."

"Thanks," Justine said. "But I'd be happy to copy them out myself if—" It suddenly occurred to her that her grandmother might have all these family recipes in her head, that she might never have written them down before.

"I'll bring them to you tomorrow morning," Charlotte went on. "In fact, you're welcome to all my recipes, dear. Just tell me which ones you want."

"Grandma," Justine said, broaching the subject carefully. "You *do* have your recipes written down somewhere, don't you?"

Charlotte laughed. "Good grief, no."

"No!"

"I've been cooking for over seventy years. The recipes were taught to me by my mother and, well, I never thought it was necessary. I certainly wasn't going to forget them."

"What about the raspberry vinaigrette salad dressing?"

"Oh, that one," Charlotte said with a sigh. "I got it from a newspaper article around 1959. I've changed it through the years."

"Grandma, would you write them out for me? *All* of them?"

"Of course." Her knitting needles made soft clicking sounds as she continued to knit. "Actually, that's an excellent suggestion, Justine. I'm sure Ben will approve, too. He always says I should publish a cookbook, you know. He loves my peanut butter cookies." She preened just a little.

"And your cinnamon rolls."

"I think that man married me for my baking."

Justine laughed at the absurdity of her comment. One look at Ben Rhodes, and anyone could see that he was crazy about Charlotte.

"Now tell me more about the tearoom," Charlotte said conversationally.

Justine smiled. "Well, there's been a change in plans."

"Oh?" Her grandmother stopped knitting for a moment.

Justine uncrossed her legs and leaned forward. "Seth and I couldn't tell anyone until all the details were settled.

The builder, Al Finch, contacted us a few weeks ago and asked if we'd be willing to sell the property. He said he might have a buyer."

Silence followed her statement. "I thought you and Seth weren't interested in doing that."

"We weren't, especially if it meant that a fast-food franchise would be built on the waterfront. But this is the best part, Grandma. The man who inquired about the land, Brian Johnson, is a friend of Al's. He's owned a number of restaurants through the years. He retired but got bored. Seth and I met with him and we were both impressed. Brian said he'd like to rebuild The Lighthouse the way it was. He even wants to keep the name."

"But that was *your* restaurant," her grandmother protested.

"True, but he's willing to pay us for the name and everything."

Her grandmother paused again, as if she needed time to absorb the news. "Are you going to do it? And what about the tearoom? Where will you build that?"

Justine explained that Al Finch had shown them a piece of commercial property off Heron that he owned and was planning to sell. The location was perfect for The Victorian Tea Room. "We signed the papers earlier this week."

There was another moment of silence.

"You aren't disappointed in us, are you, Grandma?"

"No," her grandmother assured her. "I think this is wonderful news."

So did Justine. All the hard work they'd put into The Lighthouse wouldn't go to waste now. Seth had given the new owner his suggestions on how to rebuild the restaurant, and now that she was no longer involved, she looked forward to seeing it emerge from the ashes.

"It's happened so fast."

"It has," Justine agreed, "but it feels right. This new location is much better for the tearoom and there's more parking. I can't believe how all of this practically fell into our laps."

"I'm pleased for both of you," her grandmother said.

"I am, too." Justine gazed longingly into the backyard. Seeing Seth with Leif brought her a feeling of contentment, of satisfaction. This was what she'd always wanted, what she'd hoped for in her marriage.

"I should get home," Charlotte said. "Ben's probably wondering what's keeping me." She finished her iced tea, put her knitting back in her bag and stood up.

"It's wonderful to see you, Grandma."

"You, too, sweetheart." She kissed Justine's cheek. "I'll start writing down those recipes. I'll do my best to remember them all, so if I forget any, let me know." She frowned. "I'd better go through the ones I cut out from magazines, too. And the ones I was given at wakes."

"Isn't that where you got your fabulous coconut cake recipe? At a wake?"

"Yes—Mabel Austin's. Back in '84."

Justine grinned at this, but she supposed that a great recipe wasn't the worst memorial someone could have.

"I'll just step outside and say hello to Seth and Leif," Charlotte murmured as she carried her empty glass to the sink. "My goodness, that young man is growing. I don't remember him being nearly that tall."

"Seth or Leif?" Justine asked with a laugh. It was true; Leif was tall for his age, but then his father was a big man.

"Leif, of course," her grandmother said, obviously missing the joke.

"By the way..." Justine opened the patio door. "We're barbecuing chicken tonight and I'm using a recipe I got from you."

"The one with soy sauce and honey? I picked that up at a wake, too."

Justine couldn't hold back a smile. "Whose wake? Do you remember?"

"Of course I do," she answered in a dignified voice. "Norman Schultz. 1992. Or was it '93?" With that Charlotte walked outside.

Penny and Leif ran toward her. Knowing he needed to be gentle with his great-grandmother, Leif pulled up short and then stood still, giving Charlotte the opportunity to hug him. Penny, however, felt no such constraint. With one sharp command, Seth controlled the dog, who promptly sat. After she'd finished chatting with Leif, Charlotte leaned over to stroke Penny's fur. She gave Justine a final wave, then Seth walked her out to her car.

When he returned to the kitchen, he asked, "Is that for me?" motioning toward the glass of iced tea on the counter.

"Oh, sorry," Justine said. "I was about to bring it to you when my grandmother arrived." She removed an ice-cube tray from the freezer. "Here. I'll add some ice."

"Thanks," he said, pausing to take a long drink of the tea. "Did you tell her we sold the property?"

"I did."

"What did she think?"

Justine grinned. "That we're too brilliant for words."

Seth took another swallow of the tea. The ice cubes tinkled cheerfully as he set the glass down. "Your mother and Jack know, don't they?"

"I told her this morning. Speaking of which…" Justine grew thoughtful.

"Yes?" Seth urged.

"She didn't say she had a doctor's appointment."

"So? Should she have?"

"No, I guess not, but it makes me wonder…." She suspected there was a reason her mother didn't want her to know about the appointment, and that concerned Justine. Charlotte might have said it was "routine," but was Olivia expecting bad news?

As if sensing her unease, Seth brought his arm around her waist. She felt so thankful to have her husband back. The arson had briefly changed him into an angry, vengeful man, but after Warren Saget—a local builder and onetime boyfriend of hers—was arrested, a burden had been lifted from her husband's shoulders. Seth was once again the man she knew and loved.

He held her for a long moment as though he, too, recognized how close they'd come to destroying everything that was important to them both.

"Do you want me to fire up the barbecue?" he asked as he released her.

"Please."

"Can I help with dinner, too, Mommy?" Leif entered the kitchen with Penny at his heels.

"You sure can." Justine smiled at her son. "You can help me set the table—after you wash your hands."

"Okay."

They all headed outside, and while Seth was busy on

the patio, Justine and Leif wiped the glass-topped table and adjusted the umbrella. Leif took great pleasure in carefully arranging the bright green place mats he'd chosen and the napkins with their multicolored butterflies.

When they'd finished dinner, Leif and his father cleared the table. Justine dealt with the leftovers and cleaned up the kitchen. Until recently, she hadn't realized how much she'd missed meal preparation; she'd always assumed that cooking wasn't her forte. Her mother and grandmother were the ones who enjoyed working in the kitchen. Then she'd married Seth and in those first few months while they renovated the old Captain's Galley and planned their new restaurant, Justine had taken pride in preparing their meals. She'd gone to Olivia and Charlotte for recipes and ideas, and for the first time as an adult, she'd connected with her mother in ways she never would've thought possible. Her relationship with her grandmother, always good, grew even closer.

"I talked to my grandmother about recipes," she said.

"Recipes?" Seth repeated, washing his hands. "For the tearoom?"

She nodded. "You know, I've rediscovered how much I actually enjoy cooking."

Seth blinked. "Hold on a minute. You *enjoy* cooking?"

"Yes." She rolled her eyes at his feigned shock.

"Answer me this," her husband teased. "Exactly who was standing over a hot barbecue this evening?"

"Seth Gunderson, flipping a few chicken breasts on the grill is *not* cooking."

"It is as far as I'm concerned."

"You're being ridiculous."

"Am not." He laughed, then caught Justine around the waist.

She laughed, too. Everything was going to be better now. In fact, it already was.

Four

Rachel Pendergast dumped a load of towels in the washer at the Get Nailed salon. Adding the soap, she closed the lid and turned the dial, waiting to be sure the water had started. She was taking advantage of a break between customers to deal with the laundry, a chore that needed to be done every day. When she left the small lunchroom she discovered her best friend, Teri, sitting in the chair at Rachel's station.

"Teri!" Rachel couldn't restrain her excitement. It'd been less than a month since she'd seen her but it *felt* longer. Not only did she miss Teri, but Nate, her navy boyfriend, had recently been transferred to San Diego.

Teri slid off the chair. She held her arms wide and they hugged and giggled like teenagers. The salon just wasn't the same without Teri's wisecracks and her caustic but funny view of life. Rachel had missed chatting with her about Nate. And Bruce.

"Thank heaven you're back at work," Rachel cried. Looking Teri in the eye, she said, "You *are* back, aren't you?"

"We'll see. I need to talk to Jane first."

Rachel was sure there wouldn't be any problem getting Teri on staff again. "Jane's at the bank. She'll return any minute."

Rachel didn't really understand why Bobby had insisted Teri leave her job. She knew there'd been some kind of threat against Teri, although she assumed it actually had more to do with Bobby.

Two men had confronted Teri in the parking lot, and soon afterward, Bobby had asked her not to work at the salon until he got everything straightened out. Although Jane had hired a perfectly adequate replacement to fill in, the other woman wasn't Teri.

"I finally managed to convince Bobby that either I went back to work or I'd go insane," Teri explained, smiling over at Jeannie who was cutting a young woman's hair nearby.

"Where's Bobby?"

"At home," Teri said. "I love that man to distraction, but I couldn't stand his overprotectiveness." She paused, glancing over her shoulder. "The only way I could get him to agree was to promise I'd have James drive me to and from work. James is supposed to be my bodyguard."

"James?" Rachel couldn't believe it. Bobby's driver was no bodyguard. First of all, he was as thin as a beanpole without any apparent muscle. If Teri found herself in danger, she'd probably end up saving James.

"So, can you stay this afternoon?"

"I can until I talk to Jane, but after that I'll need to get back to the house. Otherwise, Bobby's likely to send out a search party." She laughed at her own joke. "Bobby isn't overjoyed about me working, but he understands that I like my job and want to be here."

"I'm glad he's decided to be reasonable."

"Trust me, I am, too," Teri said with a sigh of relief.

Rachel looked closely at her friend, struck by how lovely Teri was. She'd always been impulsive, gregarious and outrageous. A little cynical, too, especially about men and relationships. And then she'd met Bobby Polgar. She remained her larger-than-life self, but over the past few months she'd changed. She'd become…softer, Rachel thought. More hopeful, less cynical. And it was all due to Bobby.

Only love could explain the way two such dissimilar people had fallen for each other. A deep, true love, the kind that changed people for the better. The kind that offered acceptance and trust. Bobby came alive when he was with Teri. Anyone who'd ever met him or seen him in front of a chessboard would acknowledge that he was a genius and a bit…she cast about for the right word…*eccentric.* With Teri, he became human—likeable, and on occasion even funny. Although he usually didn't mean to be. He was simply naive in ways that were endearing.

Whether she and Nate had a love like Teri and Bobby's, she didn't know. She suspected they needed more time, and this enforced separation wasn't making their situation any easier.

"So," Teri said, sitting down in the chair again and crossing her legs. "Bring me up to speed. You miss Nate?"

Rachel nodded. "A lot," she said, feeling bereft without him. Talking on the phone helped, but it wasn't enough. "He calls me almost every day."

"Like Bobby used to?" Teri asked.

Rachel laughed. "Not quite. Nate phones when he can, and that's usually in the evenings." While courting Teri,

Bobby had faithfully phoned at precisely the same hour every day, Pacific Standard Time, regardless of where he happened to be.

"What about Bruce?"

"What about him?" Rachel asked, her voice sharper than she'd intended.

"Are you seeing him?"

"No!" she returned vehemently. Bruce, a widower, had become a friend and his daughter, Jolene—well, Jolene was special to her. In many ways Jolene reminded Rachel of herself as a girl. She, too, had lost her mother at an early age; she'd been raised by an aunt who'd died a few years ago. Jolene needed a female influence in her life, and that was the role Rachel played.

"Why do you say *no* as if it's the most repugnant thought imaginable?" Teri asked. "You make it sound like dating Bruce is something you could never even consider. We both know that isn't true. The two of you are just so well suited."

Rachel frowned. "What makes you say that?"

Teri shook her head, implying it should be obvious. "It's like you're already married. That's what anyone seeing you together would think if they didn't know better. You practically finish each other's sentences."

Rachel dismissed that observation with an airy wave of her hand. Teri was fond of Bruce, which made her partial to the idea of Rachel's being involved with him. "We're friends," she said firmly. "That's all."

Teri cocked her head. "He's kissed you."

Rachel rolled her eyes. "Do you have a hidden camera? Are you watching every move?"

"No," Teri said. "You told me about it."

"I did?"

"It's true, isn't it?"

"Well, yes, but it was a—"

"Friendly kiss," Teri finished for her.

"Sort of." In retrospect, she thought Bruce might've wanted it to be more. His kiss had come as a surprise, but as kisses went, it was nice. She mulled that over and decided *nice* was a weak description. *Nice* sounded so bland, like unsalted popcorn. That wasn't really how she'd felt about it—but maybe it was all she *wanted* to feel. "I like Bruce, don't get me wrong, just not in that way."

"You mean it?" Teri asked.

"Don't you remember when I first started spending time with Jolene? Bruce made it abundantly clear that he had no interest in getting involved." She wasn't likely to forget the look on his face the day Jolene announced that she'd chosen Rachel to be her new mother. Bruce had nearly swallowed his tongue. He'd wanted it understood that he had no romantic intentions whatsoever. Rachel had taken him at his word. She simply didn't see him in those terms. Besides, she *had* a boyfriend.

"I'd rather talk about Nate," she said, preferring to change the subject.

"I'd rather discuss Bruce," Teri countered.

"Why?"

Teri shrugged. "For one thing, I find him more interesting than Nate."

"In what way?" Rachel asked coldly—knowing she shouldn't have responded at all.

"Well, Bruce is down-to-earth and he doesn't have an inflated ego and…and he's a good dad."

"Right," Jeannie said, entering uninvited into the conversation. She pointed her curling iron at Rachel as she stood behind her client. "Bruce called her the other day."

"To see if Jolene could spend the night on Friday." Rachel wondered how her love life had become the business of the entire salon.

"She was on the line for a l-o-o-ong time," Jeannie told Teri, dragging out the word.

"It was my cell," Rachel explained, in case anyone thought she'd been tying up the business line with a personal call.

"You did seem to be enjoying yourself. I heard you laughing."

Bruce *was* witty, or he could be. But Rachel ignored the comment. To acknowledge it would only invite further conversation and she was trying to avoid that.

"Whenever she's on the phone with Nate," Jeannie went on to say, "it's like she wants to cry."

"I miss Nate," Rachel said, throwing her hands in the air. "We're in love, and we have to be apart."

"I still think you should pick Bruce," Jeannie said stubbornly.

"Why don't we take a poll?" Teri suggested. She got up and turned in a complete circle, indicating that everyone in the salon should take part in the vote.

"This is crazy," Rachel said, refusing to listen. Teri could organize her vote, but she wasn't sticking around to participate. It didn't matter what other people thought.

She was in love with Nate and had been from almost their first date, which she'd bought at the Dog and Bachelor charity auction three summers ago. Okay, he was younger by five years, but that had never bothered him and it didn't bother her, either. What did concern her were his political connections; his father was a Pennsylvania congressman with higher political aspirations.

Then she'd met his mother, and that hadn't gone well. Unfortunately, Nate had been oblivious to the verbal jabs the other woman had directed at her. He thought Rachel was imagining things, but she knew. Although Patrice Olsen didn't actually say so, she considered Rachel an inappropriate choice for her son.

Teri, who'd obviously abandoned her plan to hold a run-off vote between Nate and Bruce, trailed her into the kitchen. Rachel had just slipped a frozen entrée into the microwave. The washing machine churned nearby, and the sound of sloshing water punctuated her angry thoughts.

"Don't you remember what it was like when you met Bobby?" Rachel said, whirling around to face her friend.

"I didn't want to fall in love with him."

"But you did."

A sigh escaped Teri's lips. "Bobby made it impossible not to. I'll never forget the night he brought me a dozen romantic greeting cards, flowers and about fifty pounds of expensive chocolate."

Bobby had been trying to romance Teri, and according to his "research," that was the way to do it. Naturally, being Bobby, he'd gone completely overboard.

"How could I turn him down when he asked if he could kiss me?" Teri said plaintively.

"You couldn't," Rachel agreed.

"What can I say? The man swept me off my feet."

"You feel about Bobby the way I feel about Nate," Rachel said and hoped Teri would leave it at that. All this talk about her and Bruce had unsettled her. She didn't want to think of Jolene's father as anything more than a friend.

"No, you don't," Teri said softly. "You forget I know you, Rachel, probably better than anyone else here. We've been friends for a long time."

Rachel grew even more uncomfortable. She opened the microwave and took out her lunch. Steam rose from the entrée as she gingerly lifted it onto a small plate and carried it to the two-person table.

"I know Nate wants to marry you."

Rachel had shared that information with Teri and regretted it now. "Your point is?"

"My point is if you truly loved him, you wouldn't have hesitated. You would've accepted his proposal, packed up your life and followed him to San Diego. You didn't."

"Oh, honestly, Teri, if you're gauging my feelings on that, you're completely off-base."

"Am I?"

"Yes," she snapped. Sitting down at the table, she reached for a napkin and smoothed it over her lap. "Would you mind if we discussed something else now?"

"I guess."

"Good." She picked up the fork and sampled her first bite.

Jeannie stepped into the compact kitchen. "Listen, about Bruce Peyton—"

Rachel set down her fork with a clang, interrupting Jeannie's statement, whatever it was. She didn't want to hear his name again. If it wasn't Teri, it was some other friend or colleague. People just wouldn't let the subject drop and frankly she was bored with it. "What about him?" she asked with exaggerated patience.

Jeannie opened the small refrigerator and grabbed a bottle of cold water. "A couple of my clients are hot to trot with him."

"I beg your pardon?"

"He's not hard on the eyes," Jeannie said, twisting off the cap and taking a deep swallow. "They've been noticing him…."

"Good for them," Rachel murmured, returning to her lunch. "I hope it works out for him and whoever he's dating."

"I don't think he's dating anyone," Jeannie told her.

"I have no idea." That wasn't actually true. Jolene kept her informed, and while Bruce did go out on occasion, those dates had never amounted to anything.

Jeannie left the lunchroom, but Teri stayed. After a moment, she gently pressed Rachel's shoulder.

"You'll know," she murmured. "When it's the right man, everything will be clear and you'll wonder why it took you so long to see what was already there in front of you."

"That's how it was with you and Bobby?" she couldn't keep from asking.

A joyful smile softened Teri's face. "I promised myself I wouldn't marry him. He had James deliver this huge diamond but I wasn't going to do it. I had absolutely no intention of marrying Bobby Polgar. Good grief, I hadn't even been to bed with him and here he was insisting I marry him."

Rachel smiled at the memory of Teri's misery the night she'd come to see her. Miserable and in love and so afraid she'd ruin Bobby's life if she married him.

But Rachel could see, even then, that they were meant

to be together. Bobby knew it, too, because he refused to let her go. Teri had figured it out fast enough; Rachel could only take hope from that.

Jane walked in just then, breaking into Rachel's musing. The happiness that lit her face when she saw Teri was all Rachel needed to know. Teri would be back at the salon where she belonged.

Five

Linnette McAfee's heart was broken. She'd been in love for the first time in her life and it was over. Just like that. *Over.* Cal had gone off to rescue wild horses and while he was away, he'd fallen in love with Vicki Newman, the local vet.

Linnette still couldn't understand how it had happened—and yet, she could. It was her. Something was wrong with her. Not Cal. Not Vicki. Her. Fresh tears filled her eyes as she indulged in this bout of self-pity.

The doorbell chimed and she jumped at the sound. The last thing she wanted now was company. It could only be one of two people—her mother or her sister, Gloria—and she wasn't in the mood to deal with either of them.

Everyone was angry with her because she'd decided to leave Cedar Cove. Her friends at work, especially Chad Timmons, had said that if anyone left, it should be Cal. Well, he wasn't leaving, and Linnette didn't have it in her to watch Cal and Vicki together and pretend her heart wasn't broken. All right, she was overreacting. She was being overdramatic. But she didn't care.

The doorbell chimed again, longer this time. She couldn't ignore it, so she wiped the tears from her cheeks and forced a smile. It crumpled the instant she saw her mother.

"Hi, Mom."

Corrie McAfee opened the screen door and stepped into the second-floor apartment. With comforting, cooing sounds, she put her arms around Linnette. "Oh honey, I'm so sorry."

"I know, I know." Despite her efforts to be strong, Linnette buried her face in her mother's shoulder. Sometimes a girl needed her mother and Linnette wasn't too proud to admit it.

"Let me make some tea," Corrie said, leading her into the kitchen.

While Linnette sat at the small table and pulled one tissue after another from the box, her mother set a kettle of water on the stove.

"I was hoping to leave before this," Linnette blubbered between hiccuping sobs. She wanted her mother to understand that she wasn't going to be talked out of moving. "But the clinic needs me until a replacement can be hired and trained."

"You *are* going to stay a bit longer, aren't you?"

Linnette didn't have any other choice. She couldn't let the clinic go short-staffed; she'd worked there since it opened and the place meant a lot to her. But her job wasn't the only problem. She'd signed a lease for the apartment and it was either pay the rent or find someone to sublet. That very day, she'd posted an ad online and in the local paper. She'd also talked to a rental agent. Unless she managed to get someone to take over the lease, she'd have to stay much longer than she wanted to.

"I can't stand to see you hurting like this," Corrie said, taking two mugs from the cupboard. "This is as hard on me as it is on you. I don't know *what* Cal was thinking."

"Oh, Mom! Cal can love anyone he wants." Even after he'd ended the relationship, she couldn't stop defending him. That was another reason she had to leave. Linnette still loved Cal, and because of that, she wanted him to be happy. If it meant he was with another woman, then…then she'd simply leave.

The kettle whistled and steam shot into the air. Her mother removed it from the burner and poured the boiling water into the waiting pot, then added tea leaves. When she'd finished, she carried the pot of steeping tea to the kitchen table.

Years ago, when Linnette was a schoolgirl, her mother had made tea for her whenever she was sick. But it wasn't the flu or a stomachache that bothered her now, and she seriously doubted a cup of tea would ease her aching heart.

"I've decided to put my things in storage," Linnette said. She'd been considering what to do with her furniture for some time. Not that she had much to store. At first she'd assumed she could keep her belongings in her parents' basement, but then she realized it was her responsibility, not her parents'.

"Dad and I can keep them for you," her mother offered, exactly as Linnette had known she would.

"No, Mom, this is what I'm doing." It would be easy to let her mother talk her out of her plans. The whole process would start with something small, some favor like the one she'd just suggested, and then gradually, Corrie would wear her down. Next thing she knew, Linnette would be staying in Cedar Cove.

Her mother seemed surprised by Linnette's persistence and shrugged her shoulders. "If you're sure."

"I am," Linnette reiterated.

Corrie reached for the teapot and filled both their cups, muttering, "It's a waste of good money."

"Perhaps."

"So..." Corrie tensed. "Where do you plan to go?"

"I don't know yet," Linnette said noncommittally.

This news appeared to startle her mother. "You mean to say you're just heading out the door with no destination in mind?"

Linnette nodded. "I guess so."

"That's so unlike you." Corrie looked even more distressed.

"I'm sorry, Mom, but..." Linnette didn't know how to finish her response; she had nothing reassuring to say.

Her mother was right. Acting this impulsively was unlike her. She craved structure, needed it. Once she'd decided to become a physician assistant, she'd listed all the required courses, and calculated how long it would take to obtain her degree. Then, with the full force of her determination, she'd set out to achieve it. Never before, not on a trip or in life, had she left without a road map. Until now.

"In other words, you're running away," her mother said anxiously.

Linnette had no intention of denying it. "You could say that." She took a sip of tea and not surprisingly it burned her mouth. She set down the mug.

"Do you think that's wise?"

"Probably not. I'll admit it's not a rational decision, Mom. I'm responding to pain. I'm fully aware that none of this makes sense to you or anyone else. All I can tell you is that leaving *feels* right."

"Cal should move," Corrie said in a stubborn voice.

"Mother!"

"He doesn't have family here and you do."

"No one has to move anywhere," she said. "I'm the one who wants to get out of Cedar Cove."

"Then go," her mother said. "But don't do it like this," she pleaded. "Request a leave of absence from work. Take however long you need. But to quit like this, pack up your belongings and move out of your apartment, it's so…"

"Drastic?" Linnette inserted.

"Yes, drastic," her mother agreed. "I can't imagine why you feel the need to flee like this with…with your tail between your legs. *You* didn't do anything wrong."

"Cal and Vicki didn't either. I'm walking away because I'm the one who's hurting."

"And therefore the one least qualified to be making this kind of decision," her mother said.

"Mother, don't you see…" Linnette began. She sighed. "It's time for me to do something that's more…out of my comfort zone. My life is so regimented, so…so, I don't know, so perfect."

"In other words, you're looking for a way to screw it up?"

That made Linnette smile. "No. I'm looking for a way to escape. I'm seeking adventure," she said grandly.

"But you've always been so responsible."

"Exactly my point," Linnette told her. "I'm tired of meeting all these expectations."

Her mother's eyes narrowed. "Your father and I never meant—"

"Mom." Linnette leaned across the table and placed a hand on her mother's arm. "It's not your expectations I'm talking about but my own. I'm the one who put them on myself. As of right now, I'm taking a long, hard look at my life. I'm setting out to discover what I really want. All I know is that it isn't in Cedar Cove."

Her mother seemed about to break into tears. "And you have to run away from your family?"

"Yes." It was the simple, straightforward truth.

"Oh." Corrie picked up her tea and her lips trembled as she bent to take a sip.

Linnette understood how difficult this was for her mother. "Think about the positive side, Mom," she said, forcing a note of cheerful optimism into her voice.

"What's positive about my daughter running away?" Corrie asked.

"Well, this'll be a wonderful opportunity for you and Gloria to get to know each other without me there always directing the conversation."

Her mother's eyes widened. The situation with Gloria remained awkward, although everyone was trying to make her feel like part of the family. Gloria had been given up for adoption as an infant and then found her biological family. She was a full-blooded sister Linnette had never known she had—or at least not until two years ago.

A little while before that, Linnette had moved practically next door to her own sister and they'd struck up a friendship. Gloria had been a tremendous comfort to Linnette since her breakup with Cal.

"I love you both equally," her mother said in low tones. "I always have."

"Of course you do, Mom, but you don't really *know*

Gloria. Like I said, this is your chance to bond without me being there." So far, it'd always been the three of them. Now, both Gloria and their mother could benefit from some private time together. Without Linnette who, as she readily acknowledged, tended to be the center of attention.

She finished her tea and, feeling a little stronger—perhaps the tea *had* helped—she brought her cup to the sink. Her mother stood, too. "I should go. Your father expected me back at the office half an hour ago."

"I'm surprised that he didn't call your cell."

Corrie smiled. "I suspect he knew where I was."

She was probably right. Linnette admired her parents' marriage and the way they understood each other, the way they worked together. It was what she wanted for her own marriage and was determined to have one day.

Her mother left soon afterward. Linnette hugged her, and they both managed to smile, despite Corrie's disappointment. Everything she'd said was true, and yet nothing was going to change. Linnette instinctively knew she'd made the right decision. She needed to leave Cedar Cove.

She rinsed out the cups and set them in the dishwasher. She'd just returned to her packing when the doorbell rang again. It would be either her brother, Mack, or Gloria, she figured. Most likely Gloria.

But Linnette was in for a shock. Vicki Newman, the woman Cal loved, stood on the other side of the screen door. For a long moment the two women did nothing but stare at each other.

"I hope you don't mind that I've come," Vicki said shyly, her brown eyes imploring Linnette.

"Does Cal know you're here?" Linnette couldn't help glancing over the woman's shoulder. Then she looked back at Vicki, with her plain face—there was no other word for it—and her carelessly braided hair. And yet Linnette had begun to realize why Cal loved her so much. For one thing they shared a view of the world, including their passion for animals; Vicki was a veterinarian and Cal a horse-trainer who worked for Grace Harding's husband. The way it had all happened, though—Linnette still found that hard to believe. But she respected him for caring so deeply that he was willing to stand up to the barrage of criticism directed at him because of the pain he'd caused Linnette.

In response to Linnette's question, Vicki shook her head. "Cal wouldn't like it if he found out I'd stopped by."

Knowing him as well as she did, Linnette agreed. Unlatching the screen door, she pushed it open to allow the other woman inside.

As Vicki walked into the apartment, her gaze darted about the room, taking in the boxes that littered the floor. "So it's true. You *are* moving."

Linnette ignored her comment and gestured toward the sofa. "Would you like to sit down?"

Vicki declined with a shake of her head. She gazed down at the carpet. "I heard you were leaving, and I just wanted to tell you how…how sorry I am."

"Sorry that I'm leaving?"

"No…sorry that I hurt you."

"Don't worry about it."

"I…" Vicki looked up then and seemed to reach some decision. "I've been in love with Cal for a long time," she said. "Long before he met you. He didn't know it and I…I didn't know how to tell him, so I said nothing. I never thought he could possibly love me."

"It's because of Cal that you volunteered to help with the mustang rescue, isn't it?"

Vicki nodded. "Well…partly. The cause is important to me too, of course. Anything to do with horses…"

"I understand." After a brief silence, she asked, "You knew about me?"

Vicki nodded again. "I *tried* not to love him."

Linnette wasn't sure of the other woman's purpose in confronting her. Perhaps she felt guilty. Perhaps because of that she was hoping Linnette would yell at her, curse her, condemn her for taking the man Linnette loved. A week earlier, that was exactly what might have happened. Not now. "I'm the one who's trying not to love him," Linnette whispered.

"I'm sure there'll be lots of other opportunities for you. You'll find someone else to love—someone who'll love you," Vicki said urgently. "But for me…" She cleared her throat. "I communicate better with animals than I do with people. I always have. As soon as I met Cal, I felt we should be together. He has the same feeling about animals."

Linnette suddenly had a sharp clear memory of the time she'd come to visit Cal and overheard him crooning to an injured horse. He hadn't known she was there. Linnette had felt as if she was intruding on a private moment, a private world.

"Cal's asked me to marry him," Vicki said in a low voice. "I want to…"

"Then you should," Linnette said.

"We both feel so guilty."

"Don't, please." She reached out to touch Vicki's arm. In the beginning she'd hated this woman, but she no longer felt that way. "I want you both to be happy."

"You mean that?" Vicki asked, frowning.

"With all my heart." Linnette took a deep breath. "If you've come looking for my absolution, then you have it."

"Can I tell Cal we've talked?"

Linnette nodded. "You're right, you know. I *will* find someone else." For the first time she actually believed it.

Six

It was the Saturday evening of the dreaded family dinner.

Teri couldn't stop fidgeting. She checked the ham roasting in the oven, along with a huge casserole of scalloped potatoes. She'd chosen fresh green beans for the vegetable; they were simmering on the stove. Although it was summer, ham had always been served on special occasions, and Teri wasn't about to break with tradition. The table was set with her formal dishes—even the concept of "formal" and "everyday" dishes was a new one for her—and sparkling crystal glasses. Nothing but the best for Mom, Christie and the gang, she thought with no small degree of irony. Against her better judgment, Teri was introducing her family, such as it was, to her husband.

"Bobby," she called, leaving the kitchen and pulling off the apron she'd donned to protect her pale-green shirt. She'd worn it for confidence, since Bobby loved that color on her. When he came toward her, she drew in a calming breath. "Remember what I told you?"

Her husband regarded her blankly.

"About Christie."

Judging by the blank look he gave her, he didn't recall a word. She'd wanted to warn him so he'd be prepared. Her sister, slim and lovely, would do everything in her power to attract him—and steal him away if she could.

Teri suspected that Christie had coerced Johnny into arranging this meeting just so she could prove yet again that any man would prefer *her.* Christie was thinner, prettier, sexier, and she made sure Teri knew it. Not for a minute did Teri discount her sister's charms.

She sighed at Johnny's naiveté. She didn't really blame him for engineering this…this fiasco-to-be; her little brother desperately wanted them all to live in peace and harmony—as though they actually *liked* each other.

She sighed again. "My family will be here any minute."

Bobby stared back at her, then slowly smiled. "I love you, remember."

"*I'm* not the one who needs to be reminded." Christie could be subtle while she was busy flattering some unsuspecting man. She'd be completely absorbed in Bobby, hang on his every word. He'd fall for it, too, she thought grimly. It seemed that every guy she'd loved had been lured away by her sister. Whenever Christie met any man in Teri's life, he was no longer interested in her. Even if Christie had a boyfriend at the time, she had to take her sister's, too.

No one had mattered to Teri as much as Bobby. If Christie assumed she could waltz into Teri's home and play her games, then her little sister had a real surprise awaiting her.

"Tell me their names again," Bobby said.

"My mother's name is Ruth and her husband, my stepfather, is Donald." Teri had to stop and think. "No, sorry,

Johnny phoned and told me Mom's left Donald and now she's planning to marry Mike. I haven't met him yet." She shook her head. Out of seven men, Ruth had yet to pick a decent one as far as Teri could tell, and she doubted Mike would be the exception.

"Ruth and Mike," Bobby dutifully repeated. "And your sister's Christie."

"Christie Levitt." She bit out the name, hoping she didn't sound as angry as she felt.

He nodded.

"I told Mom we wouldn't be serving any alcohol."

"Okay." Bobby studied her.

Bobby could be completely oblivious to what was going on around him—the time of day, the weather, even what month it was. However, when it came to Teri, he seemed to notice more than she sometimes realized.

"Is your sister like you?" he asked.

Now, that was an interesting question. Christie wasn't like her, and yet she was. Two years younger, Christie had tagged after her for the first twelve years of Teri's life. Anything Teri had, Christie wanted—and generally got. Teri could say without hesitation that their mother had always favored her younger daughter. And yet Christie was capable of kindness on occasion, which Teri found all too easy to forget. She knew enough about human nature to understand that she and Christie shared an insecurity that probably stemmed from their mother's selfishness and neglect. Ruth might have preferred Christie and spoiled her but both girls had suffered. They just expressed their insecurity with contrasting kinds of behavior.

"Well, in some ways Christie and I *are* alike," she conceded.

"Then why are you afraid?"

"Concerned," she said. She had to learn to trust her husband. The biggest test would come this very evening, and she'd know once and for all if Bobby truly loved her.

"Does Donald play chess?" he asked next.

"Mike," she corrected. This time around, her mother hadn't bothered to introduce the new man in her life. Well, for that matter, Teri hadn't introduced Bobby, either—but for entirely different reasons.

"Does Mike play chess?" He revised the question.

"I don't know." Teri loved Bobby all the more for asking. He wasn't comfortable in social situations and didn't handle them well. For the most part he avoided even small gatherings; they tended to overwhelm him.

The doorbell chimed, and Teri felt herself tense. "This is going to be a *perfect* dinner," she said aloud. Maybe voicing the words would make it happen, although she was pretty sure she sounded more sarcastic than hopeful. The last time the entire family had been together was two Christmases ago, and it'd been an unmitigated disaster.

Ruth and Mike were already drunk and in the middle of a pointless argument when Teri arrived for Christmas dinner. Johnny was late and their sister had left in a fit of anger, furious over something trivial. Teri was stuck refereeing between her mother and her worthless fiancé.

She'd done her best to be festive and cheerful, and all she got in return was anger and resentment. No one else, apparently, was interested in celebrating anything. Because she'd wanted to see Johnny, she'd waited until he got there; she'd spent an hour talking to him, then went home, glad to make her escape. That year, she'd spent the rest of Christmas Day propped up in bed with a good book and a large chocolate bar. She'd felt guilty about abandoning Johnny to their lunatic family, but she couldn't have been happier to get away. Yet, here she was, willing to try all over again.

When she opened the door, Christie stood on the other side. Teri should've known her half sister would show up right on time. She looked awestruck—and envious. The house was impressive, Teri had to admit.

"Some digs you've got here," Christie said. "Mom and Mike are parking the car and they're going to have a smoke before they come in." Her gaze immediately shot past Teri and flew to Bobby.

"Hello," she cooed and practically shoved past Teri in order to greet Bobby. "I'm Christie." She held out her hand, and when Bobby moved to shake it, she deftly slipped into his arms for a gentle hug. "We're family, after all," she said, smiling up at him with undisguised admiration.

Bobby extricated himself and stood beside Teri, resting his hand on her shoulder. "Bobby Polgar."

"I know all about you," Christie told him. "I read your story on the Internet. You're, like, the most popular checkers player in the world."

"*Chess,*" Teri muttered. Reaching for her husband's hand, she gave it a squeeze. "Bobby plays chess."

"Oh." Her sister's face fell. "Well, I remembered it was one of those board games."

Unlike Teri, her sister was tall with curves in all the right places, and she knew how to use them. Her blouse was cut low in the front, displaying an almost indecent amount of cleavage. Bobby, bless his heart, didn't seem to notice.

"Shall we sit down?" Teri suggested. Dinner was ready, so there was nothing to distract her in the kitchen. The last thing Teri intended to do was give her sister time alone with Bobby.

They walked slowly into the living room, then sat and stared at each other. They were like aliens from different planets meeting to negotiate a peace settlement—like on *Star Trek,* Teri thought. Except there was no Captain Picard to guide them. Silently Teri pleaded with Bobby to say something. Anything. He cast her a helpless look in response.

Teri clutched his hand as if it were a lifeline that connected her to the mother ship as she drifted around outer space.

"I'm surprised my sister caught such a handsome man," Christie said in a bright voice.

"Surprised?" Teri repeated, gritting her teeth.

"Handsome?" Bobby repeated at the same time.

Teri glared at him. *Not Bobby, too.* Her heart sank.

"Handsome *and* rich *and* famous."

"My husband the checkers player." Teri stared up at Bobby with an exaggerated starstruck expression. For further effect, she batted her eyelashes.

Bobby looked uncomfortable and confused.

Christie laughed softly. "Don't tell me you're worried that I'd try to lure Bobby away from you. My goodness, Teri, are you really that insecure?"

"I…I." She hated to admit that she was—that they both were. Her sister's need to compete, to win, brought out the very worst in Teri, especially when there was a man involved. Christie knew her deepest fears and manipulated them. And Teri allowed her to do it. That was a pattern she recognized but couldn't explain. Maybe it was simply habit, all those years of playing certain roles, feeling certain emotions.

Christie hadn't been in the house two minutes and already Teri hated her—and hated herself.

Clearing her throat, she decided then and there that she wouldn't play the role Christie always assigned her. The loser. The unattractive one. The rejected woman. "You can try all you want," she said with a look of unconcern. "My husband loves me, and I trust him. So go ahead, little sister. But it isn't going to work."

Christie blinked, obviously taken aback by Teri's directness.

"Maybe I'll do just that," she murmured. "We'll see what happens."

Rather than watch, Teri excused herself to check on their dinner. She'd made her stand and now she had to step back and trust her heart—and her husband. Finding busywork in the kitchen, she gave Christie ten full minutes.

When Teri returned, Christie seemed more than a little befuddled.

"I don't suppose you have any beer?" her sister asked.

"No, I didn't think it was a good idea to have alcohol around when Mom's going to be here."

"I could use one."

Teri caught her husband's eye and, to her utter astonishment, Bobby winked. Teri grinned and so did he. Bobby *knew*—and he'd put Christie in her place. Teri had no idea what had gone on while she was in the kitchen. But in that moment all she wanted to do was throw herself at her husband and make love to him, regardless of who was in the room.

Her husband recognized her look, and his eyes briefly flared. They shared a smile and an unspoken promise. He'd get his reward later.

Teri's mother and Mike showed up next. As soon as her mother walked inside, she oohed and aahed over the house. After introductions were exchanged, she turned to her older daughter. "Teri, this is just lovely. Give me a tour, would you? I want to see every room." She brought one hand to her throat as she roamed from living room to kitchen to dining room, commenting on each feature. Like an obedient puppy, Mike silently trailed behind.

"Teri's got the bucks now and she can flaunt it," Christie said. The words had a deflated quality that Teri chose to ignore.

Johnny arrived last and a genuine smile lit up his face when he saw Teri. He immediately hugged her and whispered, "It's not so bad, is it?"

"Not bad at all."

"Great."

Her mother left to go to the car and returned with a case of beer. "This is Mike's and my contribution to dinner," she said, setting it down on the kitchen counter. Before Teri could protest, Christie had pulled out a bottle, twisted off the cap and taken her first swig. Ruth and Mike followed in quick succession.

Johnny met her eyes and shrugged. There was nothing either of them could do now.

The evening deteriorated from that point on. Ruth and Mike, along with Christie, sat in the living room and drank beer while Teri served appetizers they mostly ignored. Bobby and Johnny gamely swallowed cheese puffs and shrimp.

"I baked a ham," Teri announced. Bobby got up and stood behind her, as if protecting her from harm.

"I hope everyone's hungry," Johnny added, joining them. "Looks like Teri's been cooking all day."

She'd taken real pride in this dinner, but that was beside the point. She smiled gratefully at her brother.

"It looks like she's been eating all day, too," her mother said, and seemed to find herself exceptionally funny.

One hand on her hip, Teri said, "No more beer for you, understand?"

Ruth's head came back as though she'd been struck. "What did you say?"

"I said this is my house and if you want to drink, you'll do it elsewhere."

"Fine, I will." She stood and the still-silent Mike stood with her.

Although she'd threatened to leave, Ruth didn't seem to be in any rush. "You think you're so smart because you're married to this hotshot checkers player," her mother spat. "Just because you've got money doesn't mean you can tell people how to run their lives."

Everyone froze, and then Bobby stepped forward. Without saying a word, he picked up Ruth's handbag.

"What's he doing with my purse?" she demanded.

Marching into the entry, Bobby set her mother's purse down by the front door.

"Are you kicking me out?" Ruth cried. "I can't believe this! My own daughter's asking me to leave her home." She glanced around the room, seeking support and finding none. Then she headed toward Mike, grabbing his arm.

"I thought you said you were leaving anyway," Christie commented.

"Yeah, Mom," Johnny said cheerfully as he held open the front door. "You drink, you go. That's Teri's rule."

Ruth hesitated in the doorway. "Don't think I'm going to forget this, Teri. One day you'll need me, but I'll tell you right now—you can forget it." With her chin so high she was in danger of tripping over her own two feet, Ruth walked out with Mike once again trudging obediently in her wake.

There was a startled silence. Teri felt like weeping; she'd known something like this would happen, although she'd suspected Christie rather than her mother would cause the scene.

"Are you going to leave, too?" Teri turned to ask her sister.

"No." Christie hiccuped. It was obvious that she'd already had too much to drink. A glint of admiration shone in her eyes. "I've never seen you stand up to Mom that way," she muttered. "I wish I had the guts to do that."

Teri blinked, hardly able to believe what she'd just heard. She'd actually confronted their mother any number of times. Apparently Christie hadn't been around to witness it—probably too busy dating one of Teri's old boyfriends.

"We should all sit down and eat," Johnny said after a moment. "It'd be a shame to let a perfectly good dinner go to waste."

"I agree," Bobby said.

To her surprise, the meal went smoothly. Without complaint, Christie switched from beer to tap water. The two of them talked in an unusually friendly fashion. Comfortable with each other, Johnny and Bobby chatted about chess, cars and *Star Trek.* Bobby was polite toward

Christie but conveyed in unmistakable terms that he wouldn't be swayed by her many charms.

"Would anyone like dessert?" Teri asked, her mood hovering close to joyous. She'd always known that she'd married a wonderful man, but he was even more wonderful than she'd realized. Every time she thought about the matter-of-fact way he'd delivered her mother's purse to the front door, it warmed her heart. Bobby wasn't about to let anyone insult his wife. He hadn't spoken a single word, but his message was clear. She couldn't wait to show him her love and gratitude, and from the gleam in his eyes, Bobby knew exactly how she intended to do that.

Christie must have noticed the look they'd shared because she followed Teri into the kitchen. "He loves you," she murmured.

"He does." Teri started to load the plates into the dishwasher. "No man's ever loved me like that."

"Where'd you meet him?"

"Not in a bar," Teri said pointedly.

"I thought you'd say that." Christie rinsed off the dishes and handed them to Teri.

Teri couldn't remember ever working side by side with her sister before. Not as an adult, at any rate.

"He's a decent guy, you know," Christie said thoughtfully. "I'm not likely to meet someone like him."

Teri had to agree that she'd been fortunate. "Don't be so sure," she told her sister. "Think positive."

Christie snickered. "A lot of good that'll do me."

Teri made a pot of coffee while Christie sliced the homemade coconut cake. Together they carried dessert into the dining room.

Half an hour later, Johnny prepared to leave for Seattle.

He hugged both of his sisters and as he walked out, he gave Teri a thumbs-up.

"We'll drive you home," Bobby said when Christie told them it was time for her to leave as well.

"Oh, no, I'm fine," Christie insisted. "I'll walk."

Bobby wouldn't hear of it. "James is outside waiting."

"James?" Christie asked, glancing at Teri for an answer.

"James Wilbur, Bobby's personal driver."

"Oh." Christie struggled with little success to hide a smile. "I guess that would be all right."

Teri and Bobby escorted her to the vehicle. James, looking distinguished as usual, stood by the passenger door, waiting to open it for her.

"La-di-da," Christie said, clearly impressed. She inclined her head. "Thank you, James." Giggling, she gestured regally. "Home, James."

Without cracking a smile, James held the door and Christie slid inside. As soon as she was seated, she lowered the tinted window. "Wow, this is really something." She sounded about ten years old, and Teri was touched by this glimpse of a more innocent Christie.

"Come and visit us again," Bobby said.

"I will," Christie promised. Then, with an exaggerated flourish, she pressed the button to raise the window.

When James pulled onto the drive, Teri leaned against her husband. "That was nice of you."

"Yes."

It was just like him to acknowledge his own generosity. But then—why shouldn't he? "So," she said. "What do you think of my family?"

"I like Johnny."

"I know."

"And Christie."

Her defenses immediately went on alert. "You…like… Christie?"

"I do, but it's you I *love.*"

"Excellent answer, Mr. Polgar."

Bobby chuckled. "I'm tired. Let's go to bed."

Teri knew it wasn't sleeping he had in mind. "It's too early."

"No, it isn't," he said. "In fact, it's two or three hours later than I would've liked."

Oh, yes, Teri Polgar loved her husband. At least as much as he loved her….

Seven

Grace Sherman Harding cradled the sleeping infant in her arms. The overwhelming love she felt for this tiny being was almost more than a single heart could hold. This was her new grandson: Drake Joseph Bowman. She smiled; that was quite a handle for such a small baby.

She'd experienced the same sense of wonder when she'd held Tyler and Katie as newborns.

"Is he still sleeping?" Maryellen asked, bringing two glasses of lemonade into the living room.

"Oh, Maryellen, he's so precious." This had been a difficult pregnancy for her daughter. Maryellen had spent the last five months bedridden. Both Grace and Cliff had done what they could to help, but it wasn't enough. Thankfully, Jon's parents had come from Oregon and were able to visit every day; otherwise, Grace didn't know how Maryellen and Jon would've managed. Not with a three-year-old underfoot and Jon working all hours to support his family.

"Drake was worth every second of discomfort," Maryellen said.

"How's Katie doing?" Grace asked.

Maryellen sat down on the sofa opposite Grace's chair. "She's enthralled with being a big sister. Jon and I were afraid she'd show signs of jealousy. But so far, she hasn't."

"Good." The baby's eyes fluttered open and he stared up at Grace. Some might say she was imagining things, but she was sure he'd smiled at her. Grace smiled back. "Hello, handsome boy."

"I see he's awake and I'll bet he's hungry," Maryellen said. "He probably needs a diaper change, too." She reached for her son, and Grace watched as Maryellen changed him out of a soggy diaper into a fresh one.

"How's Kelly doing?" Maryellen asked when she'd finished.

Grace's younger daughter was due in the next two weeks.

"She envies you," Grace said wryly. "She's definitely ready for this baby to be born."

"The last two weeks of this pregnancy were the longest of my life," Maryellen said as she nestled her son to her breast.

It was a joy to see her daughter this content. Suddenly Grace felt an intense sadness that took her completely by surprise. Dan was missing so much. Her first husband had been dead for six years now. After his disappearance, Grace had met Cliff Harding; once Dan's body was recovered—with his suicide note—she'd allowed herself to find happiness in loving Cliff. Earlier that year, she'd finally married him.

When Dan had first gone missing, Grace had been sure she'd never feel contentment again. She didn't sleep, didn't eat and was scarcely able to function. Only recently had she begun to understand the kinds of demons that had

chased her husband and compelled him into such a drastic solution.

Kelly had always been close to her father, and his disappearance had been hardest on her. She'd been pregnant with Tyler at the time, utterly convinced her father would return for the birth of his first grandchild. Until the very end, Kelly had believed Dan would have a perfectly rational explanation for disappearing.

"Mom?" Maryellen said. "Is something wrong?"

Grace smiled despite her sadness. "I was thinking about your father and how proud he would've been of his grandchildren."

Maryellen looked away and, when she turned back, her eyes brimmed with tears. "I think about Dad a lot. I miss him. I didn't expect I would.... I was so furious with him for what he did. Now...now I'm not. I just feel so sad for him and what he's missing."

Grace leaned forward. "I miss him, too. We'll never fully understand why he chose suicide, and there's no point in trying to find a logical reason. He wasn't himself." And hadn't been for years, she thought but didn't say.

"I know."

Grace heard sounds from upstairs indicating that Katie had awakened from her nap. "I'll get her," she told Maryellen, wiping the tears from her own cheeks as she walked up the stairs to collect her granddaughter.

Still tired and a little cranky, Katie crawled into her grandmother's arms and pressed her cheek against Grace's shoulder. Moving carefully on the steps, Grace carried her granddaughter back to the living room. She settled down on the sofa again and held Katie close.

"I heard the art gallery isn't doing so well," Maryellen

said. She met her mother's gaze. "Lois phoned the other day and said sales are way down."

Lois Habbersmith had taken over as manager when Maryellen had to quit. Grace knew that Maryellen had always had reservations about Lois's ability to cope with the job's responsibilities. Her daughter's instincts had proved to be right. Lois was overwhelmed, and the gallery seemed to be suffering. Grace hated to see all of Maryellen's hard work erode.

It was at the gallery that her daughter had met Jon Bowman. What a blessing he'd been to Maryellen—to the whole family.

"There's talk that the gallery might have to close," Maryellen murmured. Grace recognized frustration as well as sadness in her daughter's voice.

"That would be a real pity."

"I think so, too, but I can't go back to work." Maryellen sighed. "I'd like to, but it's impossible. Besides, I'm managing Jon's career now. With two children under four, plus getting Jon's photographs out to the various agents, I have all I can deal with."

"I know," her mother said. "The gallery's not your obligation anymore."

"It's just that I put so much time and energy into the place," Maryellen said regretfully. "It really bothers me to see it failing. I'm positive that, given half a chance, it could be profitable again."

Grace believed that, too. None of the artists her daughter had worked with depended on income from The Harbor Street Gallery as their sole support. But sales there had supplemented many of the local artists' revenue, including Jon's.

Katie squirmed down from her lap, and Grace took her into the kitchen to let the little girl choose her own afternoon snack. Katie decided on a graham cracker and juice.

When she returned, Maryellen had finished nursing Drake. "Olivia came by yesterday with a gift for the baby."

Olivia and Grace had been best friends nearly their entire lives. Before Grace could comment, her daughter continued. "She said something interesting." Maryellen studied her closely.

Grace had a feeling she already knew what this was about. "Does it have to do with Will Jefferson?"

Maryellen nodded.

Slowly expelling her breath, Grace sat down. Will was Olivia's older brother. In high school Grace had a huge crush on Will, but he'd hardly known she was alive. He'd gone off to college, married and moved to Atlanta. She'd married Dan and stayed in Cedar Cove.

Decades later, after Dan's death, Will had contacted Grace to tell her how sorry he was. Their e-mail relationship had started out innocently enough. Then it turned into an affair in every sense but the physical—and that would've happened within a matter of weeks. Grace wasn't blameless by any means; she knew Will was married. He'd lied, though, and said he was divorcing his wife, Georgia. Because she so badly wanted to believe him, she'd agreed to meet him in New Orleans, where they planned to share a hotel room. She was mortified when she'd learned, quite by accident, that Will had no intention of leaving his wife—for her or for any other reason. Fortunately, she'd found out before she went to Louisiana.

That betrayal had nearly destroyed Grace's relationship

with Cliff Harding. Over time, he'd forgiven her for the pain she'd brought him. Now she considered herself the luckiest woman in the world to be his wife.

"Olivia told me he's divorced—and that he's moving back to Cedar Cove," Maryellen said, still studying Grace.

"I heard he might do that," she said through numb lips.

"Why *now?*" Maryellen demanded.

Grace could only shrug. Apparently, seeing other women was nothing new to Olivia's brother. Grace wasn't his first indiscretion and she wasn't his last. Finally Georgia had had enough and filed for divorce. Now, after nearly forty years of marriage, she wanted out.

"You aren't going to see him, are you?" Maryellen asked.

Grace shook her head adamantly. "Not if I can help it." In fact, she intended to do whatever she could to avoid Will Jefferson. The problem was, he hadn't taken her rejection lightly.

He'd come to Cedar Cove once before, hoping to talk his way around his lies and her objections. There'd been an ugly incident, and Cliff had become involved. Just remembering it made Grace want to bury her face in her hands. Until Will had reentered her life, she hadn't realized how quickly she could lower her principles or how stupid she could be when it came to love. Or, more accurately, infatuation.

"Does Cliff know?"

Grace shook her head again. She should tell him. That went without saying, but even while she acknowledged it, Grace told herself she wasn't quite ready. She'd do it, of course. Just not yet. The time wasn't right.

Getting past how she'd misled Cliff—no, how she'd lied to him—had been a major hurdle in their relationship.

Unfortunately, his first wife had cheated on him, so Cliff recognized all the signs. He'd heard the excuses. This was a path he wasn't walking twice. It'd taken Grace months to prove herself to him. Now she was unwilling to put her marriage at risk over a man who meant absolutely nothing to her. His lies had destroyed any feeling she'd had.

The sound of a car coming into the driveway interrupted her thoughts.

"Daddy's home," Maryellen announced for Katie's benefit.

Scrambling out of her chair, Katie ran toward the door, her face lit up with joy. "Daddy, Daddy!"

Jon entered the house and swept the three-year-old into his embrace. With her arms wrapped tightly around his neck, Katie smeared kisses across her father's cheek.

"How are my girls doing?" Jon asked.

Maryellen looked up at him and smiled. "Your son might take exception to being called a girl."

"Oops," Jon said and, leaning down, he kissed the baby's head. "I keep forgetting about you." He chuckled at his own joke.

Maryellen gazed at the baby, gurgling contentedly in her arms. "Let's remind him around two this morning, shall we, Drake?"

"Hi, Grace." Jon greeted her with a lazy grin. "Good to see you."

"You, too."

"Did my parents come by?" Jon asked as he walked over to the kitchen counter and sorted through the mail.

"This morning," Maryellen told him. "They decided to stay in town until the end of the month."

He nodded.

"Daddy, Daddy, come see." Katie grabbed her father's hand, pulling him toward the puzzle she'd completed before her nap.

Seeing that the young family was busy, Grace decided to leave. She put a casserole in the oven, then said her farewells and kissed both her grandchildren.

By the time she pulled into the yard at her home with Cliff in nearby Olalla, she still hadn't decided what she should do about Will Jefferson. Sooner or later her husband would learn that Will was retiring in Cedar Cove. If she mentioned the fact, it might place more significance on the event than warranted. She didn't care where Will Jefferson chose to live. He could take up residence on Mars if he wanted to.

But by the same token, *not* telling Cliff might make it seem significant in a different way—as if she had something to hide.

When Cliff heard her car, he came out of the barn, smiling. Buttercup, her golden retriever, wandered over from her perch on the front steps, plumy tail wagging.

Her husband opened the car door for her. "Welcome home," he said.

Grace slipped her arms around his middle and kissed him warmly. When they broke contact, Cliff leaned his head back. "Wow! What did I do to deserve this?"

"Nothing out of the ordinary."

Arm in arm, they strolled toward the house. "You're late," he said casually.

"I went to see Maryellen after work."

"Ah."

"Missed me, did you?" she asked with a teasing smile.

Grace suddenly realized that if she told Cliff about Will, he'd suspect she was with the other man anytime she was late. She *couldn't* bring herself to tell him. And yet… Eventually he'd find out. What then?

Eight

Troy Davis walked into the house and dejectedly tossed the mail on the kitchen counter. He hadn't even bothered to look at it. He already knew it was nothing but junk with a couple of bills thrown in. Just like it always was. He felt bored, depressed, lonely. In fact, he was downright *crumpy,* a word Sandy had invented—*grumpy* plus *cranky*—to describe him when he was feeling low. Whenever she'd said it, he'd had to smile.

Sandy. He missed her, missed her so much.

Although she'd been in the nursing home for two years, he'd gone there almost every day after work and weekends, too. The nursing home had become an extension of his own home and, apart from his job, visiting Sandy was his routine, his life. Now that she was gone he had time on his hands. Time he didn't know how to fill.

Turning on the television, he sat in his favorite chair and watched ten minutes of a Seattle news broadcast. There had to be more to life than this…this emptiness. Because Sandy had required so much of his time, he'd never developed hobbies. He supposed he could now, but he couldn't think

of a single thing that interested him enough to devote his efforts and resources to. This didn't bode well for retirement.

Restless, he got up and wandered into the kitchen. He'd been preparing his own meals for years now. Generally he picked up something easy at the grocery store or got takeout from a fast-food place. He'd learned basic cooking skills and mastered the microwave. He could barbecue a steak, nuke a potato and pour salad dressing over lettuce with the best of 'em. Nothing fancy, though.

His stomach growled, reminding him that he should eat. But even the thought of a T-bone steak didn't excite him. With no energy and no inspiration, he opened the bread drawer and pulled out the peanut butter and jelly. The bread was relatively fresh, and the peanut butter would provide some protein—something Sandy constantly used to harp on. Good enough. He'd make do with a sandwich.

Sandy would be horrified to see him eating over the kitchen sink. But that way, if the jelly dripped, he didn't have to worry about wiping off the counter.

His wife had been a real stickler about sitting down for meals. He felt guilty as he wolfed down his dinner staring out the window into the backyard. When he'd finished, he chased the sandwich with a glass of milk. It smelled a little sour and he should probably check the expiry date. On second thought, better just to empty the rest of it down the drain.

Moving to the counter, he flipped up the lid of the garbage can—the "circular file," as Sandy used to joke—and started sorting through the mail. As he'd suspected, the top three pieces were advertisements. Without reading any of the chance-of-a-lifetime offers, he flicked them

into the garbage. The fourth piece was the water bill and the fifth was a card. Probably a belated sympathy card. They were still trickling in.

The return address read Seattle, but *F. Beckwith* wasn't a name he recognized. A friend of Sandy's? He stared at it for a moment and set it aside while he looked through the last few pieces. Then he picked up the envelope, tore it open and removed the card. His gaze immediately went to the signature.

Faith Beckwith.

Faith Beckwith? Troy didn't know anyone named Beckwith. He'd known a Faith, but that was years ago. He glanced at the opposite side of the card and read,

Dear Troy,

I was so sorry to hear about your wife. How very special she must have been. I've almost forgiven her for stealing you away from me.

My husband died three years ago and I truly understand how difficult the adjustment can be.

Faith Beckwith was the married name of Faith Carroll, his high-school sweetheart. Faith had mailed him a sympathy card? He smiled and almost before he could rationalize what he was doing, Troy reached for the phone. Directory assistance gave him the Seattle number he sought and without hesitation he dialed it.

Not until it began to ring did he consider what he should say. He'd never been an impulsive man. But he didn't need to think about what he was doing. Instinctively he knew this was right.

"Hello," a soft female voice answered.

"Faith, this is Troy Davis."

The line went silent, and Troy felt her shock.

"Troy, my heavens, is it really you?"

She sounded exactly the same as she had when they were high-school seniors. Back then, they'd talked on the phone for hours nearly every night. They'd been in love. The summer after their graduation, he'd gone into the service. Faith had seen him off with kisses and tears, promising to write every day, and in the beginning she had.

Then the correspondence had abruptly stopped. He still had no idea what had gone wrong. Soon afterward, a friend told him Faith was dating someone else. It'd hurt, the way she'd handled their breakup, but that was easy to forgive now. They'd both been so young. Besides, Troy wouldn't have married Sandy if Faith hadn't severed their relationship. And he couldn't imagine his life without Sandy….

"I got your sympathy card," he said, explaining the reason for his call. "How did you know?"

"My son lives in Cedar Cove," Faith said. "I was visiting him and the grandkids, and I saw the *Chronicle*. I always read the obituaries and…"

"That's where you read about Sandy?"

"It is. I'm really sorry about your loss, Troy. I wasn't sure you'd want to hear from me. That's why I didn't mail the card right away."

Troy didn't know what else to say until he glanced down at the sympathy card and reread her short message. "What did you mean when you said Sandy stole me away?" His memory of their breakup was quite the opposite. Faith had dumped him.

Her laugh drifted over the phone. “Come on, Troy. You have to know you broke my heart.”

“What?” He shook his head in bewilderment. She couldn’t have forgotten the callous way *she’d* treated *him.* “As I recall, you’re the one who broke up with me.”

There was a silence. “How can you say that?” she said. “You quit writing to me.”

“I most certainly did not,” he returned. He’d always wondered what had happened and wasn’t too proud to admit she’d hurt him badly. But none of that was important anymore. Hadn’t been in years.

“Hold on,” Faith said. “One of us seems to have developed a selective memory.”

“That’s what I was thinking.” Strangely, Troy found he was enjoying this. He knew beyond a doubt that the selective memory was Faith’s—but he was willing to forgive her.

“Yes,” she said, “and it’s not me.”

“Well, then,” he said, “let’s review the events of that summer.”

“Good idea,” she concurred. “Practically as soon as we graduated from high school, you went into basic training.”

“Right.” Troy was with her so far. “I remember clearly that you promised me your undying love when we said goodbye.”

“I did and I meant it.” She spoke without hesitation. “I wrote you every single day.”

“In the beginning.” He’d lived for Faith’s letters, and when she’d stopped writing he hadn’t known what to think.

“Every day,” she reiterated, “and then you stopped writing.”

“Me?”

"Yes, you."

Troy grew quiet. "I didn't stop writing you, Faith."

"I didn't stop writing you, either."

"I phoned," he said, "and your mother said you were out. Later, someone else told me you were seeing some other guy. I got the message."

"I didn't date anyone other than you until after I left for college that September."

The silence seemed to hum between them.

"My mother," she breathed slowly. "My mother was the one who took out the mail every day and collected it, too."

"She didn't like me?" Troy couldn't remember Mrs. Carroll being particularly hostile toward him.

"She liked you fine, but she thought we were too young to be serious," Faith said. "I made the mistake of telling her I hoped you'd give me an engagement ring for Christmas."

The irony was, Troy had planned on doing exactly that.

"You mean to say you believed I'd just stopped writing?" Faith asked. "Without saying a word? You honestly believed I'd do that to you?"

"Well, yes," Troy admitted. "Just like you believed I'd given up sending *you* letters."

She hesitated, then reluctantly agreed. "Did you try to get in touch with me when you finished basic training?" she asked. "You came home on leave, didn't you?"

"Of course I did," Troy told her. "I went to your house—that was in late August—but by then you'd already left for college. I wanted to talk to you, but when I asked for your new address, your mother said it was probably best not to contact you."

"My mother," Faith groaned. "I never suspected she'd do anything like that."

"I didn't, either."

They both seemed at a loss as to what to say next.

Finally she whispered, "You broke my heart."

He hadn't come out of the relationship unscathed, either. "You broke mine," he told her.

Faith exhaled softly, then said, "It seems my mother has a great deal to answer for."

"Is she still alive?" Troy didn't figure there was much point in dwelling on the sins of the past.

"No. She died ten years ago."

"Despite everything, our lives worked out well, didn't they?" he said. "Maybe not the way we expected, but…"

"Yes," Faith said. "I met Carl at Central Washington and we got married in 1970."

Funny little coincidences. "Sandy and I were married the same year. In June."

"What day?"

"The twenty-third. What about you?"

"The twenty-third."

This was too weird. They'd each been married on the same day and in the same year—to someone else.

"Children?" he asked.

"Two—a boy, Scott, and a girl, Jay Lynn. Scottie lives in Cedar Cove, like I said, and teaches at the high school. Jay Lynn's married and the mother of two. She's currently a stay-at-home mom. What about you?"

"One daughter, Megan. She works at the framing shop down by the waterfront."

"Oh, my goodness! Scottie just had her frame a picture I gave him of his great-grandparents. It was taken in the 1930s on the family farm in Kansas."

Their lives had intersected more than once. And in the

last few years, she'd visited town to see her family; they could have run into each other at any time, yet never had.

"So you're the sheriff these days," Faith said.

"Yeah, Cedar Cove's always been my home. I never wanted to live anywhere else. There aren't that many of us from our graduating class around anymore."

"I heard about Dan Sherman's death," Faith told him. "Poor Grace. Scottie called me when his body was discovered."

"That was a rough one," Troy said. He knew Dan but they'd never been close friends. "Grace is remarried—to a local rancher." He paused. "You'd like Cliff. He's a down-to-earth, no-nonsense kind of guy."

"What about Olivia?"

As he recalled, Faith and Olivia had been fairly good friends in high school.

"I always meant to keep in touch with Olivia, but life sort of crowded in."

"Olivia married a guy called Stan Lockhart when she graduated from college. They were divorced the year their son died."

"I knew she'd become a judge but I hadn't heard that she'd lost a child. Or that her marriage broke up."

"It all happened more than twenty years ago now. You never attended any of the class reunions, did you?" He should know; he'd been to every one.

"No. What about you?"

"Unfortunately, yes." Troy would've preferred to avoid them, but it was hard since he lived in town. And he'd been one of the senior class officers, so people expected him to plan the event. Against his will, he'd done it for most of the reunions, thanks mainly to Sandy and her organiza-

tional skills. His daughter had helped with the last reunion. He'd rather have stayed home.

"You were going to be a nurse, weren't you?"

"I was…am," she said, correcting herself. "Although I don't work in the medical field now. I burned out about ten years ago." She hesitated, as if uncertain she should continue. "I write a little but it's no big deal. Articles about health, that sort of thing."

"Really? I'm impressed." Troy had never been good at putting his thoughts on paper. Other than crime reports, of course, and that was a matter of getting the facts and stating them clearly.

"Don't be. I dabble at it." He could almost see her shrug. "I guess it's a way to use some of my medical background."

They chatted for another few minutes and then there didn't seem to be anything more to say. Troy searched for something to keep Faith on the line. All he knew was that he didn't want to break the connection for fear it would be half a lifetime before they spoke again. If ever…

"How often do you get to Cedar Cove these days?"

"Not a lot. But Scottie's been encouraging me to move back to town and I'm considering it." She paused. "Why do you ask?"

"I was thinking," he said, shifting uncomfortably on his feet, "that we could get together the next time you do."

"Okay," she said immediately.

"We could have coffee and pie at the Pancake Palace." They used to go there on dates, only it'd been a soda and fries.

"Not Coke and French fries?"

"You remember that, too?" he asked.

"Of course I do. We always shared both. I liked more salt than you did."

"Do you know when you'll be in town?" he pressed.

"I could come next Saturday," she said, "if that's convenient."

It *was* convenient. In fact, it couldn't have been better.

Nine

This was the last day of Anson Butler's two-week leave from army training. In the morning he'd be flying to the east coast for advanced study in computer technology, working with army intelligence. Allison Cox was proud of him, proud of his success and determination. And she dreaded not being able to see him for another eight weeks.

Her parents had been wonderful to him. Together, as a family, they were sending Anson off with a big barbecue dinner. Even Eddie, her annoying younger brother, had helped decorate the patio with streamers and balloons. All their friends from school would be there, even the ones who'd believed Anson had been responsible for the fire that burned down The Lighthouse restaurant. He'd forgiven them, and if Anson could, then so could she.

Allison had baked a cake that afternoon and was putting the finishing touches on it—smoothing out the chocolate frosting, adding candied flowers. After that, she'd go and pick up Anson at his mother's place.

"You invited Mrs. Butler, didn't you?" her mother asked.

Allison nodded, although she knew even before issuing the invitation that Cherry Butler would refuse. The truth was, she'd never been much of a mother. "Cherry said she'd think about it." Allison would definitely prefer it if his mother decided not to come. Cherry's presence would be uncomfortable and, especially if she drank, she was almost guaranteed to embarrass her son.

The kitchen door opened and her father came in from the garage. "Looks like there's a party going on here," he teased.

"How'd it go with Allan Harris?" her mother asked, referring to a local attorney who'd asked to meet with him, despite the fact that this was Sunday afternoon.

Allison's parents exchanged a brief kiss.

Her father started to loosen his tie. "Martha Evans died last night."

Her mother's face went soft with sympathy. "I'm sorry to hear that."

"Rosie, she was more than ninety years old and ready to go."

"You're the executor of her estate?"

Zach nodded. "Allan asked me to notify Martha's family, none of whom live in town. They'll be making the funeral arrangements."

Allison watched as her father sighed. "Martha's lived on her own all these years. Pastor Flemming's the one who found her body. He'd been going over there once or twice a week to check on her."

"He's a good man."

Allison liked Pastor Flemming, too. Everyone did.

"Charlotte Rhodes has offered to organize the wake."

"When will Martha's family—"

Her mother didn't get a chance to finish the question before Eddie shouted through the open sliding glass door. "Should I light the barbecue?"

"Not yet," Zach answered. "I want to change clothes first."

"Eddie!" Allison cried, irritated by her brother's impatience. "I haven't even gone to pick up Anson yet."

"All right, all right. I was just trying to help."

"We appreciate that, Eddie," Rosie said, mixing chopped green pepper and tomatoes into the lettuce greens. She turned to Allison. "Perhaps you should drive to Anson's now."

"In a minute," Allison said, arranging tiny silver pearls on the border of Anson's cake.

"Be sure and let his mother know she's welcome to join us."

"I will," Allison promised. With a last critical look at the cake, she collected her purse and the car keys and headed out the door.

Anson's mother lived in a trailer court off Lighthouse Road. Allison remembered the first time she'd met Cherry Butler, who'd been if not hostile, certainly unwelcoming. Even she—his *mother*—had believed Anson was responsible for the fire.

Anson's disappearance had been difficult for Allison. She hadn't known where he was, whether he was safe, what he was doing. To learn that he'd enlisted in the army—well, that had come as a complete shock.

Allison pulled into the trailer park, following the dirt road to the last single-wide trailer at the back of the lot. When Anson didn't step outside after a minute or so, she turned off the engine and climbed out.

Before she could walk up the three steps, the door opened and Cherry Butler stood in the entrance. She wore a short skirt and a skin-tight sweater. Her hair had been dyed coal-black. Leaning against the door jamb, she held a cigarette loosely in one hand and glared at Allison. Slowly she raised her cigarette to her crimson lips and inhaled.

"Anson's not here," she announced when she'd finished blowing the smoke upward.

"Oh."

"Don't look so worried." Cherry seemed to enjoy her discomfort. "He's with Shaw. He should be back any minute."

Shaw was one of Anson's best friends and her friend, too, and she realized that Anson would want some private time with his buddy before he left.

"He did it for you, you know." Cherry puffed at her cigarette again. "I didn't want my son in the military. He knows that. Some recruiter fed him a crock and he believed it. Now see what's happened."

"Anson told me he liked the military."

"Sure he does. You'd like it, too, if you could hide away all safe and sound while the police are searching for you."

Allison stared up at his mother and wished she knew what to say. A moment passed in awkward silence.

Then, gathering her courage, Allison resolved to speak her mind. "You're Anson's mother." She took a step closer. "You should be *proud* of him, Mrs. Butler—"

"Didn't I tell you the first time you came by that I ain't never been a Mrs. Anybody?"

"Ms. Butler." Allison tried again. "I meant what I said.

Anson's the only one in his basic training class who was selected for this specialized course. He's smart and... and...I love him. You might think eighteen's too young to understand about love, but I know what my heart feels."

Cherry Butler exhaled a thin line of smoke. "Listen, Abby."

"Allison!"

"Whatever. You just pine your little heart out for my son all you want. He's leaving, and my guess is he'll find some other girl soon enough. Men are like that, so do yourself a favor and forget about my son."

"Forget Anson," Allison repeated incredulously. "I could *never* do that."

Cherry laughed. "Suit yourself. But take my word for it—he'll break your heart. He's no different from any other man. Look at me. I was such an idiot, I actually thought his father would marry me when I told him I was pregnant." She paused to take another drag on her cigarette. "Couldn't do it, though, 'cause he already had a wife."

"Anson isn't like that."

"Believe what you want." She shrugged carelessly. "One thing I'll say about Anson. He's got his daddy's brains. Sure as hell didn't get 'em from me."

Allison badly wanted this evening to be special for Anson. She took a deep breath. "It would mean a great deal to Anson if you'd come to the party." She loved Anson, so she was willing to put aside her own preferences. If, despite everything, he wanted his mother there—and he did—Allison would try to persuade her.

"Party, is it?" She cocked her eyebrows as she flicked the lit cigarette onto the dirt road.

"A farewell party," she elaborated.

Cherry shook her head. "You won't need me for that."

"Anson would like you there," she said. "Please, Mrs.—Cherry."

Again his mother declined, shaking her head. "I got things to do."

"What could be more important than sending Anson off to his new course?" she asked, not understanding how his mother could feel so little pride or concern.

Allison glanced up as a car came toward the trailer, leaving behind a trail of dust. She recognized Shaw's old Chevy Malibu. He dropped Anson off, waved to Allison, and pulled out again. They'd see him later at the party.

"Sorry I'm late," Anson said, smiling at Allison and then his mother.

"I was just inviting your mother to join us," Allison said pointedly.

"And I was just telling your girlfriend I got better things to do than go to some rich man's house and make nice."

"It won't hurt my feelings if you'd rather stay here," Anson said, not meeting his mother's eyes.

"I didn't figure it would," Cherry told him.

Allison felt him stiffen at that response. Then he turned deliberately away. "Come on, Allison, let's get out of here."

"Bye-bye," Cherry said with a flippant wave. She moved inside the trailer and pulled the door shut.

As soon as his mother was gone, Anson cast Allison an apologetic look. "How long did I keep you waiting?"

"A couple of minutes, that's all."

"Did she get on your case?"

"About what?"

"Me and the military."

Allison shrugged. "Not really."

Anson released his breath. "She blames you."

Allison wasn't worried. Cherry could blame her, for all she cared.

"The military's my way out, Allison," he said as if he needed to explain his motivation. "Without it I wouldn't have a chance of getting an education. Cherry doesn't seem to grasp that."

"I know." Anxious to leave now, she tugged at Anson's hand. "Come on, let's go."

They both climbed into the car and Allison left the trailer park. She drove cautiously to avoid the kids and dogs playing in the dusty roads.

"Is your family expecting us right away?" Anson asked.

"I...I suppose. Why?"

He sent her a quick, secretive smile. "Can we go to the waterfront for a moment?"

"Sure. Anywhere in particular?"

A slow, happy grin spread across his face. "Somewhere private."

Allison did take her eyes off the road then. She knew a good place down Lighthouse Road and went in that direction. The tide was out, so she pulled onto a stony area near the beach, glancing around to make sure it was as deserted as she'd expected it to be.

There was no one around.

Anson got out of the car and Allison did, too. When he joined her, he took her hand; together they walked the

short distance to the water. A log had drifted up onto the shore and they stepped over it, making their way along the pebble beach. A pair of long-legged herons waded in the shallow water and seagulls cawed overhead.

"I'm sorry you had to wait for me," Anson said again. "I know what my mother's like."

"It's okay." Allison didn't want to waste their last day discussing his mother.

"I planned to be back sooner, but I needed Shaw to take me someplace."

Anson reached inside his pocket and removed a small jeweler's box, which he flipped open. Inside was a silver ring with a single blue stone. A sapphire, Allison guessed.

Anson stared down at it and then at her. "I wanted to give you this before I left."

Her throat instantly clogged with tears. "Oh, Anson."

"I want you to have something from me to wear so you won't forget me."

"Anson, there's no chance of that! I won't forget you." She hadn't before and she wouldn't now. She'd meant what she'd told his mother; she loved Anson.

"You're going off to college. You'll be surrounded by all those smart, good-looking guys."

She would've laughed if her tears hadn't made it impossible. "Haven't you figured out yet that you're the only guy I care about?" She managed a brief smile. "And, Anson? You're smarter and better-looking than any of them."

He looked up then, his eyes warm with love. "I adore you, Allison. You're my whole world. I don't know what I would've done without you these last few months. You were all that got me through basic training." He held out the small velvet box. "May I put this on you now?"

She gave him her hand and he slid the ring on her finger. "It fits," he said, sighing with relief. "This ring is a promise from me to you that I won't even look at another girl while I'm away."

"I promise I won't date anyone else, either." She stretched out her hand, turning it this way and that. "The ring is beautiful, Anson. My favorite color. It's *perfect.*"

"I had to guess at the size."

Allison threw her arms around him. "I love you." They clung to each other for a long moment. When he kissed her, she felt as if she'd spun off into some new galaxy, unknown to anyone but them. It was hard to break away from him, hard to remember that they were in full view of the road and anyone who happened to drive by.

"Thank you, Anson," she said softly, gazing down at her ring again. "This is so thoughtful. It's so *you.*"

"I wish it was the Hope Diamond."

"In my heart it is." Allison would treasure this ring all her life. She didn't want him to go, especially so far from Cedar Cove, but at the same time, she knew this was an unmatched opportunity for him. She wouldn't take it away from Anson for anything.

Anson locked his arms at the small of her back and leaned his forehead against hers. "Wait for me."

Allison nodded. "I'm not going anywhere. I'll always be here for you, Anson. Always."

He kissed her again. They separated reluctantly and, holding hands, walked back to the parked car.

In the morning Anson would be gone.

Ten

When Teri left the mall Tuesday evening after work, she found James waiting for her. Her husband's driver, following Bobby's instructions, drove her to and from the salon; Bobby seemed to think she was safer that way. James stood outside the car near the passenger door, waiting for her. "Good evening, Miss Teri."

"Good evening, James." The minute she'd slipped inside the vehicle, she took off her shoes and rubbed her aching feet. She'd had a lot of clients and hardly any breaks.

"Did you have a good day?" he asked in a solicitous voice.

"Yes, thanks." Generally James wasn't very talkative. For some reason he'd been more sociable the last few days.

"I thought it was commendable of you to invite your family for dinner last weekend."

Well, it'd been an experience, that was for sure. "It's nice of you to say so."

He dutifully closed the car door before walking around

to the driver's side. About halfway home, Teri noticed that James kept glancing at her in the rearview mirror.

"Is something the matter, James?" she asked, finding his behavior curious.

"Wrong, miss?"

"You keep looking at me."

"Sorry, miss, it's just that you and your sister don't resemble each other at all."

Teri snickered. "She's my half sister and she got the beauty while I got the brains." Teri wasn't convinced that was an accurate assessment, but it sounded good.

"She is beautiful," he murmured.

Surprised at the comment, Teri studied him for a moment. It had never occurred to her that James might be romantically interested in her sister. But why not? And why wouldn't Christie be interested in him? He was single, employed and attractive in his own way. A considerable improvement over the men she usually chose.

"James," she said. "Don't take me directly home this evening."

"I beg your pardon, Miss Teri?"

"Take me to my sister's house."

"She lives in an apartment."

"Okay, her apartment then." Teri hadn't been in contact with Christie in quite some time and certainly hadn't visited her current home.

"Should I let Bobby know?"

"No, we'll only be a few minutes."

James sat up a bit straighter. "Whatever you say, miss."

"James, call me Teri."

"Yes, miss."

The drive took a few minutes, so Teri asked James

about her husband. Ever since the threat, he'd hardly left the house. But every day, regular as clockwork, he sat in front of the chessboard. How he could concentrate without men on the board was beyond her, but what did she know?

"How was Bobby's day?" she asked. Teri was more concerned about her husband than she wanted to let on. He'd become withdrawn lately. The fact that he sent his driver to escort her to and from work told her he was almost paranoid about her safety. He hated it whenever she left his sight. Clearly there was more to this threat than she'd known. Bobby knew, though, and he wasn't taking any chances. Teri loved her husband; because of that, she wasn't about to let some goon blackmail him, using her as bait. She needed to find out what was going on and take action.

James didn't respond to her question right away, which implied far more than anything he might have said.

"He stayed in the house all day, Miss Teri."

"Do you know why he hasn't played in any tournaments lately?" she asked, deciding to force the issue.

"No—Teri." He drove into the parking lot of the apartment building on Beach Road and turned off the engine. "Your sister's in the bottom-floor unit, number 102," he told her.

"Thank you, James."

He was out of the car and opening her door before Teri had even managed to unfasten her seat belt, then waited by the vehicle while she walked toward her sister's place. The stretch limo had caught the attention of several residents and half a dozen children came toward James, full of questions.

Christie answered her knock with a soda in her hand. She blinked in astonishment when she saw Teri.

"What are you doing here?" she asked.

Teri shrugged, feeling a bit awkward. "I came by to see how you're doing." That was the truth—or part of it. She genuinely wanted to reestablish a relationship with her sister. She also thought that encouraging a relationship with James could benefit them all.

"You care?"

"I wouldn't be here if I didn't. I'm inviting you to dinner."

Christie eyed her suspiciously. "Again? Aren't you worried that I might hit on your precious Bobby?"

She was and yet she wasn't. She trusted her husband. Of all the women in the world, he'd chosen to fall in love with *her.* Bobby Polgar might be many things but fickle he wasn't, and any fear or jealousy she'd felt had evaporated in the warmth of his love.

Teri grinned. "You can try, but it won't get you anywhere."

Christie straightened when she saw James standing outside the car with kids swarming around him in the parking lot.

Teri noticed her sister's reaction right away. "I'll send James to pick you up tomorrow. Shall we say six?"

"I guess that'd be all right." Christie acted as though she was doing Teri a favor.

James held the car door for Teri when she returned. "I hope you won't mind picking up my sister for dinner tomorrow night," she said.

"Not at all, Miss Teri. It would be my pleasure."

She had the distinct impression that he meant every word.

The rest of the ride to Seaside Avenue took place in

silence. When James let her out, the front door opened immediately and Bobby exploded out.

"You're all right?" he demanded, grabbing Teri by the upper arms. His eyes raked over her as if checking for injury.

"Bobby, of course I'm all right. Why wouldn't I be?"

"You're late."

Instantly Teri felt guilty. She should've phoned or had James call Bobby, as he'd suggested. "I asked James to drive me to Christie's."

There was unmistakable relief in her husband's eyes. He hugged her, holding her close. With her arms around Bobby's neck, Teri looked deep into his eyes. She saw in him such love it made her want to weep—and she saw something else. She saw his fear. Bobby was afraid for her. Afraid someone would take her away from him.

"Let's sit down and talk," she said, leading him into the house.

They both sat on the elegant leather couch, and Teri slid close, leaning her head against his chest. "I need to ask you a question."

"What is it?"

"I need to know why you're keeping a constant watch over me."

He frowned. "So I can be sure you're safe." He seemed to feel that should be obvious.

"I *am* safe, I promise you. But if you've received a threat, then we should deal with it together. We could go to the police or—"

"No!" He shook his head and withdrew his hand from hers.

Something had happened. His body language made

that clear. “Bobby,” she whispered, turning to face him. “You’d better tell me.”

His expression was completely deadpan. He didn’t speak, simply shook his head again.

Teri’s chest tightened and she rose onto her knees, holding his face between her palms. “Bobby, listen to me. I’m your wife and married people communicate with each other. Whatever’s going on, I need to know about it. You should tell me. That’s what married people do.”

He shifted uneasily.

“Ever since that day those two men showed up at Get Nailed, you’ve been acting weird. Something happened and you’re carrying the weight of this problem all by yourself. I have to know what’s bothering you.” When he didn’t respond, she said, “They threatened me, didn’t they?”

He didn’t answer.

“Bobby! I realize you’re trying to protect me and I love you for it, but you’re miserable and because you’re miserable, so am I.”

He still wouldn’t look at her.

“You haven’t played any tournaments in weeks. You were born to play chess. It’s your life.”

“*You’re* my life,” he countered. “Nothing is more important to me than you.”

“I can’t be happy if you aren’t,” she said gently.

Bobby closed his eyes. “Shortly after those men came to see you,” he said in a low voice, “I received a phone call from Aleksandr Vladimir.”

“Who?”

“Vladimir. He’s a Russian chess player. He asked me how you were feeling and then said he hoped you were…safe.”

That was it? "Maybe that's just a Russian way of congratulating you on our marriage," she suggested. "Or of extending his best wishes."

"No." Bobby's eyes hardened. "He was letting me know that he was behind the incident in June—with you and James outside the beauty shop."

"Okay," she returned thoughtfully. "If you feel he was making a threat, veiled or otherwise, then we need to report him to the authorities."

"No!" Bobby clenched and unclenched his fists. "I have no way of connecting him to the threat. No proof. Going to the police would put you in danger. Don't ask me to do that, because I can't." Rarely had she seen him react more vehemently to anything. His emotion, more than his words, told her how heavily this had weighed on his mind.

Before she could attempt to reassure him, Bobby kissed the side of her neck, sending shivers down her arms. "I like you more than chess," he whispered. His fingers slipped inside the opening of her blouse. "Am I communicating well?"

"Yes," she whispered when his hand cupped her breast. "Very well."

"Is there anything else you want to discuss?" Bobby asked after a long pause.

"What are we going to do about this Russian?" she asked, pushing his hands away so she could concentrate.

Bobby didn't reply immediately; he seemed to be assessing his options.

"They're Mafia?" she asked. "Russian Mafia?"

Bobby shrugged and when he spoke he avoided her question. "Vladimir's a good player, one of the best, but I'm better."

In many ways her husband was a humble man, but when it came to chess, he had complete and total faith in his abilities. That unshakable confidence in himself was what she'd found so appealing.

"Vladimir wants you to lose to him," Teri speculated.

Bobby nodded.

"You told him you wouldn't, right?"

At first he didn't respond. Eventually, reluctantly, he explained. "Vladimir implied that if I didn't lose to him, something would happen to you."

The fiery burst of anger that shot through her was overwhelming. Teri blurted out a few words that apparently shocked Bobby. "I won't *let* you lose to him," she insisted furiously.

Bobby's eyes revealed a tortured look. "The thing is, I can't lose. I don't know how to lose. All I know is how to win."

"That's why you've given up tournament play, isn't it?"

His eyes met hers, and he answered with a slight incline of his head. "Vladimir will get what he wants. The longer I resist, the lower my ranking will go. Soon he'll be ahead of me."

While Teri understood his reasoning, she also realized it would never happen. The press was demanding a match between the two men and if he refused, Bobby would look like a coward, a loser. Although he hadn't said so, her husband knew it, too.

Eleven

"Olivia! It's a girl," Grace Harding all but shouted through her cell phone.

"Kelly had the baby?" Olivia sounded groggy, as though she'd been asleep. If so, she was awake fast enough, and seemed as excited as Grace herself. This was one of the great things about having a best friend like Olivia. You could call her at any hour of the day or night. You could share bad news or good, and she'd always know what to say.

"I woke you up. I'm sorry." A quick glance at her watch showed that it was eleven o'clock. Tears of joy made wet tracks down her cheeks. "Kelly phoned at nine to tell me she was in labor. I got here just in time to welcome little Emma Grace into the world."

"Emma Grace," Olivia repeated slowly. "What a lovely name."

"She's gorgeous." Grace couldn't stop talking. "She's got the biggest, bluest eyes and—"

"Meet me at the Pancake Palace," Olivia broke in with a laugh. "We should celebrate."

It wasn't champagne Goldie would be pouring—more like decaf coffee. She'd probably bring them each a slice of coconut cream pie, as well.

For years Olivia and Grace had attended a Wednesday-night aerobics class, followed by coconut pie and coffee. This was tradition. The pie and coffee were their reward for stretching and sweating and leaping up and down. More importantly, Wednesday night was their time to catch up.

Even though they'd seen each other just the night before, it seemed right to share this moment with Olivia, who'd been a constant in her life since grade school.

"I'll be there in half an hour," Grace told her. She felt too keyed up to drive home and try to sleep, anyway. It wasn't every day a woman had a brand-new granddaughter.

The next call she made was to Cliff; she remembered that he was in the barn, so she left a message. Then she phoned Maryellen, who of course already knew, and finally she drove from the birthing center in Silverdale back to Cedar Cove.

Grace's heart soared as she rounded the curving road that edged the Cove. The lights of her hometown welcomed her, and she smiled as she drove past the library and down Harbor Street to the Pancake Palace. This had been their hangout, hers and Olivia's, ever since high school.

Funny, those afternoons didn't seem that long ago.... They were both grandmothers now, but inside they remained the high-school girls they'd been back then, confiding secrets and gossiping about their friends.

The Pancake Palace had changed little in all those

years. The menu was still the same; only the prices had increased. The booths had been reupholstered a number of times, but they were the same red vinyl as they'd been in the days of their youth.

Olivia's car was in the parking lot and Grace could see her through the restaurant window. She was in *their* booth, the very booth where Grace had whispered her dreaded secret when they were high-school seniors. Olivia was the only person who knew Grace was pregnant when they graduated. Grace hadn't found the courage to tell her parents until Dan had said he'd marry her. Then and only then had they broken the news to her family.

"You look far too young to be a grandmother," Olivia said when Grace slid into the upholstered seat across from her.

"Five times over." She had four of her own and was a stepgrandmother to Cliff's granddaughter, April. And yet it wasn't so long ago that she'd despaired of ever becoming a grandmother at all. That was when Maryellen was divorced and seemed to have no intention of marrying a second time. Kelly had wanted children but couldn't conceive.

Now both her daughters were mothers, each with a boy and a girl—a wealth of happiness that overwhelmed Grace whenever she thought about it.

"Tell me everything about Emma Grace," Olivia said.

"She's a beautiful baby," Grace began, "with lots of blond hair, those blue eyes and a scrunched-up red face." She smiled at the memory of holding Emma. "She's got a powerful pair of lungs, too."

Goldie, their favorite waitress, approached the table, carrying a pot of coffee in one hand and two pieces of coconut cream pie in the other.

"Didn't I see you here yesterday?" she asked as she set down the plates. "And it's later than your usual nine-fifteen."

"I'm a grandma again," Grace announced proudly.

"Congratulations!" Goldie poured their coffee. "The pie's on the house, girls." She hurried off to see to another customer, one of the few so late at night.

"How's Kelly doing?" Olivia asked, reaching for her fork.

"Excited. Jubilant."

"That's exactly how you were when you had Maryellen and Kelly."

"And you with Justine and Jordan," Grace reminded her, "and then later with James."

Sadness flashed in Olivia's eyes at the mention of Jordan, the son she'd lost.

"Okay," she said a moment later, rebounding quickly. "Now that both Drake and Emma have made their appearance, it's time."

"Time for what?"

"Time—" Olivia pointed her fork at Grace "—to plan your wedding reception."

Grace instantly felt guilty about putting this off. She'd been so involved with her daughters and the births of the grandchildren that she'd delayed the reception again and again. "It's been so many months now, I don't think—"

"Nonsense," Olivia countered, cutting her off. "Your entire family needs to celebrate. All the grandkids are healthy and happy. And you're married to a wonderful man who adores you." As if she'd suddenly realized Cliff wasn't with them, Olivia sat up and looked around. "Speaking of Cliff…"

"He's at home, or more accurately, in the barn. Sunshine decided to deliver her foal, so Cal and Vicki are both with him. It's Sunshine's first and Cliff wants to be sure everything goes okay."

Olivia smiled softly. "A night of births…"

Grace nodded, feeling emotional. After a sip of coffee, she changed the subject. "Well, we know what my husband's doing. How's yours?"

"Jack's snoring contentedly. The phone didn't even wake him." She shook her head.

"Your Sleeping Beauty," Grace teased.

"Wait—we're mixing up our fairy tales." Olivia laughed. "All I know is that we both ended up with a happily ever after. However long that might be," she added soberly, and Grace knew she was thinking of Jack's heart attack two years earlier.

Grace could only hope he'd truly mended his high-cholesterol, junk-food ways. What she liked best about Jack Griffin, and there was a lot to admire, was the fact that he loved her friend. They were two of the most mismatched people she could imagine. And yet…it worked.

"Set a date for the reception," Olivia urged her. "And I'll help as much as I can."

Grace nodded. Olivia was right; it was time to celebrate her marriage. They were never going to find a date that suited absolutely everyone. That was why they'd gotten married during a library conference Grace was attending in San Francisco. They both had busy lives, and so did their children. But instead of fitting their schedules to everyone else's, they'd simply eloped. It was a spur-of-the-moment decision, and Grace had no regrets.

Except one. She hadn't realized how upset everyone

would be with her and Cliff. Even Olivia felt hurt. Cliff and Grace hadn't meant to exclude anyone; all they'd wanted was to be together as husband and wife. A wedding reception would allow their family and friends to celebrate to their hearts' content.

"How about two months from now? I'll confirm with Cliff and let you know." Grace dug into her pie, savoring the first bite. Coconut was her favorite although it was probably a bad choice from a health point of view. On the other hand, was there a *good* choice when you were talking about pie?

Olivia set down her fork and wrapped one hand around her mug. She stared into her coffee. "I thought you should know. Will's in town. Mom called me this evening."

Grace's heart slowed to a dull, irregular beat. "Oh."

"He showed up at Mom and Ben's earlier today."

"Okay." This wasn't the most intelligent response, but she couldn't come up with anything else to say.

"Where's he staying?" she finally mumbled.

"With Mom and Ben for now." Olivia looked down at the table. "Apparently he's going to look for an apartment."

"You…you didn't mention my house is for rent, did you?"

Olivia's gaze shot to hers. "No way! You mean it's still vacant?"

The house felt like a weight around her neck. A young navy couple, Ian and Cecilia Randall, had rented it on a month-to-month basis; they'd barely moved in when they received word of a transfer to San Diego. The rental property had sat empty for two and a half months.

The rental agent had told her that with the *George*

Washington leaving port, the market was glutted with available properties.

"He isn't planning to rent a house, thankfully."

Grace pushed the pie away, her appetite gone. "If Will knew my house was available…" She didn't finish the thought.

"I'm not going to tell him," Olivia assured her. "And I'm sure Mom won't, either."

Grace leaned her elbows on the table. "My biggest fear is that Will might make trouble between Cliff and me," she confessed.

"I'll admit that's on my mind, too," Olivia said. "Mom doesn't seem to think so, though."

"She's spoken to Will about it?" Charlotte wasn't one to shy away from an uncomfortable subject. Grace was grateful for the older woman's wisdom. Grateful, too, that she'd confronted her son and his sudden need to return to Cedar Cove.

"Mom told me that Will claims he has no intention of pestering you."

Grace hoped that was true. Even after she'd broken off their relationship, Will had attempted to get in touch with her, to explain away his lies and tell her fresh ones. She'd nearly lost Cliff once because of Will; she couldn't risk that happening a second time.

"Does Cliff know?" Olivia asked as if reading her thoughts.

"I've been meaning to tell him, but I haven't done it yet."

"Grace!"

"It's just that we're so happy and I don't want anything to upset that."

"Knowing Cliff, he'd be far more upset if he learned Will's living in Cedar Cove and you didn't tell him."

"I *will* tell him, I promise." She'd do it as soon as she got home. This was too important to leave to chance. She wouldn't jeopardize her marriage over someone as deceitful and dishonorable as Will Jefferson.

They finished their coffee and stood up to go, leaving a bigger than usual tip for Goldie. As they started walking to the door, Olivia gave her a hug. "Congratulations, Grandma."

"Thank you, my friend."

Olivia yawned. "Now let's go home and get to bed. I have to be at work in the morning."

"Me, too." Grace wasn't sure she'd be able to sleep. First, there was the birth of Emma Grace and now this distressing news about Will Jefferson. Olivia had warned her weeks ago, but Grace hadn't believed Will would actually do it. Hadn't believed he'd dare. Yet here he was.

The light in the barn was off when she pulled into the yard and parked in her usual spot. Grace figured Cliff must be in the house. She hoped he hadn't gone to bed.

"Is that you, Grace?" he said, coming to meet her in the entryway, accompanied by the dog.

"It's me." She stooped to pet Buttercup, then walked into her husband's arms. After a lengthy hug, she asked, "How's Sunshine?"

"Fabulous. She has a handsome son and she's doing well. How's Kelly?"

"She has a beautiful daughter and she's doing well, too."

He chuckled and hugged her again. "Little Emma Grace—she couldn't have a nicer name."

Grace smiled. "Olivia and I celebrated with pie and coffee at the Pancake Palace."

"That's what your message said."

"Olivia insisted we set a date for our wedding reception so I suggested mid-October. Is that okay with you?"

"Sure—as long as this is something you want to do."

She nodded. "I want the world to know I've got the best husband in the world."

Cliff kissed the top of her head. "I'm the lucky one."

"You think so, do you?" Try as she might, Grace was unable to stifle a yawn.

Slipping his arm around her waist, Cliff led her down the hallway to their bedroom. "You must be exhausted."

"I thought I'd be too keyed up to sleep, but…"

Cliff yawned, too. "I thought the same thing. Come on, honey, let's go to bed."

She should tell him now, Grace realized. But because they had so much to celebrate, she decided she couldn't. Not then. Perhaps in the morning. Right now they were both too tired. They were happy. To destroy the evening with news of Will Jefferson just seemed wrong.

All she could do was pray that Cliff didn't learn it from anyone else.

Twelve

"Can Rachel take me shopping?" Jolene asked for the sixth time.

"I said that would be fine," Bruce muttered, leafing through the *Cedar Cove Chronicle.* He worked hard at his computer support business and needed this quiet time in the evenings. Just half an hour to regroup; that was all. Since Stephanie's death he'd developed a routine with their daughter. He got home from work, watched the news and read the paper while Jolene entertained herself with a book or a jigsaw puzzle. Afterward they prepared dinner together. Their meals weren't always the meat-and-potatoes variety, either. Some nights it was bacon, eggs and waffles. More than once they'd had cookies and milk with popcorn for dessert, but he didn't make a habit of that.

"You didn't phone her," Jolene whined.

"Why don't you?" he said. She'd called Rachel Pendergast often enough in the past. Rachel had stepped in as a surrogate mother after Stephanie's death and spent many evenings and Saturdays with them both.

At age five, Jolene had decided she needed a mother and she'd chosen Rachel. Bruce smiled as he recalled the day they'd met Rachel at the beauty salon—and how embarrassed he'd been by his daughter's pronouncement. But Bruce gratefully accepted Rachel's involvement in their lives, as long as nothing was required of him. He wasn't interested in a romantic relationship, he told himself again. He was a one-woman man, and Stephanie was that woman. Now that she was gone he had no intention of marrying again. Rachel understood that, although most women didn't. Since he was what people considered prime marriage material, various friends had taken it upon themselves to find him a wife. Bruce had been in more than his share of uncomfortable social situations with women whose objectives were explicit—if not explicitly stated. Sooner or later, they all learned that he wasn't interested.

"I want *you* to phone Rachel," Jolene said.

Bruce lowered the newspaper. "Why?"

"Because then she'll know you approve."

Bruce could see that the peacefulness of the evening was already shattered. Jolene talked to Rachel on a regular basis; the two of them seemed to get together at least once a week for one reason or another. More often now that Lover Boy had departed for San Diego. Nate Olsen was no loss as far as Bruce was concerned, although he hadn't said that to Rachel. She could date whomever she wanted.

"Here." Jolene handed him the portable phone.

"Okay, okay," he muttered. If he was truthful, he'd admit he wasn't opposed to contacting Rachel. He considered her a friend—a good enough friend to be on speed dial.

"Hi," he said when she picked up. "Are you doing anything special this Saturday?"

"What do you have in mind?"

"Jolene needs to go school shopping and she'd like you to take her."

"Count me in."

Bruce grinned at her enthusiasm. He didn't understand this thing about women and shopping. He didn't know a single one who wouldn't leap at the opportunity to dash to a mall. A sale on bedsheets, some kind of giveaway, a makeup demonstration—any excuse would do.

"What's so funny?"

"You women and your shopping."

"Listen, Bruce, you don't want to go there. Men have their own preferences. I'll bet you're sitting in front of the television right now with the remote control on the arm rest. I'll bet you're reading the paper at the same time as you're watching the TV news."

How did she know this much about his evening routine? He supposed it shouldn't surprise him. Rachel had often been to his house over the past few years and he'd been to hers. She was the only woman who'd breached his defenses. Suddenly he wondered if she was right about other men's routines being the same as his. And if she was, how had she found out?

"What do you hear from Lover Boy?" he asked.

"I wish you'd stop calling Nate that," she said, the humor leaving her voice.

"Okay, your Sailor Man," he revised. The truth was, Bruce had never much cared for Rachel's navy boyfriend. For one thing, he couldn't imagine them as a couple. For another, Nate seemed to resent the time Rachel spent with

Jolene. In fact he'd tried on more than one occasion to come between them. So far, that hadn't worked; Rachel wouldn't allow it.

"We talk almost every day. He misses me."

"Do you miss him?" Bruce asked, although he already knew what she'd say.

"Like crazy. I'm going to fly down to California to visit him soon. Or he'll fly up here for a weekend. We're miserable without each other."

Bruce had to bite his tongue to keep from making a sarcastic remark. He wasn't sure why he'd bothered to ask. Thinking about Nate Olsen and Rachel invariably put him in a bad mood, although he refused to delve any further into the reasons for that.

"What's new in town?" Rachel asked, abruptly changing the subject. "You're reading the paper, aren't you? Give me an update."

"All right," he said, looking at the front page. "The school board's bringing a new bond issue to the ballot in September. You'll vote for it, won't you?"

"Of course. Anything else?"

"There's an article here by Jack Griffin about the Harbor Street Art Gallery. Apparently the owners are closing it, at least for the winter months, and maybe for good."

"Oh, no," Rachel murmured. "Maryellen Bowman's going to feel awful about that. She's the one who built it up. A lot of local artists depend on that extra income."

"There's also a short piece about a farewell party for Linnette McAfee," Bruce went on. "Apparently her last day at the Medical Clinic is next week."

"I'm sorry she's moving away," Rachel said. "If anyone should move, it's Cal," she added indignantly.

"Who's Cal?"

She launched into a rather involved explanation of Linnette and Cal Washburn and their relationship, ending with, "He broke her heart and now *she's* leaving town?"

"Why?" That didn't make sense to Bruce, either, but then he was the last person who'd understand the whys and wherefores of a relationship. Rachel explained why *she* thought Linnette had decided to move. It still didn't make sense to him. So Linnette and this Cal broke up. So what? This wasn't junior high. Everyone should be able to coexist and behave like the adults they were.

"Martha Evans's funeral was this week," Rachel said next. "Anything in the paper about that?"

"Who's she?"

"She was an elderly woman. Around ninety. I did her hair for the funeral."

He didn't like thinking about it. "That's something you do?" he asked hesitantly.

"Of course. She was a lovely woman. I'll miss her."

"But why—"

"The funeral home occasionally hires me. And I was very fond of Martha so I wanted to do it."

They chatted for another while, joking back and forth, filling each other in on what was happening at work. When he replaced the phone, Bruce was shocked to realize they'd talked for more than an hour.

"What did Rachel say?" Jolene asked. She'd been waiting patiently, completing a jigsaw puzzle of horses grazing in a field. Five hundred pieces! He was impressed.

"She said she'd be by to pick you up at nine-thirty on Saturday morning," he said absently. An *hour.* He'd spent an entire hour on the phone with Rachel?

Something was wrong.

Bruce didn't even like talking on the phone. Five minutes, tops. Say what's necessary and hang up. He could barely remember a conversation in his entire adult life that had lasted more than fifteen minutes.

"Dad?" Jolene cut into his musings.

"What?"

"You're standing up but you're not going anywhere."

"I am?" He hadn't been aware that he was on his feet until Jolene pointed it out.

"Are you okay?" his daughter asked.

Bruce sat back down. "I—I don't know." He felt dizzy, and that was unusual for him. In fact, his head was spinning. Maybe he had the flu. *Yeah, a flu named Rachel.* Where did *that* thought come from? Squinting at his daughter, he noticed she was looking at him strangely.

"Should I call 911?"

"No." He forced a laugh. "I'm fine. I do have a question for you, though."

"Sure." She knelt in front of him, her hand on his knee. "Do you want me to get you a glass of water?"

"No, no, it's nothing." His heart felt like an oil-rig pump that had gone berserk, but he chose to ignore that. "You like Rachel, don't you?" But Jolene didn't need to answer. Rachel had taken Stephanie's place in her life. His own parents lived in Connecticut, and Jolene had only seen them two or three times. Stephanie's parents had divorced when she was young and she'd never had a good relationship with her father. Her mother had died within two years of Stephanie; she'd never recovered from the loss of her only child. So it'd always been just Bruce and his daughter. Except for Rachel…

"Dad, *of course* I like Rachel," Jolene said. "You like her, too, don't you?"

He narrowed his eyes. "What do you mean?" he asked suspiciously.

"You're not mad at her or anything?"

"No, no, everything's…fine."

The relief in his daughter's eyes quickly turned to fear. "She's not marrying Nate and moving to San Diego, is she?"

Not if I can help it, his mind shouted. With Jolene studying him intently, he shook his head and pretended nothing was amiss.

Together they made dinner. Jolene prepared a green salad while Bruce fixed tuna sandwiches. Dinnertime had been important to Stephanie. Because he knew this was something his wife would've wanted, Bruce had continued the practice of having dinner with Jolene every evening. While she described her day, he did his best to pay attention. During the summer she attended a church day camp, which she loved. She launched into a long, complicated story about a little play she was in, and he forced himself to nod and exclaim in the right places.

Summer bedtime was nine-thirty and Jolene went without an argument. He cleaned up the kitchen, then thought about going to bed himself, only he wasn't tired. After washing a load of laundry and dumping it in the dryer, he cleaned the bathroom. This burst of nervous energy wasn't a bad thing, he decided. Rare and surprising, perhaps, but nothing to be alarmed by.

Once in bed, he tossed and turned for another hour, then realized he wouldn't sleep until he'd talked to Rachel again. Her phone rang four times before she answered.

"Hello." Her voice was soft with sleep.

"It's me," he said, feeling a bit unnerved when he glanced at the clock on his nightstand and saw that it was after midnight.

"Bruce? Do you know what *time* it is?" She sounded more awake now—and annoyed.

"Sorry..."

"What's wrong?"

"When we talked earlier," he began, not knowing where to go from there.

"Yeah, what about it?"

"We were on the phone for over an hour."

His announcement was met with silence, so he forged ahead. "There's something happening between us, Rachel."

She sighed, or it could have been a suppressed yawn. "No, there isn't."

"I've never talked to a woman for that long in my whole life." He hesitated, then added, "Someone other than Stephanie, I mean."

"You woke me out of a dead sleep to tell me that?" Now her voice was incredulous.

"Yes."

"Bruce, listen, we're friends. We've been friends for years. Friends talk."

"I don't chitchat on the phone," he said forcefully. "I just don't. I never have."

"You're making too much of this, okay? It's not a big deal."

"Jolene's worried." He said the next thing that came to mind.

"About you?"

"No," he told her swiftly. "She's worried about you."

"Me?"

"Yes. She's afraid you're going to marry Nate and leave." He was worried, too, but he couldn't tell Rachel that. He'd already revealed far too much of his confusion. His feelings for Rachel were changing—or perhaps he simply hadn't recognized them for what they were.

"Bruce, Jolene and I have discussed this at length. If she mentions it to you again, tell her the person she needs to talk to is me."

"What did you say to her?" he asked. They were talking about his daughter here and he had a right to know.

Rachel yawned before answering. "I promised her she'd always be part of my life."

"So you've decided to marry Lover Boy, after all."

"Would you stop it," she chastised none too gently.

"Now I'm worried about Jolene," he whispered. It felt like he was about to lose his best friend, and depression settled heavily on his shoulders. If Rachel did marry Nate, that was exactly what would happen. She'd move away and leave them both.

"Can I go back to sleep now?" she asked.

"I feel like talking," he murmured, lying down again, the pillow nestling his head.

"Bruce, it's almost one in the morning!"

"I know. But you're awake now, aren't you?"

"Yes, thanks to you. What would you like to talk about—other than Nate and me?"

"You want to go out for dinner on Saturday night? After shopping?"

"Bruce!"

"What?"

"I want to go back to sleep. That's what I want to do."

"Oh."

"Take two aspirin and call me in the morning."

Despite himself, he grinned. "Good night, Rachel."

"Good night, Bruce," she said pointedly.

He was smiling as he replaced the receiver—even though he didn't have anything to smile about. Because Rachel might very well marry Nate Olsen, and then the emptiness she'd filled would be deeper than ever before.

Thirteen

Sitting with the other ladies at the Henry M. Jackson Senior Center, Charlotte Rhodes knitted with furious speed. Her friends chatted, but Charlotte's mind was moving as fast as her hands.

"Charlotte," Helen Shelton said. "You look like you're a thousand miles away."

"Oh..." she murmured with a start. She hadn't been listening to her friends' conversation, but the fact that they'd realized it was embarrassing. She smiled apologetically at Helen, who was a favorite of hers and another expert knitter. She was a widow, living in a lovely duplex on Poppy Lane; the two women had much in common and spent many an afternoon knitting and exchanging stories.

But at the moment Charlotte was worrying about her son and his recent move to Cedar Cove. On the surface, Will's decision to retire in Washington seemed logical, but knowing what she did, Charlotte had good reason to be suspicious.

"Bess asked if you'd check her knitting," Helen said. "I can't quite figure out what she's done wrong."

"Of course." Charlotte set her own knitting aside and studied her friend's half-finished sock. She'd discovered many an easy fix in sixty years of working with needles and yarn. When people came to her with knitting difficulties, her initial advice was always the same: *Read the pattern.* If the directions weren't clear the first time, then read them again.

She glanced at the sock pattern, which had been passed around among the knitters and looked a little the worse for wear. She found Bess's mistake quickly enough and repaired it, using a crochet hook to pick up a dropped stitch.

The ladies at this table were her dearest friends in the world, and yet Charlotte couldn't divulge her troubles to them. That just wasn't done by most women of her generation. Family problems stayed inside the family. They were not to be discussed with outsiders, and that included one's very closest friends.

She envied Olivia and Grace their friendship. There wasn't anything those two couldn't and didn't talk about. But Charlotte couldn't share her disappointment in her oldest child with anyone other than her husband. Ben might not be Will's father but he was part of her family now.

How could she tell her friends that her only son had a weak character? How could she reveal to these women that Will had dishonored his wedding vows? Not once, but repeatedly. His ex-wife, Georgia, had kept this a secret for as long as she could and then the poor girl couldn't take it anymore. Charlotte didn't blame her. If Clyde had been alive, she knew he'd be embarrassed and ashamed by Will's behavior and would no doubt have a few things to say to his son. Maybe it was just as well that Clyde had gone on to his heavenly reward rather than suffer such disillusionment about his only son.

Ben was at home when she returned from the knitters' group. He opened the front door as she approached the steps, taking them slowly and one at a time.

"You look like you're carrying the weight of the world on your shoulders," he said, taking the bag from her hand and steering her into the house. Charlotte went automatically to the kitchen.

"Would you like a cup of tea?" she asked.

"If conversation goes along with that tea."

Charlotte wasn't sure she could talk; her throat felt like it was closing. Swallowing hard, she nodded because she *needed* to talk, needed to share the feelings that pressed on her so heavily.

Ben collected the cups and saucers while she boiled water and measured out tea leaves. Soon they were sitting at the kitchen table across from each other but before she could pour the tea, he reached for her hand.

"Is it Will?" he asked.

"Where is he? Do you know?"

Ben shrugged. "He left a couple of hours ago. Said he was meeting with a rental agent to look at apartments."

"Did he say where he was hoping to move?"

"He told me he'd like to find an apartment near us, in the downtown area."

"I was afraid of that," she said starkly.

"Why?" Ben asked, sounding genuinely taken aback. "It seemed thoughtful of him to want to be close by. In case either of us needs him, he said."

"Hogwash," Charlotte sputtered.

Ben's eyes widened at her outburst.

"I know my son," she said, "and his wanting to be downtown has nothing to do with any concern for our

well-being." Her hand shook as she filled their teacups. "We aren't the *only* ones nearby," she muttered, then pressed her lips together in consternation.

Ben frowned, as if he didn't understand.

"It's Grace," she said, setting the teapot back on the table.

"Do you seriously think he's still hung up on Grace?" Ben asked. He seemed to find it far-fetched that Will would go to such extremes. "He knows she's married to Cliff, doesn't he?"

"Of course he does. But a little thing like a wedding ring hasn't stopped him in the past," she said. A sick feeling settled in the pit of her stomach. "I know my son," she said again. "He's highly competitive. That's one of the reasons he was such a success in the corporate world."

"In other words, he doesn't like to lose."

"He detests it." Charlotte could list plenty of examples from her son's youth but resisted. "He's going to move downtown and in a week or two he's going to get a library card."

"Because of Grace…"

"For no other reason," she elaborated. "He hasn't felt a need for one in the last thirty-five years. Now, however, it's going to be a necessary part of his relocation. Mark my words," she added, tapping her fingers rhythmically on the table.

"It's too late as far as Grace is concerned," Ben said. "She's happily married."

"I know." And Charlotte felt it was her duty to see that nothing ruined Grace's happiness. Grace was like a second daughter to her. Charlotte wasn't planning to sit idly by and allow her own son to destroy Grace's life. He

wouldn't succeed in seducing her again, but he was perfectly capable of interfering in her marriage, spreading innuendo and suspicion.

"Then why are you so worried?"

Before she could answer, the front door opened. In walked Will, looking carefree and decidedly pleased with himself. His eyes brightened and he smiled as he entered the kitchen. "I'm back," he announced. "And I'd love a cup of tea."

"How'd it go?" Charlotte asked. She stood automatically to get him a cup and was struck by what a handsome man he was, even more handsome at sixty than he'd been as a young man. He was tall and well-built, physically fit. He had a sense of style, too; from the time he was a teenager he'd taken care with his clothes. She remembered that he'd always been far more fashion-conscious than his peers. Recently his hair had begun to gray at the temples, giving him a distinguished look. Considering his appearance and his well-developed charm, it was little wonder that women had fallen at his feet. Even sensible women, like Grace.

"I found a small two-bedroom unit right off Harbor Street," Will told them triumphantly.

"Off...Harbor Street?"

"On the water," he said as she handed him his tea.

Charlotte knew of only one apartment complex on the waterfront. "I haven't seen a rental sign there," she said, none too pleased. Naturally Will had chosen an apartment that was practically next door to the library.

"I'm subletting the unit," he explained. "I'd prefer a more upscale place, but this will do for now."

Charlotte caught Ben's eye. He nodded, got up and politely excused himself.

She waited until he'd left the room, then confronted her son. "This doesn't happen to be Linnette McAfee's apartment, does it?"

"It sure does." He sounded surprised. "How did you know?"

"I spoke with her mother," Charlotte told him. "Corrie hates the idea of her daughter moving away from Cedar Cove." But Linnette was determined to leave, whether the apartment was rented or not.

"Well, her loss is my gain," Will said, as though it was a joke. "I should be able to move in sometime next week."

"Then I suppose congratulations are in order," she managed to mumble.

"I'll be out of your hair but I'll still be around," Will told his mother.

Charlotte didn't comment. Instead she stood and carried her untouched tea to the sink. Keeping her back to her son, she attempted to control her reactions. Turning to face him, she tried to gauge his intentions, troubled by the fact that she thought the worst of her only son.

"You're sure you're doing the right thing?" she asked tentatively.

Will wore a perplexed expression. "Of course I'm sure. Although you're both healthy, I feel it's my duty to be close by in case you need me."

"Olivia and Jack are less than two miles away."

For the first time Will seemed to notice that Ben had left the room. If he was looking to his stepfather for support, Ben wasn't there to give it to him.

"You mean you'd rather I wasn't living in Cedar Cove?" Will asked bluntly.

"I wouldn't go so far as to say that," Charlotte told him.

Will was, after all, her son and she was happy to have him there—as long as his intentions were honorable.

"Then what's the problem?" he asked, gesturing with his hands, palms up.

"The problem is Grace Harding."

"Grace?" Will repeated her name with a frown. "What's Grace got to do with any of this?" Had she not known him so well, Charlotte might have questioned her own perceptions.

"I know what you did," she said, refusing to hide her awareness of his behavior. She'd never spoken of it before, but Will needed to realize he hadn't deceived *everyone.* "That's all I'm going to say on the matter."

Will's frown deepened. "I suppose Olivia couldn't wait to come tattling," he muttered, anger shadowing his face.

"Hardly. I surmised what went on between the two of you all by myself."

Will exhaled slowly. "Let me assure you, Mother, that your concerns are groundless. I'm delighted for Grace and…her husband. I wish them the very best. Grace made her choice and while I wish she'd chosen to marry me—"

"Marry you!" Charlotte exploded. "You were married to Georgia at the time."

"We were planning to divorce," he said with perfect calm.

Charlotte knew he was lying. "Oh, Will," she whispered, her heart aching. "Do you honestly believe you can lie to me so easily? I'm your mother. I *know* you."

Will had never liked being confronted, least of all by her. He bit his lip, the same way he had as a boy. "Let me assure you, Mother, I am not interested in getting involved with Grace. I'm sincere about that. Like I said, I wish her

and Cliff happiness. Right or wrong, I lost her and I accept that. I'll step aside."

"Do you mean it?" Charlotte asked, meeting his eyes.

Will grinned, and he certainly didn't look like a man who'd deceive his own mother.

"Scout's honor." He held his arms open and when she moved into his embrace, he hugged her gently.

He disappeared again soon afterward without mentioning where he was going. Ben was in the living room reading in his recliner, with Harry, her guard cat, on his lap.

"Feel better?" he asked when she joined him.

"I…think so. I couldn't go another day without speaking my mind. I had to tell Will how unhappy I am about his behavior."

Ben set aside his book, the memoirs of Ulysses S. Grant, draping it over the arm of his chair. "Don't forget, I know what it's like to have children who disappoint you. You aren't alone in that, my dear."

He spoke from experience. Ben's son David had constant money problems and often came to his father seeking financial assistance. Wisely Ben had made it a policy not to give his son any loans until he'd paid off the money he'd already borrowed.

"In some ways I wish the problem with Will was money," she said. "He asked me to trust his intentions toward Grace. Really, I didn't have any choice but to tell him I would."

"I agree," Ben said, stroking Harry's fur from ears to tail. The cat purred with pleasure. "We'll have to wait and see."

"Yes, but what do I do if he goes against his word?"

Much as she wanted to believe that Will would do the honorable thing, deep down she suspected he wouldn't.

"Charlotte, my love," Ben said. "Don't borrow trouble. Each day brings enough as it is. Take him at his word until you have reason to doubt him. Then and only then, confront him."

She nodded. "In other words, I shouldn't cross that bridge until I come to it—and other assorted clichés."

Ben stretched out his hand. "Exactly," he said, smiling widely.

Charlotte walked over to her husband's chair and slipped her arm around his shoulders. "I'm so glad I married you. You're a man of wisdom, Mr. Rhodes."

Ben kissed her fingers. "I was smart enough to marry the most beautiful woman in the universe. Now, didn't you say something this morning about an apple pie?"

"I did," she said with a laugh.

"Apple's my favorite pie for August, you know."

"I thought that was October," she teased.

"Hmm. You might be right. But we don't want to be rigid about these things, do we?"

Unable to stop herself, Charlotte laughed again. She did love this man. She'd found love twenty years after losing the husband she'd adored. All she could hope was that her son would find a woman strong enough to love him despite his flaws. Strong enough to teach him despite his failings.

If such a woman existed.

Fourteen

He was acting like a high-school kid, Troy Davis chided himself. He'd actually started whistling as he got ready for his evening out with Faith. Whistling! Anyone hearing him, watching him, would hardly recognize him as the sober, level-headed sheriff of Cedar Cove—but he didn't care what anyone thought. This was the first Saturday night in years—yes, years—that was about indulgence, not obligation. He felt a little guilty thinking that, since he'd loved Sandy so much, but surely he was entitled to an evening of simple enjoyment. Surely he was entitled to this sense of joyful anticipation.

Faith had invited him to dinner at her house in Seattle. Late in the afternoon he shaved, then slapped on after-shave, the same brand he'd been wearing for decades. Maybe it was time for a change, he reflected. When he'd finished combing his hair, he searched his closet for a dress shirt. Not the starched-collar type; a knit one that would be considered appropriate for church on Sunday morning. Appropriate for a dinner date on Saturday evening.

Ever since that first call, he'd talked to Faith nearly every night. Usually he wasn't one to while away an hour on idle conversation, yet he and Faith were on the phone that long and sometimes longer. Then they'd hang up and Troy would remember four or five other things he wished he'd said; he'd have to resist the urge to call her right back.

They'd met a week ago in Cedar Cove for hot, greasy French fries and a diet soda—at the Pancake Palace, of course. The haunt of their youth, as Faith described it. Afterward, they'd wandered down to the marina. They chatted and laughed and reminisced. By the time Faith drove back to Seattle, night had begun to fall.

Troy had waited until he assumed she was home and then phoned, just to be sure she'd arrived safely. They'd spent almost four hours together, and another hour on the phone once Faith was back in Seattle.

They hadn't kissed. Not yet, anyway. He hadn't even touched her in more than the most impersonal of ways—fingers brushing as he passed her a drink, a hand on her elbow as they crossed the street. Frankly, he was afraid. He was determined to put those fears behind him, though, and if the opportunity arose, if the moment was right, he'd approach her for a kiss. She had to want it, too. It'd been so many years since he'd needed to read those signs.... Well, he just hoped he'd know.

Before he left the house, Troy rummaged through the bathroom looking for cologne, which, to his utter frustration, he couldn't find. His daughter had given him some for Christmas. Nice stuff, expensive. That must've been a year ago, maybe two, and he was sure he'd tucked it away somewhere in the bathroom. He'd never even opened the bottle.

Now that he thought about it, Sandy had still been living at home so it would've been more than two years. By now, it was probably ruined, anyway. Just as well; he didn't want to be too obvious. And he probably shouldn't wear competing scents, not that *he'd* really notice but women tended to have a better sense of smell. Fine. The aftershave was sufficient.

He straightened some magazines in the living room, trying to calculate when he should leave. He'd rather not show up early, which might look a bit pathetic, but getting there late might be seen as rude. Traffic and the ferry schedule made it difficult to figure out exactly how long the drive would take.

Just as he'd decided it was time to go, he heard the front door open.

"Dad, are you here?"

"Megan?" His heart sank. He hadn't said anything about Faith to his daughter. Not because he felt guilty, not really. But he wasn't sure what to tell her. It seemed too soon to describe the relationship as serious. Until he knew whether he and Faith truly had a future, he'd rather keep it to himself.

"There you are," Megan said, rounding the corner of the kitchen as he stepped into the living room, pocketing his keys. His daughter arched her eyebrows in evident surprise. "Don't you look good."

He grumbled something indistinct, wondering what he should say. His instincts hinted that Megan wasn't ready to hear about any other woman in his life.

Megan continued to study him, arms folded as she surveyed his attire. "What's the occasion?" she asked.

Troy shrugged uncomfortably. "Nothing much. I'm

meeting an old friend." Now was the time to mention that the "old friend" just happened to be female, yet he hesitated.

"If I didn't know better, I'd say you were going on a date."

Troy frowned and shrugged again.

Megan shook her head. "That's what I thought."

"What?"

"I can't picture you dating," she said with finality. She seemed to think it was too improbable to waste time discussing.

"Why not?" he demanded. He might be close to retirement age but he wasn't dead.

"Oh, come on, Dad," Megan joked. "You?"

"I might want to start dating again," he informed her. "Eventually..." He didn't find her attitude the least bit encouraging. Nor was he amused.

"No way!" His daughter looked shocked, her response even more uncompromising than he'd expected.

"Why not?" he asked.

"Mom's only been dead a short while!"

No one needed to tell him that. "I'm well aware of when your mother died." He didn't remind Megan that Sandy had been ill for years beforehand. Not once in all those years had he so much as looked at another woman. He'd been faithful to the very end.

"It wouldn't be right," Megan said stubbornly, her smile fading. "You wouldn't do that, would you?"

"Why wouldn't I?" he returned, struggling to disguise his feelings.

"Like I said, it wouldn't be right," she repeated, more loudly this time. "People would talk."

"I don't live my life based on other people's opinions," he said, his voice sharp with frustration and annoyance.

"You'd be dishonoring Mom's memory." Megan was noticeably upset. "Good grief, Dad, it's barely been two months! You don't honestly mean—do you—that you're going out on a *date?* That's just…wrong." Her eyes, so like Sandy's, filled with horror.

"No, of course not," he said, his tone as soothing as he could make it.

Megan immediately relaxed. She smiled again, unable to hide her relief. "Thank goodness. For a minute there, you had me worried."

Troy sighed. No point in asking his daughter's opinion on the matter of seeing Faith. She'd made her feelings completely clear. As far as Megan was concerned, everything should remain exactly the way it was.

"I stopped by to see if you'd come for dinner," she announced.

"When?"

"I was going to suggest tonight, but I know you've already got plans—with your friend." Her face revealed her distress. "I should've asked you sooner, but it never dawned on me that you might be doing something." She bit her lip, then made an effort to pretend it wasn't important. "That's what I get for taking my dad for granted."

More than anything Troy hated to disappoint his daughter. "What are you having?" he forced himself to ask.

"Steamed clams and fresh crab I picked up at the Farmer's Market this afternoon. Craig's got everything in a huge pot, along with freshly picked corn and new potatoes."

"What are you celebrating?"

A smile turned up the corners of her mouth. "You'll have to wait and see. Is there any way you could make it?"

Why, oh, why hadn't he left the house ten minutes ago? Then he wouldn't have been here and Megan wouldn't have known anything about his plans.

"Can you, Dad?" Her eyes shone with hope.

"I'll have to make a phone call first." The words nearly stuck in his throat. If there was any alternative, he would've taken it. Yes, Megan was spoiled; he admitted that. He guessed it was natural enough, since she was an only child and cherished by both parents. In addition to that, he and Megan had been through so much together during Sandy's illness. They'd grown close and solicitous of each other's feelings. Although Megan obviously had her limits…

"Oh, Dad." Megan sniffed and her eyes were wet with tears. "I wanted to save it as a surprise, but I can't."

"Save what?" he asked, trying to pretend that changing his dinner plans was no big thing.

"My news," she said. He could tell she was trying hard to keep her voice even.

Troy didn't know what to think.

"I'm pregnant!" she cried, and then she allowed the tears to slip down her cheeks. "Craig and I are going to make you a grandpa."

It took Troy a moment to grasp this. "You're going to have a baby?"

She nodded enthusiastically and started to laugh again, still weeping. "I'm almost two months. Can you believe it? It must've happened shortly after Mom died, when I was so upset and…and missing her so much. Don't you see, Dad?"

Troy wasn't sure what he was supposed to see.

"This baby is Mom's last gift to me."

"Your mother…"

"She sent this baby to me because she knew how lonely I'd be. Mom knew a baby would help me face the future without her."

"Oh." He was touched by how childlike she sounded—and a little worried, too.

"You're happy for us, aren't you?" she asked, reaching out and touching his sleeve, silently imploring him.

"Oh, sweetheart," he said and gathered her in his arms. "I am. I'm thrilled for you. For all of us." He paused. "Are you feeling all right?"

She nodded. "I feel wonderful. Craig's so excited. Me, too. At first I could hardly believe it. I've been on the pill ever since we got married. I just went off it a few months ago, and…"

This was information he didn't need to hear, the type of thing Megan should be discussing with her mother. But he'd been standing in for Sandy so long, it probably seemed natural for his daughter to share the intimate details of her marriage with him.

"I stopped taking them when Mom got—when it became obvious we wouldn't have her with us very much longer," she elaborated. "I just forgot…."

"I see."

"Now you can understand why I said this baby is Mom's last gift to me."

Troy patted her back. The pregnancy *was* exciting news, and Sandy, had she lived, would've been over the moon at the prospect of being a grandmother.

"What time do you want me at the house?" Troy asked.

"Seven," Megan said, breaking away from him. "I don't think doing it tomorrow night is a good idea with the clams and the crab."

Troy agreed they shouldn't delay. "I'll call my friend."

"Thank you, Daddy."

Megan hadn't called him Daddy in years. Generally it was *Dad.* "I'll see you in an hour," she said, hurrying toward the door.

"I'll be there," he assured her. Then, remembering his manners, he asked. "Do you want me to bring anything?"

"No…oh, Dad, please don't let on that you know about the baby. Craig's parents are coming, and I don't want to ruin the surprise."

"I wouldn't dream of it." So the in-laws would be there, too. Funny Megan hadn't thought to mention that earlier. Not that it would've mattered. She had no reason to think he might have made other plans, since he rarely did anything outside of work. There hadn't been room for anyone in his life except Sandy and of course Megan—until now.

Troy watched Megan pull out of the driveway and head down the street before he walked over to the phone. Without needing to look up Faith's number, he punched it in.

"Hello." She answered after the first ring, her voice cheerful.

"Hi," he said, bracing himself to tell her the unhappy news.

"Troy! Don't tell me you're in the neighborhood already. Not that it's a problem. I'm as ready as I'll ever be. I'm afraid I went overboard with dinner," she said with a laugh. "I baked fresh rolls from a recipe that was

my grandmother's. I can't remember the last time I used that recipe. Thanksgiving, I think."

"Faith..." All he could do was blurt out the truth. "Listen, I—"

"Do you remember the chocolate cake I made before you left for basic training?" she asked, not letting him finish.

"You baked a cake, too?"

"Yes. I hardly ever bake these days. There doesn't seem to be much point when it's just me. I'd nearly forgotten how much I enjoy it."

He felt dreadful. "Faith," he said, unable to hide his disappointment. "I can't come."

The line went silent.

"I'm sorry," he added, "sorrier than I can say."

"Something came up?"

He wasn't sure how much to tell her. "Yes. Something...important."

She paused and seemed to regroup. "These things happen, Troy. So much for the best-laid plans," she said lightly. "We'll do it another time."

"It's Megan, my daughter," he explained. "She just found out she's pregnant. She's invited me to dinner to celebrate."

"Troy, that's wonderful news!"

"Yes, yes, it is," he said. "The invitation came at the last minute."

"I understand," she said. "Of course you have to join your daughter and her husband."

"Will you give me a rain check on dinner?" he asked.

"With pleasure."

"I appreciate how kind you're being about this," he told

her and meant it. Faith had apparently spent the entire day cooking in anticipation of their evening together.

"Troy, have dinner with your daughter tonight. I understand completely. Don't worry about it for a second."

"Thank you." His gratitude made him feel lighthearted and almost giddy. Faith was every bit as compassionate, as *good,* as he remembered. He looked forward to seeing her again—seeing what the future held.

"It's fine. Really."

"About those rolls."

"Yes?"

"Do they freeze well?"

Her soft laugh was like balm on a wound. "They do. I'll put them in the freezer now."

"And the cake?"

"I'll take it to a sick friend of mine," she said. "Neither of us needs to be indulging in sweets, anyway."

Troy would've given just about anything to be with Faith tonight. Instead he'd smile and make polite conversation with his daughter's in-laws. It wasn't how he'd imagined this evening, but Megan was his child; she had to come first. Besides, there'd be other nights for him and Faith.

He was counting on that.

Fifteen

Bobby Polgar knew one thing for sure: he wasn't going to risk losing his wife because of a chess match. Vladimir had done his best, but Bobby was unwilling to fall in with the Russian's plans.

Bobby had to give the other player credit. Aleksandr Vladimir understood that Teri was Bobby's weakness. Nothing on this earth, not his titles, not his money, was worth putting the woman he loved in jeopardy.

"Bobby," Teri called to him from the bedroom, her voice husky with sleep. "It's the middle of the night. Why aren't you in bed?"

He could hear her moving around in their main-floor room and looked away from the chessboard he was studying. He was tired, so his thinking wasn't as clear as it should be.

Teri ambled into the den where he sat. She wore a short black nightie made of silk that instantly reminded him of the pleasures of the marriage bed. Her hair, dark brown this week, was mussed and she covered her mouth with one hand as she yawned widely.

"I woke up and you weren't there," she complained. Her gaze fell on the chessboard and she shook her head. "How can you play like that?" She sounded perplexed. "Without chess pieces, I mean."

"I play in my head."

She grinned. "Who's winning?" she asked.

Bobby frowned, not understanding her question.

"Never mind." She held her hand out to him. "Come back to bed, okay?"

Nodding, he abandoned his chessboard and returned to the bedroom with his wife. He doubted he'd be able to sleep. The moves in his head continued whether he was in front of the board or not.

Once under the sheets, Teri nestled close to his side. "Can we talk for a minute?" she whispered.

"Of course."

"I think dinner with my sister went well, don't you?"

He did, but they both knew it wasn't the meal that had brought Christie back to their home. The real attraction was James Wilbur. He'd been with Bobby for nearly ten years. Although James was employed by Bobby, he was also his friend. A true friend, one of the few. They'd always maintained a professional decorum, but they understood each other. However, when it came to the subject of Christie Levitt, James had remained suspiciously silent.

"Did you see how long it took him to get back to the house after he dropped Christie off last night?" James lived in roomy private quarters above the garage.

Bobby hadn't noticed. "That's good, right?"

"I think so." His wife giggled. "James and my sister." She sighed expansively as she rested her head on his chest. "He's certainly not her usual kind of guy."

"That's good, too."

He felt Teri's nod.

"James told me there's an important chess match this weekend," she said after a moment.

Bobby knew all about the match, which was being held in Los Angeles. He'd already made his decision. "I've declined."

"Bobby!"

The organizers were pressuring him to take part, but much as he wanted to play, as much as he needed the challenge, he couldn't.

"Bobby, there's got to be a way," Teri insisted. "I won't let Vladimir steal your title by threatening me."

It didn't matter. Bobby refused to comply with the Russian's demands. He knew he was the better player, and Vladimir knew it, too. That was the reason he'd gone to such lengths to ensure victory.

Aleksandr Vladimir had given Bobby his instructions: The next match in which they competed, Bobby was to lose. It couldn't appear deliberate; he had to fall into a trap known as the Black Hole. Once the eleven moves had been played, the game was over. So far, no one had ever escaped that trap but Bobby believed it was possible. He spent day and night reviewing those first eleven moves, looking for a back door, a way to win despite Vladimir's threat. The solution was there. He was close to finding it, which was why he couldn't sleep, why he'd spent hour after hour staring at an empty chessboard.

"James said," Teri continued, "that unless you play in this tournament, you'll lose your ranking as the top international player."

At one time, his ranking had been of supreme importance to him. That wasn't true now.

"I *want* you to attend the tournament," Teri said, snuggling up to him. Her fingers stroked his chest. "This is important, Bobby."

He shook his head, unwilling to let her sway his decision. He had to keep his queen safe. If, during the course of the competition, Bobby was paired against Aleksandr Vladimir, which would almost certainly happen, he wouldn't have any choice but to throw the game. He wasn't prepared, hadn't perfected his escape from the Black Hole.

"Bobby." She whispered his name in a throaty voice he'd come to recognize.

His answer was to turn his face away from her.

She flattened her hand against his chest, then caught his earlobe between her teeth. Sparks flew down his back and he closed his eyes. "I'll play Vladimir when I'm ready, Teri. Not yet, but soon."

He could tell by the way her body tensed that she wasn't pleased with his answer. He kissed the side of her face and brought her closer. "Soon," he promised again. When he'd figured out how to beat Vladimir at his own game *and* protect Teri.

Vladimir would be furious if Bobby didn't make an appearance at this next match. Still, the idea of thwarting the other man gave him a sense of control, however short-lived or illusory that might be.

Stretching, Teri arched her back and within minutes was sound asleep. Bobby stroked her hair. She was his queen, his love, and she mattered above all else.

Soon after, Bobby drifted off to sleep. When he woke,

the sun was bright, and he could hear his wife singing in the shower. Her talents weren't vocal, yet he enjoyed listening to her.

Waltzing back into the bedroom, still singing, Teri had the towel wrapped around her as she opened their walk-in closet. He couldn't take his eyes off her.

She stopped when she saw him watching. "You're awake," she said. "I suppose my singing's responsible for that."

He loved the fact that Teri's moods rarely fluctuated. Almost always she was happy. Optimistic. And just being with her made him happy, too.

"Would you like a good-morning kiss?" she asked, moving toward the bed.

"Please." If he was lucky, that kiss would turn into something more. He wasn't an experienced lover, but he was learning. Teri had instructed him on how to satisfy her, although she'd intuitively known how to please *him.* The enjoyment he derived from giving her pleasure still surprised him and seemed to increase his own sexual satisfaction a hundredfold.

Sitting on the edge of the bed, Teri slipped her arms around his neck and lowered her mouth to his. Even after all these months, her kisses stunned him. He couldn't think when Teri was in his arms. Bobby's way of dealing with the world was cerebral, not emotional. Only with Teri did he allow himself to feel.

When they'd finished kissing, Teri released a deep sigh. "No one told me married life would be this good. It's not the sex," she said earnestly. "Although that's terrific—don't get me wrong. It's the…being together. Trusting each other. You know?"

Bobby murmured, "Yes. I know."

"Well, I'd better get ready. Rachel and I—" She stopped abruptly and Bobby felt her anxiety.

"What's wrong with Rachel?"

Teri raised her head. "Nothing. Why do you ask?"

"You're worried about her."

"Well, I guess in a way I am."

"Why?" Bobby wished he could think of something more useful to say. But most people simply confused him. Outside of Teri and James, the only other men and women in his life were chess players like him.

"Rachel's seeing Nate soon," Teri went on to explain.

Bobby searched his mind until he remembered that Nate was the navy guy Teri's friend was involved with.

"That's good?"

His wife shrugged helplessly. "She thinks it is, but I'm not sure." When Bobby frowned, she said, "I'm positive Bruce Peyton's in love with her. Only he won't say anything…."

That was foolish, in Bobby's view. "Why not?"

"Oh, I don't know. He's a widower, and he and Rachel have been friends for years. But I can tell you that if he doesn't act quickly, Bruce is going to lose her and that would be a shame."

Bobby could understand the fear of losing someone. He loved Teri; he needed her. He'd be devastated if she left him—or something happened to her.

Teri stood up, tucking the towel more securely around her, then started toward the closet.

He wished she'd drop the towel. Bobby liked watching her body. It was soft and generous, the way she was.

"Bobby Pin," she said, whirling around. "Talk to James."

"Okay."

"I want to know what's going on with him and my sister."

Ah, so that was it. "If anything."

Teri's eyes twinkled with delight. "Trust me, my darling, there's *plenty* going on. Be discreet about it, though. Subtle."

Bobby wouldn't recognize subtle if it handed him a calling card. "I'll try."

When Teri stepped out of the closet, she was fully dressed in tailored white pants and a sleeveless blue sweater. She looked as if she was ready to walk out the door and when she reached for her purse, Bobby knew he'd guessed right.

"Isn't it too early for work?"

Teri returned to the bed. "The hair show in Seattle is today," she said. "Remember? Rachel and I will be gone until dinnertime."

Bobby didn't like the thought of his wife being out of his sight for that long. Arguing with her, however, would be pointless. He had to trust that she'd be safe, and at least she and Rachel would be together.

Leaning forward, she kissed him deeply, making him all the more reluctant to release her. "Talk to James, all right?"

"He's not driving you?"

"Not this time. Rachel's picking me up. We'll grab breakfast on the way."

"But—"

"Bobby!"

The expression on her face indicated more clearly than words that this discussion was over. Teri didn't understand

the danger she was in. Vladimir was not a man to trifle with; his one consolation was that the Russian would be in Los Angeles for the chess tournament.

Rachel arrived soon afterward, and the two of them drove off. Bobby spent his morning on the Internet following the chess match in California. More than once he had to close his eyes. The lure of the game, the competition, was as powerful as any drug. He missed it.

At lunchtime he remembered his promise to Teri and asked James to bring the car around. Bobby walked out to find his car parked by the front door, his driver standing dutifully beside it.

"Where to?" James asked, as Bobby climbed in.

"Just a few questions, James," Bobby said from the back. Teri had said he needed to be subtle.

"Yes, sir." Inside the car James had turned around, hands on the steering wheel.

"It's about Teri's sister."

The back of James's neck went beet-red. "Sir?"

"Teri was thinking of inviting her for dinner again." That was subtle, wasn't it? Bobby was proud of his artfulness.

"Very good, sir. Shall I pick her up?"

"Yes, if you don't mind."

He could see James's fingers clenching the wheel. "Of course not. When would you like me to get Miss Christie?"

"I'll let you know."

"Thank you, sir."

Bobby hesitated. "She's a lot like Teri, isn't she?"

James met his eyes in the rearview mirror. "In what way, sir?"

"She's beautiful."

James cleared his throat. "I hadn't noticed that."

A lie if ever Bobby had heard one. "Do you get along with her, James?" he asked, deciding the direct approach might work best, after all.

The other man's lips thinned. "Unfortunately not."

"Not?" Bobby was certain he'd misunderstood.

"We seem… I'm afraid, sir, that Miss Christie has taken a dislike to me."

That wasn't the impression Teri had gotten. "Is there any particular reason?"

James shifted and raised both hands. "I believe she doesn't like men who are formal in manner and who are employed as drivers."

This was shocking news. "I'm s-sorry to hear that, James," he stuttered, wondering if Christie was really such a superficial snob. If that was the case, she was nothing like Teri at all.

"Yes, sir," he stated crisply.

The two men sat in the car for a few more minutes, neither of them speaking, before Bobby realized that James expected to drive him somewhere. "That will be all, James."

"Very good, sir."

His driver emerged from the vehicle, came to the back door and opened it for Bobby, who returned to the house. He was in front of his computer, eating a cheese sandwich, when someone pounded hard on the door.

Bobby answered it and discovered James standing there. Looking pale and shaken, the driver handed Bobby an envelope. "One of Vladimir's men dropped this off. He said I was to give it to you."

A chill went down Bobby's spine as he tore open the envelope—a chill that intensified when he saw what was inside. A gold medal imprinted with the image of an angel, similar to one Teri owned.

All at once Bobby's breath caught in his throat.

It wasn't *similar* to Teri's; this *was* hers.

For a moment his vocal cords refused to work. When he finally managed to speak, he looked at James. "We have to contact Teri. Now." Uttering those few simple words required monumental effort.

James fumbled for his cell. It seemed to take him an inordinate amount of time to press the appropriate number in the speed-dial function. Bobby held his breath while he waited for Teri to respond. As soon as she did, he was able to breathe again, to speak. To move.

"Bobby!" Teri sounded excited to hear from him. "Did you talk to James about my sister?"

"Where's your angel necklace?" he asked, ignoring her question.

"Oh, Bobby, for Pete's sake, I'm wearing it." She muttered something he couldn't understand. He could hear some rustling and then she gasped. "Bobby! I seem to have lost it. I can't believe I'd misplace that. I distinctly remember putting it on…."

"This morning?"

"Yes, right after I got out of the shower. I wear it quite often. Did you find it? Is that why you're calling?"

The chill he'd experienced earlier became an icy blast that froze his blood. Bobby understood the message. Vladimir had expected him in Los Angeles, and Bobby's efforts to thwart him hadn't gone unnoticed. This was his way of telling Bobby that he could get to Teri whenever he wanted.

"Bobby, you're not answering me."

He couldn't. Instead he passed the phone to James. The only option he had was to await further instructions. When the time came, he would do what was asked of him, even if it meant walking away a loser.

Sixteen

Linnette McAfee's eyes stung as she pulled away from her parents' home on Harbor Street. The farewell with her sister Gloria earlier in the afternoon had been just as hard. They'd all kept her with them as long as they could. Her mother, especially, didn't want her to leave Cedar Cove, but in the end had accepted Linnette's decision. It might be an unreasonable one, but it was hers to make.

Linnette had listened to all of her family's arguments and she understood what they'd explained over and over again. Okay, so she was running away. Okay, so leaving town wouldn't work, wouldn't solve her problems. She didn't care.

Linnette didn't know anything about Will Jefferson other than that he was Charlotte Rhodes's son and Olivia Griffin's brother. Will had sublet her apartment and she'd felt like kissing him in gratitude. Even if he hadn't taken over her lease, she would've left Cedar Cove. His opportune appearance meant she wouldn't lose a chunk of her savings paying rent on a place she wasn't living in.

What particularly distressed her parents was Linnette's

lack of a destination. She'd drive until she was tired of driving, tired of being on the road. As her mother had repeatedly pointed out, this was the most irresponsible action of her life.

Linnette agreed. But the thing no one seemed to grasp was how *freeing* that felt, how liberating it was not to answer to anyone. All her life she'd been Ms. Responsibility. She'd gone directly from high school into college and then into the physician assistant program. From the age of five, all she'd done was study and work. No big vacations, no time off for good grades—or good behavior. Nothing.

Beyond anything else, the painful breakup with Cal had taught her that this would continue to be her lot in life unless she did something drastic. So she had.

As Linnette entered Highway 16 past Olalla, her cell phone rang. Normally she wouldn't have answered. She knew it was dangerous to drive and chat on her cell. At any other time she would've let voice mail catch the call. Not this afternoon.

"Hi. This is Linnette," she sang out, doing her utmost to sound completely happy and carefree. She wasn't, but there was a lot to be said for pretending.

"Linnette? You really did it, didn't you?"

"Mack?" Of all people, she thought her brother would understand. He hadn't been able to attend the farewell dinner at her parents' because of training obligations and she was pleased to hear from him.

"I just got off the phone with Mom," he said.

"Was she still bemoaning my decision?"

"Oh, yes." He gave a wry chuckle. "You said you were packing up and heading out, but I didn't really believe you'd do it."

That was another problem. No one took her seriously. Even her family and close friends hadn't believed she'd actually follow through. She knew why, too. Linnette McAfee had always been so darned conscientious and dependable. So goody-goody, so…predictable.

"Yup, I'm out of here," she said, forcing a note of glee into her voice.

There was a short silence. "Mom says you don't know where you're going."

"I don't. I figure I'll know when I get there."

"That isn't like you."

"Which is exactly my point."

"This sounds more like something I'd do."

"Yes, it does." She'd always envied her brother his individuality and his courage. He'd been a nonconformist from the time he was in grade school. For years there'd been trouble between Mack and their dad; only recently had father and son come to a mutual understanding. Linnette, for one, was relieved that they'd worked things out.

"Stop by and see me, will you?" Mack suggested. "I'd like to talk to you before you leave."

"I thought you were at the Fire Training Academy in North Bend," she said.

"This was our last day. Let's celebrate—I'll treat you to dinner."

Mack treat her? That was a laugh. Her brother was constantly broke. Besides, she wasn't even ten miles out of Cedar Cove and already her family was weighing her down, pulling her back. "I…I don't think so."

"Why not?" Mack demanded. "You weren't on any schedule."

"No, but…"

"Then what's the problem?"

Linnette sighed. "All right, I'll meet you—on one condition."

"I'm serious, I'll buy," her brother insisted. "Then you'll owe me."

"Mack, if you say a single word about me leaving Cedar Cove or bring up Cal and Vicki, I swear to you I'll walk out of the restaurant. Now, where should I meet you?" Since he'd offered to pay, he'd probably choose a fast-food joint.

"I promise not to say a single word about the impulsive nature of your decision."

"Fine." After a few minutes of discussion they decided to meet at a Chinese restaurant in old downtown Issaquah. Neither had dined there before, but Mack had heard good things about the food, which was said to be plentiful and cheap. *Cheap* being the operative word in this case.

Mack was sitting in a booth, sipping tea, when Linnette arrived. He saluted her with the cup when she entered. She looked forward to spending a couple of hours with her brother, but she meant what she'd said earlier. One word about her decision or Cal and she'd walk out.

Mack looked good, she had to admit. Better than just about any time in the past few years. He seemed genuinely happy, and she suspected that he'd finally found his real calling. After she'd studied the menu and they'd ordered, Mack told her about his training.

"You're qualified to be a real fireman now?" she asked.

"So they tell me."

Her brother had held any number of jobs through the years. He'd delivered mail, worked for a moving company,

been an apartment manager, a bouncer and at one time, a painter.

"Do you have a line on a job?" she asked.

Mack smiled a bit sheepishly. "Dad told me there's another opening in Cedar Cove."

"Do you seriously want to be that close to Mom and Dad?" Although Mack and their father seemed to get along now, Linnette wasn't convinced that living in such close vicinity was a smart idea.

"I don't know," her brother told her. "I'm putting in my application there and another in Lake Stevens and a third in Spokane."

Spokane was on the other side of the state, which meant that both Linnette and her brother would no longer live near their parents.

"That'll be good for Gloria, don't you think?" Linnette said. The situation in their family was an unusual one. Since Gloria had grown up with adoptive parents, she didn't have the same childhood experiences Linnette and Mack did, or the same memories; in effect, she'd been a stranger to them. The fact that Linnette was already friends with Gloria had only added to the sense of unreality. So much had happened in the past two years and now, with Cal, it all felt overwhelming.

"Gloria's going to miss you, though."

"I'm going to miss her, Mack. And Mom and Dad. And you..."

"You're going to do just fine," he told her.

"I know that." She hadn't intended to be so defiant. "I'm going to be more than fine. I'm going to be *great.*"

"You bet."

"I sound a lot like my brother, don't I?" she teased.

"More power to you."

"Power to the people!" she chanted.

Mack nearly choked on his tea and soon Linnette was laughing, too. This brother-sister bantering was exactly what she'd needed after the emotional farewell scene with her parents.

Mack set down his chopsticks and pushed away his plate of Szechuan chicken. "I had a reason for wanting to see you before you left. Besides wishing you well, of course."

Linnette stopped him with one raised hand. "I meant what I said earlier, Mack. If this has anything to do with Cal, then save your breath."

"It doesn't." He inhaled and paused for a moment, as if to gather his thoughts. "Listen, I just want you to know that if you ever need help, you can call me."

"That's really nice, Mack…."

"I'm serious, Linnette. Don't brush me off, all right? There might come a time when you're low on cash and you don't want to contact Mom and Dad."

Linnette almost laughed. For most of his adult life, Mack had lived hand to mouth. The fact that he was paying for their meal surprised her, especially since he was currently unemployed.

"I appreciate the offer, but Mack, I wouldn't want you to take out a loan on my behalf."

"It wouldn't be a loan."

"You have money?" She couldn't help sounding flippant; everyone knew Mack lived one step above poverty level.

"I have enough," he said with a shrug. "If you need anything, you call me."

"What if I need more than fifty dollars?"

"Linnette, would you stop it?"

"You have more than fifty dollars you can spare?"

He nodded.

"More than a hundred?"

Again he nodded.

"*Two* hundred?" This was fascinating information.

"More than a thousand," he said.

Linnette pressed her palms against the table and leaned forward. "This is a joke, right?"

He shook his head. "All I'm saying is that I can help you if you need it."

She eyed her brother, still unable to believe he'd managed to hang on to a thousand dollars. *Mack?* "How much?"

"Money?" he asked unnecessarily. "Why do you want to know?"

She gestured weakly. "Satisfy my curiosity."

"I have enough to provide you with a buffer if necessary," was all he seemed willing to tell her. "The transmission on your car could go out in some podunk town and I don't want you stressed out about how you'd pay to get it repaired. Call me and I'll take care of it for you."

"That'd probably cost more than a thousand bucks." She had no idea how much money he had, but it couldn't be *that* much. If Mack had won the lottery she would've heard about it. And surely he wouldn't be driving that rattletrap truck if he had any other option.

"You're not going to rest until you wrangle it out of me, are you?" Mack said, shaking his head.

"You're right."

He exhaled a sigh. "It's close to six figures."

"Get out of here!"

"I'm not joking, Linnette."

Maybe he *had* won the lottery and somehow kept it a secret. "How…when?" She narrowed her eyes. "You're not a day trader, are you?"

"Hardly," he scoffed.

"Then how did you come by that kind of money? Hey—" she said suddenly. "Did you receive an inheritance and I wasn't in the will? Grandma McAfee always did like you best."

Mack laughed outright at that. "What's the matter, don't you think I could've earned it?"

"Frankly, no."

He waggled his finger at her. "Oh, ye of little faith. Anyway, you're wrong. I bought a broken-down house, spent every penny I could scrounge to fix it up and sold it for a nice profit."

"When?"

"About two years ago."

Linnette remembered that house. It'd been a real dump, and at the time she'd assumed he was renting.

"There, are you satisfied?"

She smiled and shook her head. "You're really something."

Mack returned her grin with one of his own. "I'll take that as a compliment."

"I meant it as one." Linnette settled back against the booth and looked at her brother with fresh eyes. Not only had he held on to his money, he'd kept quiet about it until now. "I'm proud of you, Mack."

"Because of the money?"

"Yes, but there's more to it. Despite all the arguments

we got into while we were growing up, you care about me, don't you?"

Her words seemed to astonish him. "Of course I do! You're my kid sister."

"Your kid sister who's about to start a brand-new life," she told him.

"Do it with confidence, Linnette. Don't forget, you've got a safety net with me."

Everyone in her family had fought her on this decision. Everyone except Mack. He understood her reasons and had offered unexpected sympathy—and help.

He was everything an older brother should be.

Seventeen

The morning hadn't begun well for Grace Harding. She'd awakened late after a fitful night and then had to rush about the house, making coffee, collecting her books and papers, preparing for work. Cliff hadn't been the least bit helpful and had wanted her to stay in bed. His timing couldn't have been worse; she had to be at the library by nine, since she was opening for the day. She scurried about the bedroom, dressing as fast as she could, and all the while Cliff made a point of telling her that she didn't need to work. In fact, he'd like her to consider retiring.

Of course she needed to work! Grace was the head librarian, and she loved her job. She'd reminded Cliff of that on her way out the door and was almost at the library before she remembered that she'd left the house without kissing him goodbye.

Now the morning was half gone and that sense of urgency had yet to leave her. She felt disoriented and disorganized; when she arrived in Bremerton for a meeting with the selector, the librarian who ordered new books, she discovered she'd forgotten that set of notes at home. The

meeting ended up being a waste of time, and it was her fault.

When Grace returned to the Cedar Cove branch, she had to admit she was giving Cliff's suggestion that she retire due consideration. One way or another, she'd been working her entire adult life. After the girls were born, she'd taken night classes at Olympic Community College. Later she'd transferred to the University of Washington for her library science degree. Upon graduation she'd been fortunate enough to be hired by the local library.

Those early years had been good for her and Dan. He'd helped with the children and given her his support as she went back to school. Despite their financial constraints and the problems that haunted Dan, Grace knew he loved her as much as he could love anyone. It was once Maryellen and Kelly started school and grew older that his dark moods became intolerable. They hung over their marriage and family life and had grown progressively worse until the end, just before he'd disappeared.

It was difficult to think about her marriage to Dan and not feel a sense of grief and loss. Grace didn't understand why he was lingering in her mind on such a busy day.

"Grace." Loretta, another librarian, stepped into her office. "There's a gentleman out front who'd like to see you."

"Did he give you his name?"

"No, he said he's an old family friend. He came to apply for a library card."

In that instant Grace knew it could only be Will Jefferson.

"He seems friendly," Loretta added.

It was inevitable, Grace supposed, that she'd see Will

again; it was going to happen sooner or later. Squaring her shoulders, she followed Loretta out of the office.

Sure enough, Will Jefferson leaned indolently against the counter, as though he had all the time in the world. When he saw Grace, he smiled and straightened.

Olivia's older brother had been a strikingly handsome young man, and the years hadn't changed that. He still had a rakish, self-assured air. As a teenager, Grace had the biggest crush on Will. Back then, he barely knew she was alive, which was probably why she'd been so flattered when he'd shown interest in her after Dan's death.

"Grace." Will bestowed on her the warmest of smiles. "You look wonderful, as usual."

He was smooth, always had been. "Hello, Will. So you're here to apply for a library card?" She wasn't going to exchange pleasantries with him, nor was she willing to make him feel welcome. If he wanted a library card, he could get one without her assistance.

"I wasn't sure if you knew I was in town," Will continued, obviously undaunted by her curtness.

"I heard about it."

"I assume Olivia told you."

Grace didn't respond. "Is there anything I can help you with?"

"Yes, as a matter of fact, there is," Will said with all the charm at his disposal. "How about having lunch with me? We've got a few things to discuss and it would be good if we cleared the air."

This was exactly what Grace could never allow. "I don't think so. In case you've forgotten, I'm married."

Will frowned. "I'm not asking you to lunch as a date or to upset your husband. It just seems that if the two of

us are going to be living in the same town, it might be best to talk about what happened. I know you have regrets and for that matter, so do I."

He sounded sincere and for a moment Grace wavered.

"Cliff isn't the jealous type, is he?"

"Of course not," she said, refusing to let him imply that Cliff was possessive and unreasonable. "But I have nothing to say to you. Your sister's my best friend and other than that, we have nothing in common."

"All right," Will murmured. "I can accept that." He seemed disappointed. "By the way, I've rented an apartment on the Cove, near Waterfront Park."

Somehow she wasn't surprised to learn that he'd be living five minutes from the library.

"I've always been a voracious reader," he said.

In other words, he was informing her that he planned to be a frequent visitor to the library. Great. Just great.

"Let me know if there's anything you need," she muttered, "and I'll have someone on staff see to it." She wanted it understood that she wouldn't be at his beck and call whenever he decided to check out a book.

It felt satisfying to show Will Jefferson that she was completely over him, and had been for a long time. Unintentionally, he'd taught her some valuable lessons about herself. Painful lessons. Furthermore, she wasn't going to risk her marriage over him, and the sooner he realized that, the better.

"Nice to see you again, Will," she said casually. "I hope you'll make good use of the library."

"I plan to do exactly that," he told her in a low voice. He stood there as if he had more to say.

Unwilling to listen, Grace turned away from the front

desk and hurried back to her office. She discovered that her hands were trembling from the encounter. To make matters worse, Cliff still didn't know that Will had moved to Cedar Cove. She hadn't meant to keep it a secret; it was just that the subject of Will Jefferson was such an uncomfortable one between them.

That evening, Grace met Olivia for their weekly aerobics class. Afterward, her friend, who knew her so well, almost immediately asked what was wrong.

"Why do you think something's wrong?" Grace didn't look at her as she changed out of her workout clothes. They stood beside each other in the locker room, ignoring the other women around them. Grace bent down to untie her shoe.

"For starters, you didn't complain once during class."

"I never complain," Grace said righteously.

"You're joking, aren't you? From the second we get here, you tell me there's got to be a better way to stay in shape. And when we're out on the floor, you huff and puff as if you're about to keel over."

Grace straightened, hands on her hips. "I most certainly do not!"

"Do, too."

Grace couldn't keep from smiling. "We sound like we're in junior high."

"Do not."

They both laughed and headed toward the parking lot. "Cliff wants me to retire," Grace said as they walked.

"Retire," Olivia echoed. "You're far too young for that."

"It isn't about age."

Olivia stopped beside her car and gave her a questioning glance.

"Cliff would like to travel and he wants me to join him," Grace went on.

Olivia nodded, opened her door and tossed in her gym bag. "Isn't this kind of sudden?"

"Not really."

Olivia paused. "This doesn't have anything to do with Will, does it?"

"Funny you should mention your brother," Grace said, unlocking her own vehicle. "He stopped by the library this morning."

Olivia's mouth instantly tightened. "And what did he want?"

"A library card. Or so he said." Grace leaned against the side of her vehicle. "Apparently he needed my help, because he asked to talk to me personally."

Olivia folded her arms. "I'll bet he did."

"Then he invited me to lunch—supposedly to talk over what happened between us. I declined. I pointed out that I'm married now."

"He already knows," Olivia muttered.

"I said in no uncertain terms that I don't have any interest in renewing our relationship." Grace enjoyed telling her this part.

"Good." Olivia nodded encouragingly.

Grace felt pleased by her response, but she was still worried about Will and what he might do. "I don't think my being married concerns him."

"Why should it?" Olivia said in disgust. "His own marriage vows apparently didn't mean very much. According to Georgia, my brother routinely had affairs. I don't get why she put up with it for as long as she did."

Knowing she'd nearly been one of those affairs dis-

tressed Grace and embarrassed her. What a fool she'd been. How easily she'd overlooked behavior she'd known to be wrong. She'd so badly wanted to believe Will that she'd ignored every principle she'd been raised to uphold.

"He informed me that he plans to be a frequent visitor to the library," Grace continued.

"He didn't!" Olivia sputtered.

"I said that if he needed anything to let me know," Grace added, enjoying the look of confusion that crossed her friend's face.

"You didn't!"

"I did," Grace said, "and then I told him I'd be happy to have someone else see to it."

A slow smile came to Olivia. "I'm ready for some pie and coffee now."

"Me, too."

They met five minutes later at the Pancake Palace. Goldie saw them pull into the parking lot and by the time they entered the restaurant she had their coffee poured.

"Coconut cream?" she asked when Grace and Olivia walked in and sat down at their favorite booth.

They both nodded.

"What's it gonna to take to convince you to try something other than coconut?" She didn't wait for a response and, shaking her bleached-blond head, returned to the kitchen.

"I notice you sidestepped my question," Olivia said, dropping her car keys in the side pocket of her purse. "Is this talk of retirement connected to my brother's visit?"

Grace mulled over the question, a little startled by Olivia's suggestion.

"You mentioned retiring and then, in practically the same breath, you said that Will was at the library."

Had she? Perhaps those two things *were* linked and she hadn't recognized it. The idea that she might consider retirement simply to avoid Will gave her pause.

No, she wasn't that weak or cowardly. No, she would not let him interfere with her life, would not grant him that power.

Olivia reached for her coffee. "Will has a great deal to answer for," she said grimly.

"This has nothing to do with him," Grace insisted and she realized it was true.

Fortunately their pie was served just then, which signaled a change of subject.

"Mmm." Olivia savored a forkful, closing her eyes. "How'd Maryellen take the news, by the way?"

"What news?" Grace asked, glancing up from her own pie.

"You didn't read the newspaper this morning? The Harbor Street Gallery is closing the first of October."

"Oh, no." If she hadn't been in such a rush this morning, Grace would've had a chance to look at the paper. "I'd heard rumors, but I'd hoped it wouldn't come to that."

Olivia nodded.

"I'll call her tomorrow and tell you what she says." This would be a major disappointment to both her daughter and son-in-law. Maryellen had been instrumental in the success of the gallery and Jon still sold some of his work there.

Grace wished Maryellen had the time, energy and financial resources to buy the gallery herself. But right now, that possibility was completely out of reach.

Eighteen

This time Troy wasn't taking any chances—he brought a change of clothes to the office on Friday morning, and he intended to leave *precisely* at five. Regardless of the Labor Day weekend traffic, he was visiting Faith.

At five o'clock, as planned, he donned his clean pressed shirt and slacks, putting his uniform inside the garment bag he had with him. The way people stared, he felt almost naked walking down the hallway outside his office. You'd think they'd never seen him in regular clothes before, he grumbled to himself.

Now that Megan was pregnant, she seemed to need her father more than ever. He realized that despite her happiness about the baby, she was feeling vulnerable and insecure. He'd had no chance to have an extended phone conversation with Faith since Megan had made her announcement. His daughter called him several times every evening, to talk about her mother, discuss baby names, ask his opinion on all kinds of pregnancy-related questions. He even wondered, almost guiltily, if she knew about him

and Faith and was trying to thwart the relationship. But Megan couldn't possibly know about Faith.

When he left the office, Troy drove down to Southworth and discovered that the lineup for the ferry was hours long. Too impatient to wait, he drove around instead, which meant crossing the Tacoma Narrows Bridge. Traffic was bound to be heavy, but it didn't matter to Troy. He was going to see Faith. She talked more and more about moving to Cedar Cove, and he encouraged the idea.

For reasons he couldn't really explain, he was nervous. Earlier that week, when Faith had invited him to dinner, Troy had decided he'd kiss her. Okay, he'd kiss her *if* he got the signal that she wouldn't object.

He lost track of time as he drove through the steady but unobstructed traffic and was surprised to find himself at the freeway exit she'd instructed him to take.

Fifteen minutes later, he pulled up to the curb outside her house—a two-story colonial painted white with green shutters. The porch had two large columns, with a couple of wicker chairs and a glider. The lawn was well cared for and lined with flowering bushes. Sandy had liked flowers, too, and when she'd still been able to, had spent copious amounts of time maintaining their garden.

Troy stood there, staring at the house, when the door opened and she came outside.

"Troy! I'm so glad you're here."

He felt the warmth of her welcome all the way from her porch, and yet he remained rooted to the spot. The night before they'd talked for a mere ten minutes, mostly plans for tonight, but now that he was here, he seemed to have nothing more to say.

"Hi." He shoved one hand in his pocket and once again

felt as awkward as a high-school kid. With his other hand he clutched the bottle of sauvignon blanc he'd bought on the advice of a friend.

"Come in, please." Faith gestured toward the house.

He nodded. His mouth had gone dry and his tongue felt like it was glued to his teeth.

Looking around, he walked up the porch steps and into the entry, thrusting his wine into Faith's hand. The first thing that caught his eye was the carpeted staircase. Large framed photographs lined the wall going up the stairs—graduation photos of her two children, a couple of formal family shots and a portrait of her husband. He'd since learned that Carl had died of lung cancer, Troy's gaze didn't linger on the pictures. Instead, he glanced over at the living room, which was to his right. He could see that it was furnished with a sofa and a couple of matching chairs next to a brick fireplace. A few small tables. Lots of plants. That was where she led him.

"Can I get you something to drink?" she asked. "I have coffee, tea and soda." She smiled. "And wine, of course."

"Not yet, thanks," he mumbled as he sat on one of the chairs next to the fireplace. A moment of uncomfortable silence followed.

"How was the traffic?"

"Fine." He was suddenly hot and resisted the urge to unfasten the top button of his shirt.

"I was afraid it'd be bumper-to-bumper the entire way, but it looks like you made good time."

Troy had no interest in this mundane conversation. "Listen, Faith," he said abruptly. "I'd best get this over with now." He stood and paced in front of the fireplace. "My wife was sick for many years."

"Yes, Troy, I know that."

"Right." He was going over ground already covered. "There's never been anyone else."

"I'd be shocked if there had been."

Troy saw that he was making a mess of this. "I'm not eighteen anymore, Faith. I don't know about…these things."

She looked at him with such sweet innocence, it was all he could do not to kiss her right then and there. "Just tell me, would you?" he groaned.

"Tell you what?"

"Can I kiss you?"

"Oh."

"I mean, if you'd rather I didn't, I understand. But I don't want to spend the whole evening wondering—worrying about it. So tell me now. Either way is fine."

"Fine." Her hands were clenched tightly in her lap. "I think it would be perfectly nice if we kissed."

"Really?" All at once he felt lighter than air.

"Would you like to do it now?" she asked with a faint smile.

"Now?"

"I don't want you to worry about it through dinner."

He thought she might be teasing him but he didn't take offense. "If you don't mind, I'd prefer to wait."

Faith grinned. "As a matter of fact, I'd like to wait, too."

Then they had a glass of wine, and the conversation flowed as naturally as it always seemed to, everything from high-school reminiscences to the books they happened to be reading.

Because the dinner she'd made when he had to cancel at the last minute had gone more or less to waste, Troy

insisted on taking her out. With the help of an online recommendation, he'd made reservations at an upscale waterfront restaurant. The place was small and elegant, with intimate lighting and attentive waiters. Faith raved about the seafood she had, and he had to agree that his salmon, too, was exceptionally good. Afterward they went for a walk along the beach near Alki, removing their shoes and strolling hand-in-hand. He carried his shoes, with his socks stuffed inside, and felt conscious of every sensory detail—the cool, firm sand, the brilliant colors of the setting sun, her enticing floral scent.

"I didn't know what to think when you got to my house this evening," Faith told him. "You looked so stern. I had this horrible feeling you'd gone through all that traffic just to come and tell me you didn't want to see me again."

"Hardly," Troy muttered, loving the feel of her so close. Asking permission to kiss her might not have been his smoothest move, but he was glad he'd done it. Now he could concentrate on *her* and on the anticipation of that kiss.

"Might I remind you that you've already broken my heart once," she said lightly.

"You recovered."

"So did you." She paused. "Troy, we both loved our spouses, but they're gone. I'm so grateful that you and I have this second chance. Grateful and excited."

"I feel the same way. Grateful, excited *and* nervous." He shook his head. "The truth is I'm surprised I didn't throw up."

"You? Oh, come on, Troy, you've always been so sure of yourself."

"Yeah, right."

The wind carried the sound of her laughter and just hearing it made him want to laugh, too.

"I'm knitting a baby blanket for your daughter," Faith told him. "I hope that isn't too forward of me."

"Of course not. I'm sure Megan will be very pleased." Even as he spoke, Troy instinctively realized that the instant Megan learned the blanket had been knit by a woman he was dating, she'd be upset. Megan needed time before she'd be able to accept Faith, or anyone else for that matter, in his life. Maybe when the baby was born… He considered sharing his concern with Faith, but decided against it. He suddenly wondered how her kids felt about him.

He shook off his thoughts, and together they watched the final moments of sunset. *Now.* He'd kiss her now. He dropped his shoes on the sand, then gently turned her into his embrace and lowered his mouth to hers. Faith slid her arms around his neck.

This was the first time in more than thirty years that Troy had kissed a woman other than his wife. He found Faith's lips moist and warm and most wonderful of all, inviting.

When he lifted his mouth from hers, he saw that she was smiling up at him. "That wasn't so bad now, was it?" she murmured.

He frowned at her. "Not bad? That's *it?*"

"All right, lovely."

"That's a little more like it." Perhaps he should try again, he mused, and without hesitation touched his lips to hers. The same thrilling sensation stole over him. In his opinion, this was a thousand times better than *not bad* or *lovely.* It was…he searched for the right word. *Incredible*

came to mind, but Faith had to feel it, too, before he'd risk saying that.

Her eyes were still closed when he raised his head.

"Pretty good," he said in an offhand manner.

"Pretty good?" Faith echoed. "*Pretty* good?" Louder this time.

"All right, it was nice."

"Nice?" She sounded outraged.

"How about incredible?" he suggested.

Her face softened. "That's what I was thinking."

"Me, too." They scooped up their shoes, then he reached for her hand and they headed back to the parking lot. The streetlights had come on, and the usual Friday-night revelers had begun to crowd the beach.

Troy drove Faith home. Just as he had when they were in high school, he walked her to the front door.

"I had a perfect evening," she whispered. "Absolutely perfect."

"I did, too," Troy said. "How about a movie next?" he asked.

"When?"

"Monday?" He had the day off and wanted to see her again as soon as possible.

"Sure," Faith answered. "Monday's good."

"The way Sandy and I used to do it, she'd choose a movie, generally one I wouldn't have picked myself, and then the next time around, it'd be my turn."

"That seems fair," Faith agreed. "So who'll choose the movie this time, you or me?"

"You."

"That's chivalrous of you, but since it was your idea, you should go first."

"We can compromise. I'll check the paper and get back to you with some ideas."

"Okay."

They still hadn't decided whether to meet in Seattle or Cedar Cove, but that gave Troy a legitimate excuse to call her later. Not that he really *needed* an excuse…

They kissed good-night, a brief, comfortable kiss, and Troy left. As he made his way down side streets to the freeway on-ramp, he couldn't stop smiling.

The freeway traffic remained heavy, thanks no doubt to the holiday weekend. Driving back to Cedar Cove took nearly ninety minutes. As soon as he walked into the dark, silent house, he noticed the flashing red light on his phone. He checked the caller ID function; all four calls had come from his daughter. No surprise there.

It was close to eleven, too late to return Megan's call. He'd phone her in the morning, when his head would be clearer and he'd be better prepared to answer her questions. He'd tell her enough to satisfy her curiosity for the moment, but he wouldn't lie.

As he started toward his bedroom, the phone rang again. Apparently Megan wasn't going to let this rest.

"Yes, Megan," he said, recognizing the number. Who else would be calling him this late at night? Well, except for work, of course.

"It's Craig," his son-in-law said in a flat tone. "I just got back from the hospital." He hesitated and Troy could hear him taking a deep breath. "Megan lost the baby."

Troy felt as if he'd had a fist slammed into his belly. The first word out of his mouth was "No."

"I'm sorry…. We tried to reach you. Apparently you had your cell turned off."

Troy hadn't bothered to check. "I was…out."

"Megan's taking the miscarriage pretty hard."

Troy felt the sudden need to sit down. "What went wrong?" he asked, shocked by the news.

Sandy had lost two pregnancies after Megan, and both times the experience had been devastating. He couldn't stand that this had happened to his daughter, too.

"The doctor couldn't say for sure. Sometimes they can't tell."

"Is she still at the hospital?" Troy asked.

"No, she's here."

"Can I talk to her?"

"Of course."

Troy heard his daughter's tears even before she started to speak. "Daddy, where were you? We tried and tried to call, and we couldn't get hold of you." Megan was sobbing in earnest now. "I needed you, Daddy, I really *needed* you and you weren't there."

"I'm so sorry, sweetheart."

"I wanted this baby so much. This baby was Mom's gift to me and now…now there isn't a baby."

Troy didn't know how to comfort her, any more than he'd known how to help Sandy when she'd miscarried. While he'd been out with Faith, sipping expensive wine in a fancy restaurant, walking on the beach, kissing her, his daughter had been at the hospital losing her baby. His grandchild.

Nineteen

"Bobby wants me to cut my hours," Teri complained to Rachel as they walked along the Cedar Cove waterfront. They were on their lunch break and both felt the need to get out of the salon, into the crisp, fresh air and lovely September sunshine. Before long, the October rains would come and warm, bright days such as this would be rare.

"Is that what you want?" Rachel asked, tossing the leftover crust from her sandwich to the seagulls.

Teri didn't reply, and Rachel glanced up from feeding the gulls.

"Do you *want* to work part-time?" Rachel repeated.

"I don't know what I want anymore," Teri confessed. "I love my job, but I love Bobby, too, and he needs me more than Mrs. Johnson needs a spiral perm or Janice Hutt a color job."

"Then you have your answer," Rachel said, as if the decision should be an easy one.

"I don't think it's quite that simple." Feeling queasy, Teri sat on a bench that overlooked the Cove. Baskets of blooming annuals in an array of pinks and reds hung from

the lightposts along the walkway. "Bobby is so intense and, well…" She hated to say it, but she needed a break from her husband every now and then. A few hours apart from each other did them both good. Working at the salon was the perfect arrangement.

Rachel sat down beside her, and instantly a flock of seagulls gathered at their feet. She tossed the last of the bread onto the lawn, then shooed the birds away.

"This whole thing's giving me an upset stomach," Teri murmured. In fact, she felt like throwing up.

"You're pale," Rachel said, eyeing her closely.

"Darn him." She closed her eyes as a wave of nausea swept over her. "Since the hair show, Bobby's been worse than ever."

"Worse?"

"He hardly lets me out of his sight." Teri knew without looking that James was somewhere in the vicinity. He'd been assigned to watch over her whenever she was away from home. To his credit, James tried to be as unobtrusive as possible. But Teri couldn't help knowing he was there, especially when he hung around the mall, peering into the salon every ten or fifteen minutes. The other girls were used to it now and tended to ignore him.

"Get Nailed is more than my job," Teri continued. "It's a big part of my social life, too. You're there and I'd miss seeing you every day."

"Yes, but…" Rachel paused. "I'm actually thinking maybe Nate and I…" She let the rest fade.

"You really think you might marry Nate?" Teri liked the other man well enough and she knew Rachel was completely enthralled with him. But as she'd told Bobby, she was unsure this was right for her friend. Apparently

she wasn't the only one with doubts; Rachel seemed to have reservations herself, otherwise she would've moved to San Diego when Nate was transferred.

"I'm still trying to decide," Rachel said miserably. "Nate and I talk about it every time we're on the phone. He's coming to see me and I know he'll want an answer."

"So the pressure will *really* be on."

"Exactly."

"If you love him, why the doubt?"

Rachel sat back against the park bench and crossed her legs, one foot swinging. "You're going to think I'm being silly."

"Rachel, you're my best friend! I'd never be that judgmental."

"It has to do with Jolene," she said with a deep sigh. "I know what it's like to lose a mother. That was hard enough on the kid, but then her grandmother died, too. Bruce's family lives somewhere out east and they don't seem to have much contact. I'm afraid Jolene will feel abandoned if I leave now."

"How old is she again?" Teri asked.

"Twelve. She's almost ready for junior high. This is such a vulnerable age. Bruce is worried, too, and, well, I just don't feel I can do that to Jolene."

Teri understood Rachel's quandary. "But you can't base your life on Jolene."

Rachel leaned forward and uncrossed her legs. "Now you sound like Nate. Jolene's gotten to be a real sore point between us. I'm afraid to even mention her name because whenever I do, he gets upset with me."

"What about Bruce?" Teri wondered if Jolene was the *only* complication.

"What about him?"

"You know." Teri gestured vaguely, but Rachel understood what she meant.

"Bruce's been acting a little weird lately." Rachel shook her head, as if to dispel thoughts of Jolene's father. "Remember I told you he phoned me in the middle of the night?"

"Yeah, I remember." Teri really wasn't feeling well. In fact, her stomach seemed to be pitching like a rowboat in a squall. She did her best to ignore it.

"He did it again."

"When?"

"Last week. Not as late as that first night but well past the time for non-emergency calls."

"What did he want?"

"That's just it. He didn't *want* anything. We talked for a few minutes, he told me Jolene's decided to run for class secretary, which I already knew because she'd told me herself, and then he hung up." Rachel raised her hands in a questioning way. "I don't know what to make of it."

"He might be afraid you're going to marry Nate and move to San Diego."

"He didn't say that."

"He wouldn't, would he?" Teri said. Judging by her own experience, men rarely said what they meant. Neither did women, but at least they were more likely to recognize their feelings and desires; they just expressed them indirectly. Most men, on the other hand, didn't actually *know* what was bothering them. She figured this was the case with Bruce Peyton.

"He asked if he could come over this weekend with Jolene."

"I thought Nate was flying in."

"He is."

"Oh, boy."

"See what I mean?" Rachel said.

Teri nodded. She wanted to ask what Rachel had told Bruce but suddenly felt light-headed. No longer did she *think* she might vomit, she knew it.

She leaped to her feet and raced toward the women's restroom. Pushing through the door, Teri barely made it inside the stall before her entire lunch came up.

"Teri?" Rachel followed her into the restroom. "Are you okay?"

"No." She staggered out and leaned against the tiled wall.

"Miss Teri?" James called her from the doorway. "Everything all right in there? Do you need me to do anything for you?"

"Go away," she yelled as she let her head fall forward. The room had started to swim. "I've got the flu," she muttered to Rachel, who handed her a wad of tissues.

"The flu?" Rachel repeated with a giggle.

"You think this is funny?" she asked. "You ought to try upchucking your lunch and see how much fun it is."

"I doubt you have the flu," Rachel told her.

Fortunately Teri had bottled water in her purse; she rinsed out her mouth and wiped her face with the dampened tissues. "What do you mean this isn't flu? You've been watching too many episodes of *Grey's Anatomy,* haven't you?"

"Honestly, Teri, think about it. How long have you and Bobby been married?"

What should have been obvious from the first suddenly became clear. Rachel was right; this nausea wasn't due to

any flu virus. She was pregnant. Her cycle had always been irregular but now that she considered it, she hadn't had a period in two months. That should have been a sign. After all, they both wanted children and they weren't using protection.

"Teri." Rachel placed her hand on Teri's shoulder. "You look like you're going to faint."

"Miss Teri?"

"I'm fine, James. Please wait outside."

"You're sure? Should I take you to the doctor's?"

"James!"

Reluctantly he backed out of the restroom. It was a good thing no one else was in there at the moment, Teri thought. As soon as he was out of sight, she leaned against the wall again. "If Bobby's protective of me now, this news will only make it worse."

"But you have to tell him," Rachel insisted.

"I will—just not yet. He's obsessive as it is."

"Because of those two men? But nothing's happened since."

Teri hadn't said anything, not even to Rachel. Lowering her voice, she whispered, "I think it has, although Bobby didn't tell me about it."

"What do you mean?"

"The day of the hair show in Seattle."

"Yes?"

"Remember how he called me out of the blue? He was frantic and he asked me about my necklace." She pulled the gold medal out from under her blouse. She'd replaced the delicate chain at the first opportunity.

"He found it at home, right? You said you must've forgotten to put it on."

Teri shook her head. "I had it on. I distinctly remember putting it on after my shower, like I do nearly every day."

"But how would someone get it away from you without you knowing?"

"I have no idea." Teri had asked herself the same question over and over. At the hair show, she'd been bumped any number of times. The place was crowded. Whoever had taken her necklace had done it quickly and cleverly, snapping the fragile chain.

"Why would anyone do that?" Rachel asked, her own voice dropping to a whisper.

"It's another chess player," Teri told her friend. "He wants Bobby to lose, so he's threatening me in order to get Bobby to cooperate."

"You have to go to the police," Rachel said.

"Bobby won't. I've already talked to him about it. He wants to take care of this himself, his own way. He promised he'll call in law enforcement but only when he has the proof he needs. The thing is, Bobby wouldn't know how to throw a match if he tried. All his life he's been trained to win. Oh, he's lost on rare occasions but it sends him into a tailspin."

"He won't risk letting anyone hurt you, though."

Teri groaned. "I know. That's why he's stopped playing."

"And that's why he's being so protective," Rachel said with dawning comprehension. "Teri, this is awful!"

"I'd rather walk out of Bobby's life right now than allow him to give up chess because of me," she muttered, wiping tears from her eyes with the sodden tissues she clutched.

"Oh, Teri," Rachel said. "It's so wonderful to see how much you love Bobby."

Sniffling, she nodded. She did love her husband. In fact, she'd found herself weeping easily these past few weeks and she'd assumed— Oh, my goodness, the pregnancy explained her tears! No wonder she'd been so emotional lately.

News of a baby would panic Bobby. She didn't dare tell him.

"I don't have any appointments for the rest of the afternoon," Teri said, more to herself than Rachel.

"Are you going home?"

She nodded. "I think I'd better. I'm still not feeling well."

"Do you want me to go with you?"

"Thanks, but no. I plan to take a nap." Nothing sounded more appealing at the moment.

James drove them back to the salon. As soon as he pulled up in front of Cedar Cove's mall, Rachel hugged her.

"Call me after you see Nate," Teri said.

"I will." James opened the door and Rachel ran lightly out.

This weekend could change her friend's life, Teri mused. She'd either agree to marry Nate—or not. She wasn't convinced Bruce would let himself be counted out.

On the drive home, Teri nearly fell asleep in the car. When they arrived, James helped her out, his manner even more attentive than usual.

"Thank you, James. And listen, what happened back there…"

"Yes, miss."

"Please keep it to yourself."

"Yes, Miss Teri."

"I mean it." She didn't want Bobby hearing about this episode from his driver. James had probably guessed she was pregnant, and she'd rather Bobby didn't figure it out quite yet. That would just multiply his worries—and hers.

James nodded, his hand supporting her elbow. He didn't meet her eyes.

Entering the house, she went straight to the den. As she'd expected, Bobby was there, sitting in front of his chessboard.

"Hi, Bobby."

He didn't respond. His thoughts were on some chess move only he could see. She kissed his cheek and without another word wandered down to their bedroom. She quickly removed her clothes, then slipped beneath the covers. The sheets felt cool against her skin and she sank her head into the pillow and closed her eyes. Almost immediately Teri fell into the welcome oblivion of sleep.

The next thing she knew, her husband was sitting on the bed, his arm around her waist. She smiled and pressed her hand over his.

"The phone rang," he said quietly.

"I didn't hear. Was it for me?"

"It was your sister. She got your message and said she can come to dinner next week."

Teri rolled onto her back. "Did you mention that to James?"

Her husband nodded.

"Did he look happy?"

Bobby frowned, then shook his head. "No, he looked sad."

Teri sighed. She could see that James and her sister were going to need some guidance to get this romance off the ground.

Twenty

Rachel was so excited she could barely hold still. It'd been almost three months since she'd seen Nate and now they had a whole weekend together. A whole weekend! She paced outside the security area at Sea-Tac Airport, counting the minutes until he appeared.

According to the arrivals monitor, his Alaska Airlines flight from San Diego had landed. People were streaming through, so many at a time that Rachel was afraid she'd miss him.

Then he was there, standing in front of her. She let out a squeal of delight and launched herself into his arms. Her sailor man wrapped her in his embrace, swinging her around so people near them stepped out of the way, smiling. Then his hungry mouth claimed hers again and again.

"Oh, Nate, I've missed you so much."

He held her tight, drawing in several deep breaths as though desperate to take in her scent.

"I've never been on a longer flight in my life," he whispered. "I kept reminding myself that every minute brought

me closer to you." Slowly he released her until her shoes touched the floor again.

"I've got a wonderful weekend planned," she told him, laughing. He slipped one arm around her waist, carrying his overnight bag in the other. Walking side by side, they started toward the parking garage.

"What kind of plans?" He kissed her cheek as if he couldn't stop touching her now that they were finally together.

"The Puyallup Fair's on. You'll love it." It was a classic country fair, with rides, entertainment, animals and all kinds of exhibits. Rachel had often attended the fair when she was growing up; it had been one of the joys of her childhood. But she hadn't been to the Puyallup Fair in years and she thought seeing it with Nate was an inspired idea.

"Sounds like fun. Anything else?"

"Yes." It was supposed to be a surprise but she couldn't keep it to herself. "Two front-row Seahawks tickets," she informed him, feeling downright smug. One of her clients, who had season tickets, was going to be out of town when the Seahawks played the Raiders and had given the tickets to Rachel. The timing of this generous gift couldn't have been more perfect. Rachel wasn't much of a sports fan, but she knew Nate loved football.

"You're joking!"

"Nope." To prove she was telling the truth, Rachel pulled the tickets from her purse. "We might have to leave the game a few minutes early so you can catch your flight Sunday evening, but that's a small thing, right?"

"Right," he echoed. Nate hugged her again. "I *knew* there was a reason I loved you."

Rachel laughed. "Well, if that's all it takes…"

They had dinner at a Mexican restaurant in Kent that Nate had heard about from a friend. The enchiladas were the best Rachel had ever tasted. They lingered over margaritas and talked for nearly two hours; in fact, the restaurant was closing before Rachel noticed the time and suggested they leave.

On the drive over the Tacoma Narrows Bridge and home to Cedar Cove, she decided to introduce the subject of Jolene. Nate couldn't ignore the girl, as much as he might like to. Their relationship was too important to Rachel.

"Did I mention that Jolene's running for class secretary?" she said, knowing she hadn't.

"No."

He didn't say anything else.

"Bruce is helping with her campaign, and so am I." She was intentionally probing a little, hoping he'd respond with at least a show of interest.

Nate sighed and closing his eyes, rested his head against the seat, shutting her out. "Do we have to talk about Bruce and Jolene?" he asked. "Can't tonight just be about us?"

"Of course it can," Rachel told him, but his indifference to Jolene hurt.

The silence between them seemed to stretch and Rachel knew it would be up to her to break it.

"I have news, but I have to swear you to secrecy first."

"Okay." He opened his eyes and straightened.

"You won't tell?"

"I swear."

"Cross your heart and hope to die?"

"Yes, yes. Now tell me."

"Teri's pregnant," Rachel said triumphantly. "The crazy part is that *I* had to point it out to her."

"What does Bobby think?"

"Bobby doesn't know, which is why it's a secret."

"She isn't telling her own husband?"

Rachel didn't want to go into the details. "It's too hard to explain. She's ecstatic, though. I have no idea how she's kept the news from Bobby. The poor girl's sick every afternoon."

"I thought pregnant women suffered from morning sickness?"

"Not Teri. She has afternoon sickness. She hasn't managed to hold down her lunch all week."

Nate shook his head. "This pregnancy might help her lose weight, then."

"Nate!" That was an unkind comment and she wasn't going to let him get away with it. "Teri isn't fat."

"She isn't skinny, either."

"So what?" Rachel frowned at him. "That was rude of you."

For the first time he seemed to notice that she was upset. "Hey, come on, Rachel, I was only teasing. I didn't mean anything by it."

She nodded, unwilling to spend their precious time together arguing over how he viewed her best friend. These two days were going to be short enough.

"Listen, before I forget, I have a favor to ask you," Nate said, effectively changing the subject.

"Anything." They exited off the freeway to Highway 16 and then over the Tacoma Narrows. In another thirty minutes, they'd be in Bremerton, where Nate was staying with a navy friend.

"My father called me about coming home for a big political rally in October. I want you to fly in and meet me there." Nate's father was a congressman from Pennsylvania. Nate had grown up accustomed to living in the spotlight; events such as campaign rallies, political dinners, meetings with diplomats and dignitaries were part of his everyday life.

Dread filled Rachel and although she tried, she couldn't keep the reluctance out of her voice. "If you want me there, then of course, I'll arrange to join you."

"I do. This is important, Rachel. I'd like you to meet my extended family and my friends."

The initial introduction to his parents, when they'd visited the Seattle area a few months earlier, hadn't gone well. Nate evidently hadn't been aware of his mother's disapproval, although Rachel certainly hadn't missed it. While Patrice Olsen had seemed polite and charming, her message was clear. Rachel came without connections, without influential relatives or other beneficial associations. She was from a different class than the politically based Olsen clan, and Rachel was afraid she'd never fit into his family. She was convinced Patrice had someone in mind for her only son. And that someone wasn't an orphaned hair and nail tech from Cedar Cove, Washington.

"The rally would be a great experience," Nate assured her.

"Really?" Rachel knew she sounded doubtful, even though she tried not to.

"I want you to understand the responsibilities of being part of my family."

"Oh." That was straightforward enough. "Are you

thinking of running for office one day?" she asked. When they'd first met, Nate hadn't even told her his father was a congressman. He'd joined the navy as an enlisted man in defiance of his family. At the time, he'd felt the need to prove himself. Obviously that was no longer the case.

"I have been thinking about it," Nate confessed. "That doesn't mean I will, but it's in the blood, you know? Just being at one of these rallies with Dad is exciting, and I didn't realize how much I missed it until he called. There's an energy to a campaign—it's contagious. You'll see what I mean."

"Oh, Nate, I'm not the right woman for you." She blurted this out, feeling close to tears. "I hate being in the limelight. I'd be a detriment to you."

"Rachel, how can you say that? I love you—you're everything I want in a woman, a wife."

"But I'm not! How can I be? The mere thought of a political life terrifies me."

"Don't be so quick to judge. Meet me in October and you can see for yourself what it's really like. Don't be so willing to give up on us."

The possibility of not having Nate in her future was the deciding factor. "I'll do it," she said, her voice resolute.

"Thank you, babe." He reached for her hand, then raised it to his lips.

The weekend was a whirlwind of activity. Nate and Rachel arrived at the Puyallup Fairgrounds at eleven on Saturday morning and didn't leave until nearly ten that night. By then they'd experienced just about everything the fair had to offer, from cotton candy to corn on the cob and rides that terrified her. They'd attended a horse show and dog obedience trials and she'd watched a baby chick

peck its way out of its shell. At Rachel's strongly worded request, Nate purchased tickets to see one of the *American Idol* winners.

"Promise you won't tell any of my friends I actually paid to listen to someone from *American Idol,*" Nate protested.

Rachel swatted his arm. "Don't you dare say a bad word about my all-time favorite TV show."

Despite Nate's reservations, he seemed to enjoy the performance as much as Rachel did.

Sunday morning, after brunch at her place, they were on the ferry to the Seahawks game at Quest Field in downtown Seattle. The game was exciting, even for someone who didn't care much about football. The Seahawks won in the final seconds, and because the game was so close, Rachel and Nate left later than they'd planned.

She had to drop Nate off at the airport; there wasn't time to go inside with him. He kissed her long and hard, releasing her only when a security guard approached their vehicle.

"Move along, folks," he said, waving toward Rachel's car.

Nate kissed her again. "We'll be together next month."

Rachel had put the political rally out of her mind. She sighed and closed her eyes, trying not to worry about it. Nate was right—she shouldn't give up on their relationship without making more of an effort. She *could* learn to be the kind of wife he needed if he entered politics. She'd just have to learn the social niceties. The protocol. The conversation.

She waited until he'd walked through the glass doors,

then drove away with tears in her eyes. Periodically on the drive back to Cedar Cove she had to blink rapidly to clear her vision.

Her small rental house felt even smaller once she got home. She tossed her purse and keys on a shelf in the hallway and ignored the blinking red light that informed her she had phone messages.

When the doorbell rang, she groaned audibly. She wasn't in any mood for company. She debated not answering but the doorbell rang again. Someone was persistent. Not entirely to her surprise, she found Bruce Peyton standing there—looking as if he was lost and needed directions. Jolene wasn't with him, either.

"Can I come in?" he'd asked when she didn't immediately invite him inside.

"Oh, sure, sorry." She'd put him off when he'd asked, earlier in the week, if they could get together, and felt guilty about that. "I just got home," she explained. "Not two minutes ago."

"I know," he said as he followed her into the kitchen. Without waiting to be asked, he slouched down in a kitchen chair.

She wondered what was wrong, and all at once it occurred to her that this might have to do with his daughter. "Where's Jolene?" she asked urgently. "She's okay, isn't she?"

"She's roller-skating with friends." He rested his elbows on the table, then propped up his head. He looked tired.

"What's the matter with you?" She began to make a pot of coffee. Bruce could obviously use the caffeine and she needed something to do, something to work off her nervous tension.

Bruce studied her with wide blue eyes. "You're going to marry that navy guy, aren't you?"

"Bruce, honestly…"

"I know. It's none of my business."

The coffee had started to drain into the pot. Rachel waited until there was enough for a cup, then poured it into a mug, which she handed him.

"I don't know what I'm going to do yet," she said. "It's too soon."

"You love him, though?"

"Yes." She wouldn't deny it.

"He wants to marry you." He said this as though making a statement of fact.

Nodding, she filled a second mug. "If I do decide to marry Nate, we'll work something out with Jolene. She can fly out to visit us in California—or wherever we are—on a regular basis." Rachel sat across from him at the table.

"She'd appreciate that, I'm sure."

"I'd miss her. It isn't like I could just forget her."

He sipped his coffee, then held the mug with both hands and stared down at it. "I care about you, Rachel."

"Thank you," she said simply. "I care about you, too."

A smile came and went, almost before she could notice.

"Thanks," he said. "A little while ago, I realized how much I depend on you. You're a good friend."

"I consider you a good friend, too." And she did.

"Have you had dinner?" he asked.

At the game they'd had hot dogs and soda, and then later Rachel had eaten salty, greasy popcorn. In fact, all she'd had since brunch was junk food. "Not really. Want to go out?"

"Sure." The suggestion seemed to please him. "Do you have anything in mind?"

"Mr. Wok's?" It was her favorite Chinese place.

"Fine with me."

Not until she was getting ready for bed later that night did she remember Bruce's comment that he knew she'd just gotten home. He must have been parked outside her house, waiting.

Twenty-One

Christie Levitt wasn't sure what to make of Teri's sudden interest in reestablishing their relationship. As a kid she'd looked up to Teri and followed her like a shadow. Not that it got her anywhere. Teri always lost patience with her little sister, dumping her whenever she could.

It wasn't until Christie was twelve or thirteen that she discovered she had something Teri didn't, and that was beauty. Not that Teri was ugly or anything. But Christie had the looks—the classic face and shiny blond hair—and the body to go with them. She'd quickly learned to use that to her advantage, and then she'd gone about proving she could have anything and everything her big sister did. The sense of power and exhilaration she got from stealing Teri's boyfriends was addictive. Christie wanted her sister to experience a little of the frustration she'd felt when Teri used to exclude her. Rejection hurt. This was payback time—and it went on and on. Christie had never been serious about any of the guys interested in her older sister. If she'd felt remorse for her cruelty…well, she ignored it.

Her charm and beauty had never failed her until she

met Teri's husband. Bobby Polgar had simply ignored her compliments. Nothing she'd said had any effect on him. When Teri left the living room to check on dinner that first night, Christie had made her move. She'd deliberately stood and walked over to Bobby, claiming she needed help with a button at the back of her blouse.

Bobby refused, claiming he wasn't good with buttons and she should ask Teri. It wasn't so much what he said as the way he said it. Bobby wasn't interested in her. He'd fallen for Teri, and this seemed to be the one man who wasn't susceptible to Christie. He'd shown it that first night and proved it several times since.

"Home, miss?" James asked, breaking into her thoughts.

Christie sat in the backseat of the stretch limo after an early dinner at Teri's. The car was utterly ridiculous, she told herself scornfully, and yet Bobby Polgar wasn't pretentious in the least. So why this fancy car and driver? The driver, especially, was annoying.

"Take me to the Pink Poodle," she instructed. James had what could only be described as a stiff upper lip. Christie couldn't recall where she'd heard that expression—probably some BBC costume drama—but it fit James perfectly. He was devoid of personality and so polite it made her crazy. She could tell him to jump off a bridge and his response would be something along the lines of "Very good, miss."

Twice now—since that disastrous dinner with their mother—Teri had invited Christie to the house. On both occasions she'd sent Bobby's driver to pick her up and afterward deliver her home.

Spending an evening with Teri and Bobby had become

surprisingly enjoyable. They might not always agree but they were family—and she hadn't thought of Teri that way in years. Family hadn't had much meaning for her until recently, although she'd always been close to Johnny. So was Teri. They had that much in common, anyway. But until recently, Teri seemed to avoid her and, in all fairness, Christie knew why. She'd made it a habit to be as unpleasant toward her older sister as possible. For the first time since childhood, Christie saw potential in their relationship. They were moving tentatively toward something new, a kind of friendship, and that required concessions from both of them.

Teri's marriage had started it. Christie had never seen her sister this happy, this much in love. Teri's husband was a bit…unusual, but Christie discovered she rather liked Bobby Polgar.

Teri seemed to want to make up for lost time now. She was reaching out to Christie in various unexpected ways. The long-stemmed red rose that had awaited her in the car both nights was a good example. It was a nice touch, thoughtful and rather sweet.

"The Pink Poodle, miss?"

"Yes," she snapped. The tone of his voice told her he disapproved. Well, he could think what he wanted. She didn't care.

Bobby was odd, but that was understandable. He was a famous chess player. As for Bobby's driver—well, James had no excuse. He wasn't even English or anything. He just acted like someone on—what was that old show? *Upstairs, Downstairs.*

Who the hell had a driver in this day and age, anyway? Then again, Bobby probably didn't have a driver's license,

which might explain why he'd hired James. What didn't make sense was the way Bobby had James drive Teri everywhere she went. Talk about ridiculous. Still, if Bobby was going to keep the man as a full-time employee, James needed something to do. Driving Teri to the mall. Waiting around. Driving her back. Talk about *boring*.

Without further conversation, James pulled up in front of the local tavern where Christie spent several evenings a week. She tended to go there when she got off work at the Wal-Mart just outside Cedar Cove. It wasn't as though she had anyone waiting for her at home. The Pink Poodle was a friendly place; the music was lively and she could kick back and relax. James came around to the passenger door to let her out. He didn't look at her, which irritated her even more. The real reason she'd asked him to bring her to the tavern was to get a reaction out of him. She should've known she wouldn't. Other than the disapproving tone he'd used earlier, he didn't give the slightest indication of…anything.

"Thank you, Ja-ames," she said, drawing out the one syllable of his name. The desire to break through that reserve of his was nearly overwhelming. She couldn't imagine what he'd do if she suddenly kissed him. The thought produced a smile. He'd keel over in a dead faint. Or step on the gas and drive right into a tree.

Climbing out of the car, Christie headed for the tavern door without a backward glance. Most people in the crowd greeted her; she knew nearly everyone there. Without stopping to chat, she went up to the bar and ordered a draft beer.

Larry, the bartender, a middle-aged guy who was also the owner, picked up a chilled mug and automatically

filled it from one of the taps. He didn't need to ask which brew she wanted. He knew what she liked.

She sat down on a stool and they chatted for a few minutes until Kyle Jamison strolled in the front door. "Say, what's that limo doing outside?" he shouted.

"What?" Christie couldn't believe her ears. James was still parked outside!

Half the tavern moved over to stare out the smudged, wavy windows.

"Who's he waiting for?" Larry asked, his nose practically pressed against the glass.

"Good question," Kyle commented as he slid onto the stool next to Christie. She'd dated Kyle a couple of times. He was a local plumber and a decent guy. She liked him well enough but there weren't any sparks, and the relationship had gone nowhere. With most men, it was better just to be friends. She'd crossed the line more than once with guys she knew from the tavern and always regretted it.

"Say, can I get a beer over here?" Kyle asked, growing impatient with Larry, who continued to gaze out the window.

"Comin' right up," Larry muttered.

Christie waited a respectable amount of time, then casually slid off the bar stool and walked toward the ladies' room. Instead of going down the hallway, though, she snuck out the door. Her footsteps resounded on the tarmac as she approached the limo, moving quickly. She wasn't halfway across the lot when James climbed out of the driver's seat and held open the passenger door.

"What are you doing here?" she demanded.

He seemed surprised by the anger in her voice.

"I'm waiting for you," he explained, as if that was completely logical.

"There's no need to do that."

James shook his head. "Miss Teri asked me to see you home."

"Go away," she said, dismissing him with a wave of her hand.

"I'm afraid I can't do that."

Now he was *really* beginning to annoy her. "I don't want you here."

"Shall I move the car and wait for you around the corner?"

Christie wanted to groan in frustration. "No. Just leave."

He declined again with a shake of his head.

"A friend will drive me home," she insisted.

James remained stubbornly quiet.

"I want you to leave."

"Yes, miss."

Every word out of this man's mouth made her furious. "And stop calling me Miss! My name is Christie."

"Very well, Christie."

There was a silence, and they stared at each other, neither looking away.

"You're going to sit here even if I stay all night, aren't you?" she finally asked.

"Yes."

From the firm set of his mouth, she could tell he wasn't kidding, either. He'd sit in that damn car for hours without a word of complaint, patiently waiting for her to reappear.

"Oh, all right," she groaned. "You win." She went back into the tavern, paid for her beer and left.

James remained standing by the passenger door, holding it for her. She climbed in and reached for the door handle, jerking it from his hand as she slammed it shut. She glanced out at the tavern, hoping no one had seen her get into the limo. She'd never hear the end of it.

Slipping into the driver's seat, James started the engine and turned into the road.

"*Now* look what I did," Christie complained. "I ruined the rose my sister gave me." In her temper, she'd sat on it and crushed the petals.

"That rose isn't from your sister."

"Bobby gave me the rose?" That didn't sound like something her brother-in-law would do.

"No, miss, I did."

"*You?*" She was so shocked she forgot to be upset that he'd called her *miss* again.

"Yes."

"Both times?" she asked speculatively.

"Yes."

Christie frowned. "Why?" He didn't answer, so she rephrased her question. "Is there a reason you bought me roses?" She raised her voice so he'd know she expected an answer.

"I wanted you to have them."

She regarded the crushed bud in her hand. "Don't do it again, understand?"

"Very well."

"I mean it, James."

There was no response. All at once Christie felt the most compelling urge to weep. That happened once in a while, usually when she'd been drinking. This evening she hadn't even finished her beer, so that couldn't be it. Tears

gathered in her eyes and she swallowed against the lump in her throat.

"I'm going to tell Teri I don't want you driving me any-more."

"Very well."

She didn't know what made her say that. James hadn't done anything to her and yet she seemed to be looking for ways to offend him.

When he drove up to her apartment building, she practically leaped out of the car. She certainly didn't give him time to get out and open her door. She ran to her apartment and hurriedly let herself inside. Her pulse roared in her ears as she leaned against the closed door, breathing hard. When she looked down she realized she still held the battered rose. A tear fell from her cheek and landed on the red petals.

Twenty-Two

"We got a postcard from Linnette," Corrie McAfee told Roy when he came into the office after his morning walk. Her voice was a little too cheerful, and he didn't believe it reflected how she really felt.

"Where is she?" he asked. He'd ultimately sided with his daughter about making her own decision, but that didn't mean he approved of the way she'd taken off without a destination, without a plan. Nor did it mean he didn't sympathize with her reasons. Like any father, he hated seeing his child hurt.

"North Dakota," Corrie told him, studying the postcard. "A town called Buffalo Valley. Roy," she said, glaring at him. "She's taken a job as a waitress at a restaurant called 3 of a Kind. She says the owner won the business in a card game about ten years ago. What sort of place is this?"

"Apparently one that needs a waitress," he said in as casual a tone as he could manage.

"After all those years of schooling and medical training, Linnette is working as a *waitress?*"

"I know." He didn't like the sound of that, either. However, he was willing to give Linnette the benefit of the doubt and wait a few months until she found her footing.

"A waitress," his wife repeated indignantly.

"What I find interesting," he said, "is that she chose to mail us a postcard rather than call."

He and Corrie exchanged a quick, private smile.

Their daughter Gloria had once mailed them postcards, too, but hers had been anonymous with cryptic messages neither of them had understood at the time.

Corrie handed him Linnette's postcard and he read through the tightly scribbled lines. "She seems fairly happy," he said, somewhat surprised. "Apparently the proprietor's included a room with the job."

"Buffalo Bob? I don't like it, Roy. What a ridiculous name!"

"Listen, Corrie, we raised our daughter to the best of our ability. Linnette's got a good head on her shoulders. She's told us about this job and where she's living, so the least we can do is trust her judgment."

"How can you say that?" Corrie cried. "Her judgment ever since Cal broke up with her has been terrible."

"In our opinion," he pointed out.

"*Our* opinion?" she returned, her eyes narrowing. "You mean to say you thought so, too, and didn't say anything?"

Well, he'd certainly stepped into that one. Roy nodded slowly. "I didn't like the fact that Linnette chose to run away, but she felt she had to make a change, which I understand. We won't always agree with her decisions, Corrie." He put his arm around his wife's shoulders. "That's a given. We didn't always approve of Mack's

choices, either. Kids have to learn to fend for themselves. We can't get in the habit of rescuing them every time."

Roy could tell that his wife still had trouble with this, and he didn't blame her. Corrie was a nurturer, someone who tried to fix whatever was wrong, especially in her children's lives. He tended to feel that kids should face the consequences of their actions. Not just kids—everyone. Which wasn't to say he didn't miss Linnette; he did. He wanted her back home. He believed that eventually she would return, but not until she was ready. Not until she'd figured out whatever she needed to know.

Later that same afternoon, he went to the sheriff's office and saw Troy Davis sitting at his desk, the phone held to his ear. The sheriff noticed Roy and immediately gestured him inside. There was a coffeepot across the hall; Roy helped himself to a mug while Troy finished up his conversation.

When Roy came back into the office, the sheriff was off the phone. He picked up his own mug and ambled across the hall for a refill. Roy noticed a haggard, weary look on his face.

"Problems?" he asked.

Troy didn't answer right away. "Remember Martha Evans who died a couple months back?"

"The widow? Didn't Pastor Flemming find the body?"

"That's her. The family claims that several expensive pieces of her jewelry are missing."

Roy was taken aback. "You don't think Dave—"

"Of course not." Troy shook his head. "But you didn't come here to listen to my woes. What brings you to my neck of the woods?"

Roy decided not to pursue the subject of the missing

jewelry. "I'm doing legwork on a case. Gotta check some old police reports. Corrie asked me to stop in and invite you to dinner Friday night."

Troy's gaze instantly left his. "Sorry, I'm busy Friday. I've got another engagement. Thank Corrie for me, though."

"Sure. Would Saturday be better?"

Troy still didn't look at him. "I'm busy Saturday too."

Roy found this astonishing. "You seem to have an active social calendar all of a sudden." Not that it was any of his business, but Troy always used to be eager for a dinner invitation, especially after he'd moved Sandy to the nursing facility. Roy couldn't remember the sheriff ever turning him down, especially for a meal.

"I'm…" Troy seemed more than a little flustered. "I've reconnected with an old friend."

"Male or female?" Judging by Troy's discomfort, he guessed it was a woman, but he couldn't resist asking.

"Female," Troy muttered, lifting the coffee mug to his lips so that his answer was muffled.

Roy peered across the desk at him. "Are your ears getting red or am I imagining things?"

Troy scowled back. "You're imagining things."

Roy had to make an effort to suppress his smile. He, too, took a sip of coffee to hide his amusement. "This so-called friend got a name?" he asked next.

"You don't know her."

"That's a long tricky name."

Troy snickered. "Very funny."

"Is that her surname?"

"No." Troy sighed. "Enough of this nonsense. If you must know, her name is Faith."

Roy nodded in an encouraging manner. "And?"

"I haven't told Megan about her yet, so I'd appreciate if you didn't mention any of this to my daughter."

This was even more surprising than the news that Troy was seeing another woman so soon after Sandy's death. When he'd asked Roy to be one of the pallbearers, the sheriff was badly shaken by the loss of his wife, despite her long illness.

"I'm seeing Faith on Friday, then having dinner with Megan and Craig on Saturday," Troy said.

"I heard about Megan's miscarriage," Roy said. "I'm sorry."

"Thanks." Troy settled both hands around his mug. "Sandy lost two pregnancies, and both times she fell into depression."

"How's Megan doing?"

"Not well, I'm afraid. She put a lot of significance in the fact that she probably conceived the baby either right before Sandy's death or right after."

Roy nodded thoughtfully. Without meaning to, the poor girl was probably making a painful situation even harder on herself.

"Two big losses like that, one right after the other—it's pretty tough," Troy continued. "Which is why I haven't told her about Faith."

Roy leaned back in his chair. "She isn't going to hear about it from me, so don't worry."

"Thanks," Troy murmured.

The sheriff's phone rang and Roy stood to go. As he left, he heard the other man's voice take on a gentle, soothing quality. "It's okay, honey," he was saying. "We'll just…"

Roy moved down the hall, out of earshot. The sheriff was talking to his daughter.

Twenty-Three

Grace and Cliff's wedding reception would be Saturday, October 13, which still gave them three weeks to finish getting everything organized. That weekend, thank goodness, worked for almost everyone; their families and close friends would all be available. Grace was particularly excited about seeing Cliff's daughter, Lisa, and her family, who were flying in from the east coast.

Sitting at the kitchen table on Saturday morning, she went over her extensive to-do list. Decorations, catering, her outfit and hair appointment, wedding cake… A lot of details to keep track of. All the work, all the time spent organizing and making phone calls, would be worth it, though. This would be a celebration of Cliff's and her commitment, their love.

Cliff had gone into Cedar Cove to do some errands, and the house was quiet. She glanced around; everything was orderly and comfortable. Recently Grace had begun to make a few changes. Nothing drastic, though. Cliff had lived here on his own for twelve years, and the place had a distinctively masculine feel, so she'd added a few

feminine flourishes, beginning with decorative pillows on the bed. This was followed by a row of family photographs, hers and his, on the dresser. Cliff immediately approved of the pictures, but the pillows were there for two weeks before he even noticed.

"Where did those come from?" he'd asked one night as they got ready for bed.

"I put them there," she told him. "They look attractive, don't they?"

He'd thought about it for a moment and agreed, then once again assured Grace she could change whatever she wanted in the house. Still, she was trying not to overwhelm him with too many alterations and additions at once. Slowly, she went about making a few changes. A couple of oil paintings, both western landscapes she'd bought at the gallery years before, had gone up next. When she pointed them out, Cliff had nodded, obviously pleased with her choices.

Jon and Maryellen had given them a print of one of Jon's best-selling photographs as a wedding gift. It showed snow-covered Mt. Rainier against the backdrop of Puget Sound with a pink-and-lavender sunset. With Cliff's help, she'd hung that over the fireplace. He'd admired it, too, full of praise for her son-in-law's talent.

She'd just started checking the RSVPs against the list of invited guests when the back door opened and Cliff walked in.

"Hello, sweetheart. Would you like some lunch?" she asked, getting up from the table.

"I'm not hungry." Without looking at her, he walked directly to the cupboard for a mug and poured himself a cup of coffee.

It was past one, and Grace had postponed her own lunch, waiting for him, assuming they'd eat together. "Did you have lunch in town?"

"No." He kept his back to her.

Grace set her pen aside. All the warm feelings she'd experienced a few minutes earlier left her. "Are you ignoring me?" she half joked, wondering at his mood.

Finally he turned to face her. His eyes held none of the tenderness she was accustomed to seeing, and her stomach tensed. She knew what had happened.

"How long has Will Jefferson been in town?" her husband asked coldly.

"I…I don't know." This was true, in a fashion. She was certainly aware that Will had returned to Cedar Cove, but not exactly *when* he'd arrived. "Did you see him?" she asked, striving to sound nonchalant.

"Oh, I saw him. He saw me, too."

Grace closed her eyes for a second, filled with regret and remorse. She wished she'd told him when she'd first heard about it. Now she was terrified that Will would do whatever he could to drive a wedge between her and Cliff.

"You knew he was in town?" Cliff demanded.

Grace swallowed. "Olivia told me…."

"He's here to stay?"

Grace nodded reluctantly. She hadn't really meant to hide it from Cliff. But it'd become more difficult to tell him the longer she delayed. Considering his reaction now, she'd give anything to have told him the truth.

"You didn't think it was important to mention this?" he asked. His voice was calm, but Grace could feel the emotion behind his question. He felt hurt, angry, betrayed.

At this point Grace feared that anything she said would only upset him further. "I probably should have."

"Probably?"

"All right," she agreed contritely, "I *should* have mentioned it—as soon as I found out. But, Cliff, I don't—"

He didn't respond or even let her finish her remark. Holding the mug, he walked out of the kitchen. Shocked by his unaccustomed rudeness, Grace followed him to the door and watched as he crossed the yard and entered the barn. Her first inclination was to go after him. She pushed open the screen door, then hesitated. Cliff needed a few minutes alone, she thought, and so did she.

The problem, of course, was Cliff's marriage to Susan. His ex-wife had had a series of affairs, so trust was difficult for Cliff. Grace knew he *wanted* to believe in her fidelity but struggled with his experiences from the past.

She realized then that she couldn't let another second pass without setting things straight. There'd been rain the night before, but heedless of her shoes, she started across the yard just as Cliff walked out of the barn, leading his stallion Midnight. The horse was saddled, and Cliff obviously intended to go riding.

"Can we talk?" she asked.

"Later," he said curtly as he swung into the saddle.

"Cliff," she said, gazing up at him. "Please. This is important."

He stared down at her. "I'll feel better after I clear my head. We can talk then."

With a sick feeling in her stomach, she went back to the house. Sitting at the kitchen table again, she studied the guest list for the reception but couldn't concentrate.

She paced the house, transferred laundry from the

washing machine to the dryer, then decided to bake an apple pie. She hoped that by showing him how much she loved him, he'd know he had nothing to fear.

Two hours passed before he came back.

When he kicked off his muddy boots by the kitchen door, the pie was cooling on the counter. He glanced at it and, to her surprise, seemed more perturbed than ever.

"What's that?" he asked, frowning.

"What does it look like?" she asked in a teasing voice. "I baked you an apple pie."

"Why?" He maintained the distance between them.

Grace stood with her back to the counter. "I—I wanted you to see how much I love you."

"Uh-huh."

"Cliff, you're overreacting! This is ridiculous."

He raised his eyebrows. "Did I ever tell you Susan used to do that?"

"Do what?"

"Whenever I learned about her current affair, she'd bake me a pie or make dinner, which was a rarity. That was her way of telling me she was sorry. She'd promise me it was the last time, swear up and down that I was the one she really loved."

Furious that Cliff had compared her to his first wife, Grace strode over to the counter, picked up the pie and without a word, dumped it in the garbage. "I was married to Dan for more than thirty years. Not *once* in all those years did I even consider being unfaithful. Not once. How *dare* you compare me to Susan. How dare you." She choked back tears, glaring at him across the room.

"You didn't tell me about Will Jefferson," he said accusingly.

"That's such a big sin? He doesn't mean anything to me. Suggesting that I'd have anything to do with him is an insult."

He looked uncertain. "Have you spoken to him?"

"No," she snapped, then remembered the encounter in the library. "He came into the library."

"To see you?"

"He said it was to sign up for a library card."

"And you believe that?"

The phone rang and Cliff grabbed the receiver. After the initial greeting, he said, "Just a minute, please. It's the real estate agent," he muttered, bringing her the phone.

She took it from him with a nod of thanks. "This is Grace Harding," she said, astonished by how calm she managed to sound.

"Hello, Grace, this is Judy Flint from the rental agency."

"Yes, Judy, what can I do for you?" All she wanted was to get off the phone and back to Cliff. This problem was too important to be deferred; if they didn't settle it now, it would loom between them, growing more awkward all the time.

"I have a party interested in renting your house on Rosewood Lane. They've given me a check for the first month's rent."

"Wonderful."

"I'm just not sure about them...."

"Why not?" Grace didn't want to go another month making payments on a house that sat empty. She'd been forced to refinance in order to cover a debt of her dead husband's. Before committing suicide, Dan had borrowed money from his cousin, which Grace felt honor-bound to repay.

"The Smiths' references are questionable and—"

"Judy, this really isn't a good time. Can we discuss it later?"

"Well…"

"They gave you a check, right?"

"Yes."

"Then rent the house," she said, decision made.

"Grace, are you absolutely certain about this?"

"Yes," she said rashly, intent on resuming her conversation with Cliff.

"Okay. I'll tell the Smiths they can have the house."

"Thank you." Grace prepared to hang up the phone. "Bye—"

"You'll need to come by and sign some paperwork."

"Yes, of course," she said. "Thank you, Judy. Goodbye now." Before the other woman could make small talk, Grace concluded the call and put back the receiver. Turning to Cliff, she braced herself.

Cliff now stood on the other side of the kitchen. "You said you hadn't spoken to Will, then you said he'd been in the library. So you saw him?"

"Yes, and we did speak."

"You're changing your story. Again."

Grace felt like groaning with frustration. "I'd forgotten about it, and then I remembered. I wanted you to know the whole truth."

"Which is?" Cliff crossed his arms. His body language couldn't have been more obvious; he was protecting himself, warding off pain—or the threat of pain.

"Exactly what I told you," she told him, raising her voice. "Will invited me to lunch. He said it was so we could clear the air. I declined. I want nothing more to do

with Will Jefferson and he knows it. Despite that, he's trying to create doubt and confusion between us and you're letting him. I, for one, am not going to allow it. I married *you.* I love you and I want to be your wife until the day I die."

Cliff faltered slightly. After a few seconds, he dropped his arms and sighed. "I didn't have lunch. I think I might be a bit cranky."

She felt the tension seep away. Studying him, she said, "You should know I've decided against ever cooking again."

"You have?" Frowning, he eyed the chicken breasts thawing on the kitchen counter.

"If Susan cooked for you out of guilt, then I refuse to follow in her footsteps. As a result, I may very well have baked my last pie."

"No!" Cliff's protest was immediate.

"Compare me to Susan again and watch what happens."

He smiled then, for the first time that afternoon, and opened his arms to her. "I'm a jealous idiot."

"Yes, you are," she agreed, walking into his embrace. Their argument had frightened her, but the fact that Will held such power over her marriage was even worse.

"I'm sorry," Cliff whispered.

"I am, too." She clung to him, still shaken by what had almost happened. "I'm not Susan."

"I know, and I hate myself for implying otherwise. But please, Grace, don't keep anything from me again."

"I won't, I promise." She closed her eyes, listening to the beat of his heart, and for a moment all they did was stand there, in the middle of the kitchen, holding each other.

"Grace?"

"Yes?"

"Do you think that apple pie is ruined?"

She saw him look longingly at the garbage. "I'm afraid so."

Cliff's chest expanded with a sigh of regret. "That's what I thought."

She lifted her head. "However, I made two apple pies and put the second one in the freezer. I'll heat it up later."

"Thank you." He leaned down and kissed her, hands clasped at her back. "One more thing."

"Yes." She spread small kisses along his neck, taking pleasure in the intimacy they shared.

"What you said about not cooking anymore?"

"Oh, that."

"How serious were you?"

"Well…for a suitable incentive I could be persuaded to reconsider."

Cliff stroked her back slowly and with just the right pressure. "Do you have any suggestions on how I can make it up to you?"

Grace smiled at him. "I'd be more than happy to do that," she said, standing on the tips of her toes and offering him her mouth. The lengthy kiss that followed was not only satisfying, it promised much, much more.

Suitable incentive, indeed.

Twenty-Four

Linnette McAfee had been in Buffalo Valley, North Dakota, for almost two weeks. Her meager savings had run out much faster than she'd expected; gas, food and motels had taken a lot of it, and she didn't want to use her credit cards until she had money coming in.

She'd stayed off the main thoroughfares and stumbled onto this town by accident. Since it was almost lunchtime, she'd walked into the only decent-size restaurant around, a place called 3 of a Kind. Standing outside, she'd noticed a sign in the window advertising for a waitress. She was down to a couple of hundred dollars, so she decided to apply.

"You ever worked as a waitress?" asked a burly man with a leather vest and a long skinny ponytail. He had tattoos on both arms, and in other circumstances might have intimidated her. He'd introduced himself as Buffalo Bob and although he looked as if he belonged in a biker gang, his eyes were kind. Before she could answer, two small children came rushing in, calling him Daddy. Buffalo Bob scooped them up in his arms, which was

enough to convince Linnette that she had nothing to fear from him. Later, she'd met his wife, Merrily, and discovered there was a third child, an infant who kept the young mother so busy she could no longer work in the restaurant.

Linnette had some experience waiting tables. Years ago, while she was still in high school, she'd worked in a neighborhood diner.

"Do you have references?" Buffalo Bob had asked once the kids had gone upstairs and they were able to resume the interview.

"No. And I don't have a place to live, either." She might as well lay her cards on the table. The name of the establishment certainly encouraged that, she'd thought with a smile.

He'd smiled back, but then tried to sound stern. "The job comes with a hotel room. It isn't the Ritz so don't get your hopes up, but it's clean and has a television. We live here ourselves." He eyed her speculatively. "You running from the law?"

"Absolutely not!" She'd been shocked that he'd even asked such a question.

"We're not looking for trouble here," he warned.

"I'm not bringing any with me," she informed him primly.

Whatever his doubts, Buffalo Bob had offered her the job and Linnette had settled into this small town, which in many respects was like the one she'd left—with a couple of exceptions. It was smaller, and Cal Washburn didn't live there.

This was Linnette's first day off after working ten days straight and she planned to explore the area. She'd already

met a few people. Hassie Knight, who had to be at least eighty, owned the pharmacy and seemed to be the person everyone went to for guidance or advice. It reminded her of the way people in Cedar Cove confided in Charlotte Rhodes. Maddy McKenna ran the grocery; she lived somewhere outside town with her husband and two children, a girl and a little boy. Linnette had enjoyed meeting all four of them the previous Sunday and taken an instant liking to Maddy. When her newfound friend asked her to visit the ranch, the two kids seemed eager to show Linnette around, especially once they learned she'd never seen a real buffalo. "Bison," they corrected her in unison.

Maddy's husband, Jeb, was quiet, smiling readily at his wife and family, although Maddy carried most of the conversation. Linnette saw that Jeb walked with a limp, but he didn't seem self-conscious about it. He seconded Maddy's invitation to come out to the ranch.

The sky was overcast as Linnette got into her car. She and Maddy had met for coffee a few days earlier, and Maddy had given her written directions to their ranch. Linnette could hardly wait to tell Gloria about these instructions, which would definitely amuse her sister. As a cop, Gloria had heard plenty of convoluted and downright incomprehensible directions from members of the public.

According to Maddy's notes, Linnette was to drive 2.3 miles south of town, turn left at the dying oak, then follow the road until the dip and the rural route box with the black lettering. From there, she was to... Linnette flipped over the page.

The color of the sky reminded her of the flat gray of the navy vessels that congregated in the Cove. In the state of

Washington, that usually presaged rain. She was sure it meant the same thing here. Just her luck, too—her first day off.

The sky was growing perceptibly gloomier. And it was hot. The heat seemed oppressive for September, unlike home, but what surprised Linnette most was how still everything was. Even with her windows down, she couldn't hear any birds. The road was completely deserted.

Then she saw it.

A mass of black, twisting, spiraling cloud in the distance. She recognized the characteristic funnel shape of a tornado. *A tornado?* Here? Now? This couldn't be happening!

The next thought that flashed through her mind was: *What should I do?* Her medical training kept her levelheaded and calm as she analyzed the danger. Although the panic was quickly rising in her chest, she refused to give in. *Keep calm,* she told herself. *Keep calm.*

Her hands sweating, she gripped the steering wheel and pulled to a stop along the side of the road. Staying with the vehicle seemed to offer the best protection.

As she stared out the windshield, she saw that the twister was coming straight at her. If she couldn't outrun it, she'd be killed. The image of Sheriff Davis arriving at her parents' door, informing them of her death, was unbearable. Her mother had insisted Linnette was making the wrong decision. This would be the ultimate confirmation.

Barely aware of what she was doing, Linnette scrambled out of her car. Was she going to die? It looked that way, she observed in some remote part of her brain. She'd never survive this. Already the wind was strong enough

to throw her to the ground, carry her away, hurl her into the next field—or the next county. The only reason she was still upright was that she held on to the open car door. Her hair whipped painfully about her face.

Then, out of nowhere, another vehicle crested the hill, roaring down the road toward her. This truck was obviously trying to outrun the tornado. It came to a screeching halt beside her.

"Get in!" the man yelled and flung open the passenger door.

Linnette leaped into the vehicle. Half in and half out of the truck, she clutched the dashboard as he took off again. she'd just managed to clamber all the way in when the man slammed on his brakes again and the passenger door banged shut.

"Get out!" he yelled.

Hardly able to open the truck door against the force of the wind, Linnette threw the full weight of her body against it until the door flew open. The man, already out, grabbed her around the waist and dragged her into a large culvert beside the road.

"We're going to die," Linnette told him, astonished by how calm she sounded. That serenity quickly evaporated when the wind hit. Crouched down though they were, the violence of it dashed them both to the ground. The noise was like a jet engine roaring through a tunnel.

Linnette screamed in sheer terror. The man, this stranger, clasped her by the waist and held her against him, his arms around her, protecting her. The roaring of the wind was horrendous. Painful.

Then, without warning, it was gone.

Linnette's ears hurt, and she wasn't sure if that was

because of the terrible sound or the change in barometric pressure.

"Well, we're not dead," the man said to her.

"No." She looked up at him and into the bluest eyes she'd seen other than Cal's. The sudden memory brought a rush of tears.

"Hey, everything's all right."

"I know." That didn't stop the tears, though.

He broke away from her and reached in his back pocket for a clean white handkerchief. She'd never met anyone who carried a handkerchief before.

His thoughtfulness only induced more tears. Not ladylike sniffles, either, but wrenching sobs that made her shoulders shake. To add to her embarrassment, she started hiccuping, too, as she and her rescuer sat in the culvert side by side, their knees bent.

"I'm Pete Mason," he said. "My brother and I own a wheat ranch about ten miles down the road. I was going into town for supplies."

"Linnette McAfee," she said between sobs.

"Are you hurt?"

"No." She took a deep, shuddering breath. "I was in love, you know, really, truly in love, and then Cal dumped me. He went away to…to rescue mustangs and fell for the vet. The thing is, they're perfect together."

"I see."

Clearly he didn't. "And…and my brother has all kinds of money he's never told anyone about."

Pete stared at her. Linnette had no idea why she couldn't stop talking; despite her best efforts, the words continued to spill out. "I left Cedar Cove—my hometown. I basically just packed my bags and drove off. People

thought I was an idiot and…and maybe I am. Even my mother, my own mother, said I was making a terrible mistake."

"Linnette…"

"I thought I knew all about love and I don't… I don't know anything."

In an obvious attempt to comfort her, Pete laid his arm across her shoulders.

Wiping her nose with his handkerchief, Linnette took a wobbly breath. "I have no idea why I'm telling you the most intimate details of my life. I've worked for Buffalo Bob and Merrily for almost two weeks and haven't told them any of this."

Maybe she was having some sort of emotional breakdown. Maybe the tornado and her extreme fear had pushed her over the edge of sanity. How else could she explain what had come over her? She'd never reacted like this to anyone before. Here she was, divulging her private life to a complete stranger.

"Will you be okay if I leave you here for a minute?" Pete asked.

She nodded. "Sure. I'll be fine." But that wasn't true, and when he half stood and started to leave the culvert, she got to her feet and followed him. Walking low to the ground, they cleared the culvert.

As soon as they reached the road, Linnette gasped. It looked as if someone had burned a trail through the land, displacing the earth and everything around it. Then she realized her car was nowhere to be seen.

"My car!" she cried in shock. Had she stayed with it as she'd originally intended, she would've been hurled into the air….

"You saved my life," she said. "You saved my life! If you hadn't come along when you did, I'd be dead now."

"Another two minutes and we both would've been goners."

Pete's truck was tipped on its side about two hundred feet down the road.

"What do we do now?" she asked helplessly.

"Either we walk back to town or we wait for someone to drive by," Pete told her. "I say we wait."

"Okay." She really didn't know what else she could do, anyway. And he was the one who was familiar with these roads, this land.

They sat down on a patch of flattened grass. Now that the adrenaline had subsided, she felt weak, exhausted. Looking at her rescuer, Linnette saw that Pete was well over six feet. Tall enough so she had to tilt her head back. He was lean, too. He'd been wearing a cowboy hat when she first saw him, but that had long since blown away.

He wasn't what you'd typically describe as handsome. Yet there was something compelling about his appearance, especially his brilliant blue eyes.

His cheekbones were strongly defined, and his nose looked as if it'd been broken once. The dimple in his chin drew her attention, too. All in all, she had to admit she found him attractive.

At least an hour passed before someone drove through. As they sat there, chatting in a desultory manner, she began to feel more and more uncomfortable in Pete's company. Fortunately, he didn't remind her of the way she'd blurted out all the embarrassing elements of her life—like the fact that Cal had dumped her after falling in love with Vicki. Still, it hung between them.

The rancher who drove them into town dropped Linnette off at 3 of a Kind. By then she had trouble even meeting Pete's eyes. Most humiliating was her realization that, while she couldn't stop babbling, Pete hadn't shared a single detail of his own life. The sum total she'd learned was that he lived on his family's ranch. For all she knew, he could be married with a houseful of children. Not that she was *looking* for a romance. She was running away from one and had no plans to involve herself in another.

"Thank you again," she said over her shoulder. She waved at the rancher and at Pete, who'd lowered the passenger window of the pickup.

"Like I told you, Dennis Urlacher can tow your car back to town," he called out to her. "He'll give you a fair estimate on repairs, too."

"Yes, thanks, I appreciate that." Red-faced, she hurried into the restaurant. At this point, her car was the least of her concerns. They might never even find it. The damn thing could be in the next county by now or at the bottom of some lake. Linnette was just grateful she wasn't inside it.

"You okay?" Buffalo Bob asked from the tavern side of the restaurant. "Merrily was worried when she remembered you were driving to the McKenna place today. We heard there was a tornado warning out there. You see anything?"

Rather than launch into a long explanation, Linnette simply nodded. Doing her best to look composed, she walked past the men sitting at the bar and made her way to the stairs that led to the second floor. Dashing up the steps, she ran down the long hallway to the very rear of the building, where her room was situated.

She threw herself on the bed, breathing hard, torn between relief at surviving and humiliation at her own disclosures.

Thirty years from now, her experience in the tornado would be a wonderful story to relate to her grandchildren—if she had any. Naturally, Linnette would embellish it a bit, add some humor. At the moment, however, she could see nothing amusing in the circumstances. Nothing whatsoever.

A few days went by, and the traumatic events of that morning were relegated to the back of her mind. She refused to linger on them. Every time she thought about the tornado and everything that followed, her face heated up as if she had a bad case of sunburn.

Her parents had phoned, of course, after seeing images of the destruction on the TV news, and so had Maddy. She'd briefly described what had happened—without mentioning Pete. Everyone praised her clearheadedness and quick action, which made her cringe with guilt. Fortunately, she hadn't seen Pete since that fateful day.

Then on Sunday afternoon, while she was waiting tables by herself, he sauntered into 3 of a Kind. He saw her and inclined his head in recognition. Choosing a corner table, he pulled out a chair and placed his Stetson—obviously a new one—on the empty seat beside him.

With no other alternative, Linnette brought him a menu and a glass of ice water.

"Good to see you again," Pete said, smiling up at her.

Not trusting herself to speak, Linnette bit her tongue and nodded.

"What did you find out about your car?" he asked as he opened his menu.

"It's a write-off," she told him. There was major structural damage. One side was crushed when the car landed against a tree a few fields from where she'd stopped. Most of the glass was shattered and the damage to the frame was extensive. Although Linnette complained every month when she wrote out a hefty car insurance payment, she was grateful for it now. According to the adjuster, she had the go-ahead to order a new car.

"I'm glad," Pete said, glancing away from his menu. He chose the meat loaf and mashed potato special.

"What about…your truck?" It seemed only polite to ask.

He shrugged. "A few dents. I figure they add character."

She liked his attitude.

"Just like a broken heart adds character to a person…"

Glaring at him, Linnette jerked the menu out of his hands and stomped off to place his order. How dare he say that to her! Pete might have saved her life, but that didn't give him permission to embarrass her.

She'd never talk to him again, Linnette decided. Ever.

Twenty-Five

Jack had three steaks ready for the grill when Olivia got home from the courthouse Thursday afternoon. They rarely ate red meat anymore; however, they'd invited Will to dinner, and she knew her brother's favorite was T-bone steak. Besides, she had a few questions for Will and she wanted him in a good mood when she asked them.

No doubt Jack was pleased with the menu. Olivia kept a careful eye on her husband's diet. After his heart attack, Jack had promised to abstain from fast food and late hours. He left the newspaper office as close to five as he could these days and often got home before she did, which was a real switch from the way things used to be.

"Hi, Jack," she greeted him, setting her purse on a small table in the hallway alcove, just as she did every night.

"Out here," Jack called. He had a Reba CD playing and the volume was loud enough to rattle the windows. She was surprised he'd heard her at all.

Moving into the kitchen, Olivia found her husband preparing a salad. He'd arranged pale green Boston lettuce

and baby spinach leaves in a large glass bowl, which sat on the kitchen counter, along with two ripe tomatoes and a cucumber fresh from her garden.

"Do your talents never cease?" she teased, sliding her arms around his middle. She hadn't realized how deeply she loved this man—who'd come into her life nearly twenty years after her divorce—until he'd almost died. Now she appreciated every day she had with him. Every *minute.*

"I picked up a bottle of a new spray-on salad dressing," he was saying. "There was a coupon in the *Chronicle* and I used it. I think we'll like this one."

He handed her the bottle of Italian dressing and she glanced at the label with an appropriately enthusiastic comment. Who would've dreamed that Jack Griffin, editor of the *Cedar Cove Chronicle* and renowned junk-food fanatic, would care about low-fat salad dressing? Certainly not Olivia.

"You're spoiling me," she said with a laugh.

"Well, actually, I was thinking I'd get you happy and then lure you into my den of iniquity."

"Den of *iniquity?* Den of books and stacks of paper is more like it." Olivia loved the banter between them. "Anyway, after all this time you should know you don't need gifts of salad dressing to get me into your arms."

Jack turned and enfolded her in his embrace, kissing the tip of her nose. "The things you say to me, woman, it's a wonder I don't seduce you right here on the kitchen floor."

"And let my brother find us?" she asked.

Jack scowled. "Oh, yeah. I forgot for a minute—Will's coming to dinner."

"Don't forget, I need to talk to him…."

"And you want me to conveniently disappear."

"If you don't mind?" She sighed unhappily. "It's just that this might get awkward."

"I'm happy to retreat to my den," he said, waggling his eyebrows in Groucho Marx fashion.

After a quick kiss, Olivia went into the bedroom to change while Jack finished making the salad. When she returned he'd poured two glasses of iced tea.

As they waited for Will, they sat on the front porch, which overlooked the Cove. The waters were a clear blue and, for September, surprisingly calm. Sitting side by side on the glider, they sipped their tea and enjoyed the quiet of early evening.

"How was your day?" Olivia asked, grateful for these few minutes alone. Will's arrival would transform this peaceful mood into one of tension.

"I had lunch with Seth," Jack said. "Ran into him at the deli. I had vegetable soup and a multigrain bagel with low-fat cream cheese," he added righteously.

"Well, I had lunch with Justine." She smiled. Her daughter had been full of news about the sale of the waterfront land and their purchase of a commercial plot off Harbor Street. Everything had come together so smoothly, Justine was convinced this was meant to be. She'd talked about collecting Charlotte's special recipes. Justine planned to use them in the tearoom, which had pleased Charlotte no end. In fact, during their last conversation, Olivia had learned that her mother was finally writing down all her recipes. Although friends and family had been asking for ages, Justine had given her the inspiration she needed.

"Seth told me the permits have been issued and construction on the tearoom should start in the next few weeks."

"Justine said the same thing."

They both paused to savor their tea. Olivia loved the serenity of early autumn. Summer had lingered in the Pacific Northwest, but soon the rains would come. The days would grow short and the bleakness of winter would begin to descend. At the end of the month, Jack would store the barbecue in the garage for the winter and put away the patio furniture. Hard to believe on a lovely night like this. Knowing how few such evenings remained made it even more special.

"Seth said he'd decided to keep his job with the boat broker," Jack told her.

Olivia already knew this, and felt it was a wise decision. She said as much.

"Oh?" Jack questioned. "Why's that?"

"He's doing so well, and…" She hesitated. "I don't suppose it would do any harm to tell you."

"What?"

"Justine's pregnant."

"That's great!" He paused, frowning and obviously puzzled. "Seth didn't say anything about that."

"He doesn't know yet. Justine is telling him tonight." Justine's pregnancy was wonderful news to Olivia. Not so long ago, she'd begun to lose hope of ever having grandchildren and now, like Grace, she'd have four. Her youngest son, James, who was in the navy and lived in San Diego, had two children and soon Justine would, as well.

After a few minutes, Jack kissed the side of her face. "You're very quiet all of a sudden. Any particular reason?"

Olivia finished her tea. "I was thinking about Jordan," she said. The son who'd died the summer he was thirteen. More than twenty years had passed since his death, and hardly a day went by that she didn't think about him. Her thoughts were especially poignant at times like this, when she learned she was about to become a grandmother again. What would've happened if Jordan had stayed home from the lake that day? It was a question that still haunted her, maybe even more so now that her children were adults. What kind of person would Jordan have been? Would he have a family now? How different would her own life be? Her ex-husband, Stan's? Justine's? Even James's? They'd all been profoundly affected by Jordan's death.

"I can hardly imagine it," he murmured.

"A mother never forgets," she said simply. The pain wasn't as intense as it'd been during the first few years after Jordan's death. Still, at special moments like today's lunch with Justine, it was as if the loss had just occurred.

A car rounded the bend and she recognized it as her brother's. Jack saw the car, too. Standing, Jack and Olivia walked down the steps to greet their guest.

Will joined them. "Thanks for the dinner invite," he said, then kissed Olivia on the cheek and shook hands with Jack.

"I should be the one thanking you," Jack said. "I'm getting steak for the first time in a month of Sundays."

Olivia cast a disparaging look at her husband. "Ignore him."

While Jack got Will a glass of iced tea, Olivia led her brother onto the porch, where they sat on two of the wicker chairs that lined the wide veranda. She'd initially planned to have their conversation after dinner, but decided sooner

was better. Jack brought out the tea, eyed Olivia and then excused himself, telling them he wanted to start the barbecue.

"It's nice here. Really peaceful," Will commented, relaxing in his chair. He looked out over the Cove, where a pair of herons waded in the water, seeking dinner.

"We love it."

Will nodded, then sipped his tea.

Olivia plunged into the murky waters of her brother's obsessive behavior. "Grace mentioned that you stopped by the library the other day."

Will didn't respond right away. "I thought she might've said something," he finally muttered.

Olivia wanted to get to the point. Surely Will knew why she felt the need to talk to him. "You're aware that she's married, aren't you?" she asked bluntly.

"Of course." Will sighed and shook his head. "It isn't what you think, Liv. I made a fool of myself over her the last time I was in town. I regret that. The whole situation was unfortunate."

That was putting it mildly, although Olivia chose not to say so. Her brother had tried to provoke a fistfight with Cliff Harding, which was almost a joke. Cliff outweighed Will by at least fifty pounds and was in much better physical condition. The incident had mortified Grace, and Olivia had been outraged by her brother's childish behavior.

"Exactly why are you in Cedar Cove?" she demanded. "Because if it has anything to do with Grace, I'm telling you right now, neither Mom nor I will stand for it."

Her brother seemed about to argue, then appeared to change his mind. "I know stopping by the library wasn't a good idea."

"No, it wasn't. You're my brother and I love you, but Grace has been my best friend my entire life and I will not allow you to interfere in her marriage."

"I know." Will leaned forward and exhaled slowly. "I see now that inviting her to lunch wasn't the best way to go about any of this. All I wanted to say was that I'm sorry for…well, for everything. I wish her happiness."

"You have to admit, moving to Cedar Cove looks pretty suspicious."

He shrugged uncomfortably. "I thought about it quite a bit, Olivia, but I really didn't have anywhere else to go. I needed a change. God knows Georgia deserved a better husband, and it just seemed easier to start over someplace familiar. Mom's here and you're here. The two of you, plus your kids, are the only family I've got."

"You don't intend to make any trouble for Grace?"

"No," he returned with such vehemence that Olivia felt she had to believe him.

"What I'd like," he continued, "is to buy a business or start my own, I haven't decided which. Cedar Cove is home. I have the skills—and the cash—to make a contribution to this community."

"I'm glad." Olivia wanted to trust that what he said was true.

"Have you heard of anything that might be appropriate?" he asked.

Olivia thought for a moment and then inspiration struck. "Oh, my goodness! This is perfect."

"What?" Will's eyes widened with excitement.

"The Harbor Street Art Gallery. I just found out it's going to close. You've always had an interest in the arts."

He nodded eagerly at that, and she remembered how, years ago, he used to take very good photographs. He'd always bought paintings, too, supporting up-and-coming artists. "The gallery was doing well until Maryellen Bowman had to quit," Olivia went on to explain. "The woman who replaced her just didn't have the eye or the business savvy Maryellen does."

"Would I be able to hire Maryellen back?"

"No, but you wouldn't need to. You could manage it yourself. The community needs this art gallery and I really think you're the right person." The more she thought about it, the more Olivia warmed to the idea. "Talk to Maryellen. I'm sure she'd be willing to help you as much as she can. Keep in mind that she's a new mother, so her time is limited. She's also Grace's daughter, but that shouldn't matter—should it?"

Will looked pleased, disregarding the comment about Grace. "I'll call her first thing in the morning. I can get her number from you?"

Olivia nodded. "She can give you the contact information for the owners, too."

"Great."

They smiled at each other in mutual understanding, and Olivia's heart felt lightened.

As if on cue, Jack reappeared. "The grill's ready."

She and Will walked into the house.

Jack took the three T-bone steaks out of the refrigerator. While they watched, he rubbed both sides with olive oil, a grilling trick he'd learned from an interview with a local chef. Collecting the silverware and plates, Will and Olivia followed him outside.

The phone rang and for a moment, Olivia was tempted

not to answer. At the last second, she hurried into the house and grabbed it.

"Olivia, it's your mother," Charlotte announced.

As if Olivia wouldn't recognize her own mother's voice.

"Hello, Mom."

"I'm not interrupting your dinner, am I?"

"No, no, not at all. What can I do for you?" From the way Charlotte spoke, Olivia could tell she was worried. "Is anything wrong?"

"No," Charlotte murmured. "I don't think so, but… well, I felt I should say something. I don't want to cause any problems or borrow trouble, but I think forewarned is forearmed, don't you?"

"Mom, what are you talking about? Has anything happened?"

"Well, not yet, but I wonder if you should speak to Grace and Cliff."

Olivia didn't need any more information to figure it out. "This is about Will, isn't it?" Little did her mother know that her brother was on their patio at that very moment, talking to Jack.

"Will stopped by the other day and while he was here he saw a piece of mail on the kitchen counter. Although the envelope was addressed to Ben and me, Will didn't hesitate to take the card out and read it. I suspect he noticed the name on the return address." Her mother was getting upset now and her words were rushed.

"Who was the card from?" Olivia asked calmly.

"It wasn't a card exactly. It was an invitation to Grace and Cliff's wedding reception."

All at once, everything her brother had said came under

suspicion. Olivia was no longer sure she could believe his assertions that he'd put the past behind him.

"I told him how happy Grace and Cliff are," Charlotte continued. "He just kept looking at the invitation and I'm afraid...well, if you must know, I'm afraid he was memorizing the details."

"Mother, do you seriously believe Will would come to the reception uninvited?"

"Honestly, Olivia, I have no idea *what* to believe. I can't imagine that any son of mine would be so forward or so rude, but then I don't really know Will anymore."

"Don't worry, Mom, I'll take care of it."

"I don't want Will to do anything that would embarrass Grace and Cliff. He's made a pest of himself more than once."

"Don't worry, Mom," she said again. "I'll take care of everything."

"Thank you, dear. I feel much better now."

While she had her mother on the phone, Olivia shared Justine's news, which ended their conversation on a positive note. Before she hung up, Olivia confirmed that she'd handle the situation with Will.

She realized, as she replaced the receiver, that even a year ago, her mother would never have come to her over something like this. Charlotte was beginning to show her age. Olivia shouldn't have been surprised, and yet...

Until recently, her mother had seemed invincible, full of life and energy. She'd led a group of senior citizens against city hall, single-handedly held together the knitting group and organized any number of charitable enterprises. For the last three years she'd been the president of the garden club. Suddenly Olivia saw her mother in a

new light. Older, growing fragile, overwhelmed by concerns that wouldn't have intimidated her a short time ago.

As Olivia was about to turn away, she noticed the flashing red light, indicating a message.

Jack walked into the house to get her. "The steaks are done."

"I'll be there in a minute." She reached for the pencil and pad she kept by the phone and pushed the recall button.

"Ms. Lockhart-Griffin, this is the Women's Diagnostic Center. We're calling about your mammogram. Would you please contact our office at your earliest convenience? Our office hours are from eight to five, Monday through Friday."

Olivia stared at Jack as dread clutched her stomach.

"It's probably nothing," he said in what seemed like a determined effort to reassure her.

"If it was nothing they would've sent a letter the way they normally do," Olivia whispered. "Something must've shown up on my mammogram."

Instantly Jack was at her side. "We'll phone them tomorrow, Olivia. Together. No matter what it is, I'm with you."

She nodded numbly. "We'll talk later." For now they had company and she didn't want this to get to her mother. Charlotte had enough to worry about without adding a cancer scare to her concerns. No, they'd get through dinner with Will and deal with the phone call once he'd left.

Twenty-Six

Teri realized she couldn't keep her pregnancy from Bobby much longer. Everyone at the salon knew—even her sister had guessed—but Teri still hadn't told her husband. With good reason. If Bobby was protective of her now, and he was almost obsessive about it, this would only make matters worse. She didn't want to give up her job; she enjoyed it and as a gregarious, friendly person, she needed the social outlet the salon provided. Even Bobby had noticed a change in her spirits since she'd returned to work.

Teri had some serious concerns regarding her husband. He wasn't happy, and she knew why. He needed to play chess. He missed the game, the challenge and even the travel. When they'd first met, he'd been involved in chess matches around the world every few weeks.

When she questioned him, he assured her there were no significant matches scheduled now or in the near future. More importantly, he told her, he wasn't ready. That meant Bobby didn't feel prepared to face the Russian player he'd mentioned earlier.

Teri was so unfamiliar with the game and with the chess world that she didn't know how to communicate with him about it. She might be married to a champion but she understood chess about as well as he grasped the basics of a good haircut. What she did know was that he should be playing—just like she should be working at her own job.

The telephone rang and Teri automatically answered it. Bobby rarely heard the phone, especially if he was studying chess moves, which he did every day. It was her sister.

"Haven't heard from you in a while," Christie said conversationally. "Everything's all right, isn't it?"

"Oh, sure." Teri had no intention of sharing her concerns with Christie, although their relationship had definitely improved.

"I was thinking I should have you and Bobby to dinner soon, you know, reciprocate for the times you've had me over."

The invitation surprised Teri and pleased her. Originally she'd invited Christie back in the hope of encouraging a romance between her and James. Lately, though, she'd come to enjoy Christie's company. For the first time in her adult life, she felt like she had a real sister. As for the romance Teri had hoped to see between Bobby's driver and Christie, nothing had come of it.

"We'd love to have dinner at your place," Teri told her. "Let's arrange something soon."

"Have you told Bobby about the baby yet?" Christie asked, her voice falling to a whisper.

"No, no," she said in the same chatty tone. "Of course I'll bring something. I wouldn't dream of letting you make the whole meal on your own."

"Bobby's listening?" her sister guessed.

Probably not, but Teri wasn't taking any chances.

She was about to say goodbye when her sister said, "Uh, Teri…" There was a pause. "Listen, don't read anything into this, but I'd like to ask you a question."

"Sure."

Christie seemed to hesitate again. "It's about James."

Teri straightened and, catching her husband's eye, gave him the thumbs-up signal. When Bobby frowned and shook his head, she mouthed the words, "I'll tell you later."

"What do you want to know?" Teri asked, returning to her sister.

"Well…just some information. He's so…odd. What can you tell me about him?"

Teri had never really asked. James was James, and she'd heard very little about his background. He seemed too private for nosy personal questions. "He's Bobby's friend as much as he is his driver."

"What does he do all day? When he isn't driving you or Bobby around, I mean."

"Well, sometimes he waits for me at the shop—doing his bodyguard thing. Why do you ask?"

"I'm curious, that's all. It's not like I'm interested or anything, you understand?"

"Of course not," Teri said, glad Christie couldn't see her smile.

"In fact, the last time he took me home, I told him I didn't want him to drive me again."

"Oh." Bobby hadn't said a word to her about that, and Teri suspected James hadn't mentioned it to him.

"He didn't do or say anything to upset you, did he?" Teri asked.

"Nothing bad, if that's what you're talking about, but he…he brought me a long-stemmed red rose. Twice."

Teri didn't think that was so terrible. "How sweet," she murmured.

"Why would he do something like that?" Christie demanded.

Teri had been right all along. James *was* attracted to her sister and, if she was reading Christie correctly, her sister was attracted to him. But Christie was afraid in exactly the same way Teri had been when Bobby had first started paying attention to her.

"Do you want me to ask him about the roses?" Teri asked.

"No! Please don't."

"Okay."

"I don't like him."

Teri arched her eyebrows. "Really?"

"He's so…refined. It makes me uncomfortable. He calls me *miss*. That's such an outdated term! And he…he insists on escorting me to my door. Except the last time," she rushed to add, "when I didn't give him the chance."

"I know his mother was English and his father an American." That much she'd heard from Bobby once.

That didn't seem to be the information Christie was looking for.

"Do you want me to say anything to Bobby?" Teri asked. "Tell him you'd prefer not to have James drive you?"

Her sister hesitated briefly, then murmured, "Maybe not. I guess it doesn't really matter."

They ended the conversation soon after. When she hung up, Teri did a little dance around the kitchen, grinning madly. Bobby watched her, smiling, too.

"What's that all about?" he asked.

"It's working, Bobby Pin! Christie has definitely noticed James."

"Good."

"He brought her a rose."

Bobby frowned in disapproval. "Just one?"

"Trust me—one was all he needed. Only…she's afraid."

"Afraid?" he repeated.

Teri walked over to where he sat, climbed into his lap and slipped her arms around his neck. "I was afraid, too. Don't you remember?"

"All I remember is how frightened I was that you might not love me."

His words melted her heart. "Oh, Bobby, I've always loved you."

"I'm glad," he said simply.

They exchanged a few very gratifying kisses, and then Teri left to make dinner.

She'd just begun frying hamburger for one of her comfort-food casseroles when she started to retch. The aroma of cooking meat triggered a nausea so severe, she immediately rushed to the downstairs powder room. Thank goodness for a house with four bathrooms! She didn't think she could've made it up the stairs.

Bobby must have heard, because he was in the hallway outside waiting for her when she'd finished throwing up. "Are you sick?" he asked urgently.

"I'm okay," she insisted.

"Flu? Food poisoning? Should I phone the doctor?"

"I'm fine," she said again.

"I'll call for James."

"Bobby, no!"

A deep frowned creased his face as he studied her.

"I'm perfectly okay now," she assured him. "Dinner will be ready soon, but if you don't mind, I think I'll pass."

Bobby didn't take his eyes off her and Teri sighed. She was doing her husband a grave disservice by keeping the pregnancy a secret.

"I need to talk to you," she whispered. Taking him by the hand, she guided Bobby back into the living room and urged him down onto the sofa. Then she sat in his lap again and rested her head on his shoulder.

Bobby held her close.

Teri wondered how to lead up to her revelation and then decided on the direct approach. "I'm pregnant," was all she said.

For a moment he didn't say anything, but when she leaned back to get a better look at his face, he gave her the biggest, sweetest smile, a smile of such joy that tears threatened to fill her eyes.

"I'm due in March."

He accepted the news with his usual composure. "You will be a good mother."

"I want to be."

"Childbirth will be easy. You have wide hips."

She rolled her eyes. "From what I've heard, it won't be that easy, no matter how wide my hips are. And do we *have* to keep talking about my size?"

Bobby ignored that. "I'll be there with you." He pressed his forehead to hers and laughed. "A baby," he murmured. "A *baby*." She couldn't remember the last time she'd heard him sound so happy. The stress of the

past few weeks had taken its toll on him, and she was afraid this pregnancy would only add to his worries.

Then, just as suddenly as he'd begun to laugh, he stopped. The happiness seemed to drain out of him. The change in him was so complete, so striking, that Teri instantly realized he was worried about her, frightened by the Russian's threat.

"The baby is why you've been so tired lately?" he asked anxiously. "And why you were sick?"

She nodded. "The nausea's going to end very soon—most women only have it for the first three months, and I'm almost there now. So don't worry about me. Promise you won't."

"I'll try."

"I want you to be happy." All she needed to do was look in his eyes to see the truth. Bobby was ecstatic—and at the same time, terrified.

The doorbell buzzed, and Bobby let her go. She wasn't expecting any deliveries, nor had she invited any family or friends. Although, now that she thought about it, she wouldn't be opposed to seeing Christie. Or Rachel. She felt like celebrating. Telling Bobby seemed to make the pregnancy official.

As soon as she opened the door, Teri recognized her mistake in not checking the peephole first. At least ten people stood on the other side, crowded together, each angling for position. Cameras flashed and Teri instinctively raised her hands to her face.

"Are you Bobby Polgar's wife?" someone shouted at her.

"Who are you people?" Teri shouted back.

A microphone was thrust toward her. "Can you tell us why Bobby's dropped out of the chess world?"

"He most certainly has not," Teri cried.

"He hasn't shown up at any of the matches he was scheduled to compete in for the last four months," someone else yelled.

"No one knew where to find him," a different reporter added.

"Has he been in hiding?" asked another.

Both major 24-hour news channels were represented, she saw. Their trucks blocked the driveway. "Bobby hasn't been hiding."

"Where is he?" a man asked.

Her husband moved behind her, and the cameras started flashing again.

"Bobby!"

"Bobby."

His name came from every direction. Bobby gently pushed Teri behind him, then faced the crowd of reporters.

"Have you quit chess?" one of them asked.

"Are the rumors true? Have you surrendered your crown to Aleksandr Vladimir?"

With everyone shouting questions at him, it was impossible for Bobby to answer. He held up his hand, indicating that he was willing to speak. A hush fell over those assembled.

"No comment." With that, he eased back and quietly closed the door. With his arm around Teri's waist, he led her out of the foyer. Then, as calmly as if this didn't matter at all, he called the sheriff's office and reported that there were trespassers on his property.

"Bobby," she said when he turned back to her. "You can't keep this up. You've got to play sooner or later."

"I will," he promised. "When I'm ready, but not before."

"I won't let you surrender your title to Vladimir," Teri insisted. "He's trying to use me as bait. Don't fall for it." But she knew that Bobby's concern for her was even greater now that she'd told him about the baby—just as she'd feared.

"One thing I vow to you," Bobby said, taking her hands in his and raising them to his lips. "Vladimir will never hold my title. Never."

"Someone told the press where to find you," she murmured.

"Yes," Bobby agreed, frowning. "I know who it was."

"So do I." It wasn't hard to figure out. This was Vladimir's effort to force Bobby to the chess table.

Twenty-Seven

"I'm going to be in Cedar Cove this Saturday to visit my son," Faith told Troy on Thursday evening. He hadn't seen her in a couple of weeks, although they spoke on the phone almost every night. Faith had listed her house in South Seattle, and several potential buyers had already come to see it. No offers yet, but he knew it would happen soon.

He felt both dread and excitement about Faith's move to Cedar Cove. He still hadn't told his daughter about this relationship. The guilt he'd felt after Megan's miscarriage had destroyed his pleasure in seeing Faith. Logically, rationally, he understood that being with her had nothing to do with the loss of his grandchild. Still, he couldn't forget the fact that he hadn't been available when his daughter needed him.

"I...I was hoping," Faith continued, "that I might see you while I was in town."

Troy hated to turn her down. At the same time, he dared not risk Megan finding out. Not after what had happened. "I'm very busy down at the office."

"Even on a weekend?"

He should be honest with Faith. She deserved that and he despised himself for being so weak.

"Your daughter doesn't like the idea of you seeing anyone, does she?" Faith asked bluntly.

Troy felt a measure of relief. At least the truth was in the open now, although it should have come from him. "I don't know that she ever will," he muttered.

"Why didn't you tell me?"

"I'm sorry. I should have." He sighed deeply. "I was afraid that if I told you how Megan feels, you'd suggest we not talk to each other anymore." Troy didn't think he could cope with that. Their conversations were the highlight of his day; he could hardly wait to get home because then he could talk to Faith. They must have discussed every subject under the sun—except his daughter.

"I'd miss talking to you, Troy."

"You would?" Her saying so instantly gave him hope. "But it's not fair to leave you hanging like this. I can't even promise that anything's going to change with Megan."

"Troy, it's fine. Don't worry. Everything will work itself out in time."

She sounded so confident….

"I'll see you on Saturday," Troy said, coming to a decision. As much as he loved his daughter and as much as he regretted the miscarriage, he had his own life.

In fact, he doubted he could stay away from Scott Beckwith's house, knowing Faith was in town. Now that he'd given himself permission to see her, the guilt shrank, replaced with a sense of anticipation. He'd be with her in a couple of days!

"I knit you something," she said. "I'll bring it on Saturday."

"What did you knit?" The idea of her doing this thrilled him and the happiness he felt warmed him from the inside out.

"Socks," she murmured.

"Two?"

Faith giggled. "Yes, silly."

"I have big feet."

"I remember that about you," she said in a wry voice that made him laugh. "Those high-school dances. My poor scuffed shoes."

That led to a brief reminiscence of the Friday-night dances at Cedar Cove High and the songs they'd particularly liked.

"I'm taking my son and his family to dinner," Faith said next. "Would you like to join us? We're going to D.D.'s on the Cove."

He considered the invitation and then decided to decline. It was one thing to see Faith privately, another to flaunt it. Megan would find out soon enough and he'd rather be the one to tell her. He didn't want her hearing gossip from some busybody.

"I'd better not. Should I pick you up at your son's house at eight? Will that give you enough time?" He already knew where he'd take her.... But he'd save it for Saturday night. Surprise her.

"That would be fine. Where are we going?" she asked.

"You'll see."

His mood was almost jovial as he put down the phone. Then, on impulse, he reached for his car keys and headed out the door.

He drove to the cemetery. He'd only been there once since Sandy's funeral, but that didn't mean he didn't think about her. He did, every single day. After all the years they'd been together, Sandy was part of him. She always would be. Troy wished he knew how to convey that to his daughter, how to tell Megan that his relationship with Faith or any other woman would never diminish his love for Sandy. He wasn't sure she'd accept his words. Wasn't sure she *wanted* to.

He parked and walked over the damp green lawn to the gravesite. The array of pink carnations told him Megan had recently come by. He suspected she was a frequent visitor, coming as often as two or three times a week.

For long minutes all he did was stare down at the headstone. He was tempted to speak to Sandy, tell her about Faith. But his wife wasn't there. Not the *real* Sandy, the person she'd been, the woman he'd loved. Like Megan, he believed she'd gone to heaven, released at last from sickness and pain. He couldn't imagine her anywhere else.

When he thought about it, he realized there was really nothing to tell her, other than the fact that he'd kissed another woman. What astonished him was how good he felt about being with Faith. In his heart, he believed that Sandy would approve. Megan might have a hard time condoning it, but he didn't think Sandy would object. More than that, she'd encourage him to grab hold of any chance at happiness.

The marble headstone was polished and new. He bent down to run his finger along the carved letters. *Sandra Marie Davis. 1949-2007.* That said so little about the kind of woman she'd been. Never in all the years that she'd

battled MS had she complained. Nor did she curse her lot or question God. He'd been married to a very special woman and not once had Troy forgotten that. Not while Sandy was alive and not now.

Troy pressed his fingers to his lips and touched them to the gravestone, then walked slowly back to his car. Still unwilling to return to an empty house, he decided to visit his daughter and son-in-law.

Megan flew into his arms the minute she opened the front door. "Oh, Daddy, it's so wonderful to see you."

She looked much better than she had a few weeks ago, he thought, hugging her back.

"I can hardly remember the last time you came by," she said, and he heard the chiding in her tone.

Troy understood what had kept him away. *Guilt.* He was sorry he'd allowed that to happen.

His daughter had the same gift of hospitality as her mother. He was immediately ushered into the family room and handed a cup of coffee with extra cream and sugar, just the way he liked it. Megan had dessert out and had cut him a slice of pecan pie before he could protest.

"Craig and I are going to the ocean this weekend," Megan said, carrying in dessert plates for herself and her husband.

Craig thanked her and Megan sat down beside him. "I figured we could both use a weekend away," his son-in-law explained. "So I booked us into a place at Cannon Beach."

"Excellent idea." Troy probably exhibited more enthusiasm than warranted. Not only did he think this would be good for Megan, with his daughter away, he'd be free to enjoy Faith's visit. Okay, fine, so he had his own agenda. But he didn't want Megan hurt—*and* he wanted to see

Faith. For the moment, he felt as if he'd been handed a reprieve.

Before he left, Troy got the name of the hotel where Megan and Craig would be staying. As soon as he got home, he ordered champagne for their room. A romantic weekend was exactly what his daughter needed—and so did he.

Saturday evening, Troy was dressed by five o'clock. He shaved, combed his hair, then watched the clock for nearly three hours, pacing and periodically turning on the TV to pass the time. Precisely at eight, he parked outside Scott Beckwith's house on a street close to Rosewood Lane. He was just climbing out of the car when Faith opened the screen door and stepped outside to greet him. Her son, Scott, was with her and the two of them had a brief conversation. Troy recognized Scott from seeing him around town but hadn't known, of course, that he was Faith's son.

After a quick introduction, Faith ran in to get her bag, leaving Troy to exchange awkward remarks with her son. Troy was conscious of being carefully assessed but he didn't sense that Scott disliked him or disapproved. A far cry from Megan.

He and Faith walked to his car a few minutes later. She'd worn a simple green long-sleeved dress and had thrown a lacy knit shawl over her shoulders. Her beauty left him nearly breathless.

"You look…" He struggled for the right word. "Amazing," he concluded, convinced he sounded like a tongue-tied nincompoop. Whenever he was around Faith, he had to remind himself that he was a responsible adult in a position of trust.

"You, too," she said with a light laugh. "Oh, I have your socks."

"I'll wear them every day." They'd remind him of her, not that he needed reminding.

He held open the car door for her, the same way he had in high school—the same way he had for Sandy. His father had drilled manners into him from an early age and they'd stayed with him all these years.

Once inside the car, Faith asked, "Are you ready to tell me where we're going?"

"You'll know soon enough."

"Okay." She smiled over at him.

Clutching the wheel with tense hands, Troy started his car. He wished he could kiss her right then and there, but he resisted. Not in front of her son's house! And not where Megan might *hear* about it…

After ten minutes of driving through back streets, Faith seemed to guess their destination. "Troy?"

"Yes?"

"You're not going where I think you're going—are you?"

He took the winding road up Briar Patch Hill. One surreptitious glance told him Faith had figured it out.

"Troy! This is where we used to come to neck."

"I see you remember," he said softly, enjoying the tinge of pink that colored her cheeks.

"It had the best view of the lighthouse," Faith said, her voice husky. "I'm surprised someone hasn't built a house here."

"It's county property."

"I want to know how many other girls you brought up here," she said with mock sternness.

"None." That was true. Not even Sandy. "You're the only one. Ever."

"Remember the first time we parked up here?"

Troy wasn't likely to forget. His father had let him take the car. He and Faith had gone to a basketball game and afterward they'd attended the school dance. About halfway through, he'd suggested that since he had a car, they go for a drive. Faith had agreed. They'd parked up here, on the bluff overlooking the Cove.

Troy, however, couldn't remember a single thing about the view; what he did remember was kissing Faith. Holding her… They'd returned to their favorite spot many times after that. He liked to consider this place theirs, although a lot of other couples had claimed it, too.

"What do you have in mind, Troy Davis?" Faith teased when he parked the car and turned off the ignition. It was dark now and the lights around the Cove glittered brightly, reflecting on the water.

"It's a pretty view, don't you think?"

"Lovely," she whispered.

Troy stretched his arm across the back of her seat.

"As I recall, the last time we were here, there were no bucket seats and no console between us," she said.

"We can compensate for that." Troy leaned toward her. Faith shifted closer to him and their lips met. Although it was a bit clumsy, his arms came around her and she leaned into him. The kiss was everything he'd anticipated, everything he wanted it to be.

When they broke apart, Faith's head was on his shoulder. He certainly wasn't comfortable in that position, but he didn't care. Faith was in his arms. Again.

"I think time has only enhanced the experience," he whispered.

Faith responded with a sweet smile. "I couldn't agree with you more."

Because it was too tempting to resist, Troy kissed her again. They were both breathing hard when he finished.

"I took your bra off here, remember?"

"Honestly, Troy." She sounded flustered that he'd reminded her of that. In retrospect, it'd been a comedy of errors. He'd wanted to be sophisticated, pretending he knew all about a woman's intimate apparel. As it turned out, the closure had been at the front, not the back, and taking pity on him, Faith had finally aided his addled efforts. No matter how much he'd embarrassed himself, though, the result had been worth it.

"Oh, yeah, you remember." And so did he—every detail.

"I don't suggest trying the same technique this time," she said.

"Oh?" He didn't intend to, but the memory was a pleasant one.

"I wear support bras now and they're even more complicated than the ones I wore as a teenager."

"Heaven help me." He couldn't refrain from touching her, just to see. Then they were kissing again, reveling in each other.

All at once there was a flashing blue-and-red light behind them.

Faith pulled away from him and fumbled with the front of her dress. "Oh, my goodness. Oh, my goodness." She sounded seventeen again.

Troy dragged a calming breath through his teeth, then stepped out of the car.

The young officer instantly paled. "Sheriff Davis."

"Everything's all right here, Payne."

"Yes, sir. S-sorry, sir." The kid was almost inarticulate in his desperation to escape.

"That's fine. You were just doing your job."

"Thank you, sir." The patrolman was in his car as fast as his feet would move. Within seconds, he'd driven away.

Opening the car door, Troy got back inside. Faith looked at him and they both dissolved into giggles.

Twenty-Eight

Maryellen Bowman was so excited she could barely contain herself. Two important phone calls had come that afternoon, each one bringing good news.

Nursing Drake while Katie sat next to her holding a book and pretending to read to her baby brother, Maryellen let her mind race with the possibilities for Jon and his future as a photographer.

Just a couple of weeks earlier, Maryellen had received news that had distressed her. The owners of the Harbor Street Gallery had definitely decided to close their doors. She felt as if the years she'd spent as the gallery manager, building up the clientele and forging relationships with local artists, had been for nothing. Apparently, without her there to oversee everything, sales had fallen off to the point that it was financially infeasible to continue the business. Lois Habbersmith, who'd assumed Maryellen's role, felt dreadful and blamed herself. She'd never been comfortable in a managerial position and admittedly wasn't as good with either the artists or the customers as Maryellen.

Still, Maryellen had hoped sales would pick up during the summer, but that hadn't happened. Aware of her distress, Jon had suggested she return to work part-time. The owners had wanted that, too.

Maryellen had agonized over that decision, but in the end she knew she couldn't. Not with a newborn and a toddler. Her primary concern had to be her own family. When she told Jon, she saw the relief in his eyes—but if she'd wanted to go back to work, her husband would have honored her decision. Thankfully, Jon desired the same things she did. Family came before anything else, even if that meant sacrifices.

The first call was from Will Jefferson, the brother of her mother's best friend. Will said he was interested in buying the Harbor Street Gallery and asked if he could stop by later that afternoon to discuss it. Maryellen felt slightly uncomfortable about this; Will, after all, was the man who'd come between Cliff and her mother. But if he bought the gallery, he'd make a real difference to Cedar Cove, a positive difference, and she was grateful for that possibility. So naturally, she'd agreed to the meeting, although she'd made it plain that she wouldn't be able to work for him.

The second exciting call followed within the hour. During a ten-minute conversation with artists' agent Marc Albright, Jon's financial future had changed. Marc wanted to represent Jon's work. The opportunities, he said, were endless. Maryellen had researched artists' representatives and e-mailed a number of the most reputable, then sent them samples of Jon's photographs. It had paid off.

Now Jon would be able to devote all his working time to photography. While she was pregnant with Drake, he'd

found employment taking school pictures. Maryellen knew how much he hated that, although he'd never complained. He was doing what he had to in order to pay the bills.

Her biggest fear was that the job would kill Jon's love for photography. Until the fire that burned down The Lighthouse, he'd supplemented their income by working as a chef. With that fire had gone his employment. The restaurant had provided a steady—and reasonably good—salary, so they felt the financial loss immediately.

And yet, in unexpected ways, the fire had actually been a blessing.

If not for the arson, the rift between her husband and his parents might never have been settled. If not for the fire, Jon might've been content to work as a chef and keep his photography as a sideline business.

Behind a camera, Jon came alive. His photographs of the rainforest were so vivid, viewers felt that if they reached out and touched the print, their fingers would come away moist.

Until they'd started seeing each other, he didn't often take photos of people. But after Katie's birth and then Drake's, he'd taken thousands of family pictures. Maryellen had to admit she was self-conscious about the photographs he'd done of her but when she looked at them objectively, she could see what other people did. A man's love for a woman. A mother's love for a child. Still, her favorite was a picture of his father gazing down at the infant in his arms. Joseph's craggy face, juxtaposed against the smooth, soft lines of the infant's, was so moving it could bring her to tears.

But Jon's scenic work was where he truly excelled. One

of his best-known was of an eagle in flight, wings in a graceful arc, poised above the blue-green waters of Puget Sound. Another was of a ferry crossing with Mt. Rainier in the background. An art gallery in Seattle routinely sold his work, as did the Harbor Street Gallery; unfortunately, the money he made as a photographer hadn't been enough to support their family. That, however, was about to change.

Shortly after Drake was born, Jon had begun another job as a chef, working at Anthony's Home Port in Gig Harbor. It meant he could quit his job with the photo studio, which was a plus, but the hours were a problem. Because he had the evening shift, Maryellen was alone with the children most nights. The benefit was that her husband could spend the mornings with Katie and Drake. Maryellen loved him all the more for the way he treasured their children.

She heard a car door slam and eased a sleeping Drake onto her shoulder as she went to the door. When she didn't recognize the man who stepped out of the car, she assumed it must be Will Jefferson. As quickly as she could, she straightened the living room, collecting toys, cups, books and magazines, and rushing them to the kitchen. Katie attempted to help, but her efforts only added to the general chaos.

There was a knock at the door. She opened it, slightly out of breath.

"Maryellen Bowman?" the man asked.

She nodded and nearly tripped over her daughter, who grabbed hold of her leg. "Katie," she chastised, moving the little girl out of her way. "Watch where you are." Her reprimand had no effect. Katie wrapped her arm around Maryellen's thigh and clung to her mother.

"You must be Will Jefferson," she said, choosing to ignore the child hanging from her leg.

"I am." Will smiled at Katie, who finally stepped aside. He came into the house.

Looking at the living room through his eyes, Maryellen felt compelled to apologize. "Please excuse the mess, but as you can see I've got my hands full here."

"I understand. Don't worry about it."

They sat down on the sofa and when she offered him refreshments, Will declined. Just as well, because all she had was apple juice and graham crackers.

After some casual conversation, Will produced a pad and pen and asked a series of detailed, intelligent questions. Maryellen answered them to the best of her ability. Judging by the things he wanted to know about the gallery, the local artists and the sales when she was manager, Will Jefferson would do an excellent job—if he bought the place. The fact that he lavishly praised Jon's work endeared him even more.

"I do hope you give this serious consideration," Maryellen told him when he'd finished. "The gallery's been part of this community for a long time. Everyone is upset that it's going to close."

Will glanced over his notes. "After I talk to a couple more people, including my accountant, I'm going to contact the owners and see if we can come to an agreement. This sounds like exactly the kind of opportunity I was hoping to find."

"It would be wonderful to see the gallery back the way it used to be," she said wistfully.

Just as Will was getting ready to leave, Maryellen heard another car door close. She hadn't had company in several

days and two guests in the same afternoon was certainly unexpected.

"I'd better be going," Will said, coming to his feet. He smiled at Katie again and the little girl shrieked and buried her face in the sofa.

Shaking her head, Maryellen saw him to the door and noticed Cliff Harding, her stepfather, climbing out of his truck. They stared at each other, and Maryellen remembered again what she'd heard about Will Jefferson—and her mother. Now the two men were meeting face to face. In *her* front yard.

Not sure what to do, Maryellen shut the door and stepped over to the window to watch. At first, both men maintained a respectable distance from each other. From the set of Cliff's shoulders, Maryellen could tell he was tense. But gradually his shoulders relaxed and after a few minutes, the two men approached each other and shook hands. Maryellen saw, to her astonishment, that they were smiling.

Will left first, and then Cliff came up to the house with a box of clothes Kelly had asked him to drop off for Drake. He couldn't stay. She didn't ask about his exchange with Will Jefferson; the way Maryellen figured it, whatever had taken place was their business.

That evening she received several other phone calls, including one from her mother, but she managed not to even hint at any of her exciting news. It just didn't seem right to tell anyone else before she spoke to Jon. She had to wait until Jon got home, though. Maryellen decided not to call him; he was too busy at the restaurant, and she wanted to see his face when she told him about Marc Albright. By the time the children were both asleep, she was pacing the floor, eager to talk to him.

When Jon finally walked in, it was after eleven. Generally she was in bed by then, and he seemed surprised to find her up. He looked tired; still, he smiled when he saw her.

"To what do I owe this pleasure?" he murmured.

Without hesitation, Maryellen hurried toward him, slipping into his embrace and hugging him fiercely. "Oh, Jon! I have so much good news. I just couldn't go to bed."

"I heard a rumor that the Harbor Street Gallery might have a buyer. Is that it?"

She nodded. "Will Jefferson is probably going to buy it. He stopped by to talk to me about my views on the current problems and how to resolve them. He seems very knowledgeable."

"That's great."

"I have other news, too."

Jon regarded her with a mildly puzzled expression.

"This has to do with you."

"Me?"

"Yes." She led the way to the living room. He sat down between a laundry basket piled with folded baby clothes and a stack of freshly washed towels. She remained standing. "Do you remember all those weeks I spent living on this sofa?" Although she asked the question, it was unlikely either of them would forget the long months of forced rest she'd had to endure.

"This is a trick question, right?"

"No, it's rhetorical. I spent the first few weeks worrying because there was so little I could do, and you were run ragged."

"Maryellen," he said, reaching for her hands. "That's all in the past."

"Yes, I know, and I promise I'll get to the point in a minute. Just bear with me, okay?"

"Of course."

He looked puzzled but Maryellen needed to tell the whole story and tell it her way.

"Then," she continued, "despite your own preferences, you asked your parents for help."

"Yes, but—"

"Please, let me finish." She didn't mean to cut him off, but she was nearly bursting with what she had to tell him. "I understand how hard that was for you, Jon." He'd done it for her and Katie and the baby, and Maryellen would never forget that or what it had cost him.

"Just a minute," Jon said, "before you go any further with this. I don't want you seeing me as some wonderful hero. In case you've forgotten, I wasn't happy about it."

"I know, and that makes what you did even *more* admirable." She smiled at him, tears gathering in her eyes. "Anyway, while your family was here, I occupied my time trying to get you an agent."

Jon stared up at her. "How did we move from my parents being here to you finding me an agent?"

"That's *how* it happened," she said, speaking quickly. "If it hadn't been for your father and Ellen, I wouldn't have been able to spend all those hours on the computer or making all those phones calls."

"Are you saying an agent's interested in me?"

She nodded. "More than interested."

"Who?"

"His name is Marc Albright and he's already made two tentative sales of your photographs."

"Already? What about the terms?"

"It's limited use and Jon, oh, Jon, the money is fabulous." When she told him the figure, his eyebrows shot up in disbelief.

"Limited use?" he asked. "As what?"

"One's being picked up for a print ad for an outdoor clothing franchise and the other's the backdrop for an author's promotional kit, which is being sent to booksellers and distributors."

"Which shots?" he asked, immediately curious, just as Maryellen had been. She had them ready and pulled out the two photographs for his inspection.

Jon glanced at them, then looked up, his eyes filled with shock—as if, only now, had this become real to him.

"Remember how we talked about me being your manager one day?" she asked.

He nodded.

"Well, my beloved husband, that day has arrived."

Jon smiled widely. "That's wonderful, Maryellen." He stood and hugged her, then announced that he needed a shower.

A shower? Jon wanted to go upstairs and take a shower? She'd just delivered the best news of his career and all he could think about was a shower?

Maryellen didn't allow her disappointment to show. She hadn't known Jon all these years for nothing; he needed to process this information in his own way.

When he'd finished his shower, Maryellen was in bed. Drake would wake for his feeding soon. She considered waking him now and getting it over with so she could count on a few hours of uninterrupted sleep, but that wasn't a practice she wanted to start.

The moonlight shone through the uncurtained window.

Jon kept the bedside lamp off as he slipped between the sheets. "I did hear you right, didn't I? I have an agent?"

"He's one of the top agents in the country." She smiled. "I did my research, you know."

Jon lifted her hair and dropped soft kisses on her neck.

When he stopped, Maryellen rolled onto her back and discovered him looking down at her, his head propped up on one elbow. "He'd like to talk to you in the morning," she said.

"And you only mention that now?"

She grinned and threw her arms around him. "Are you excited yet?"

"I'm getting there."

"You should be, Jon."

"He likes my work?"

Maryellen wanted to laugh out loud. "He thinks you're brilliant. And you are."

In response, Jon lowered his mouth to hers. Their kisses took on an urgency that matched their happiness, and soon he'd divested Maryellen of her nightgown. When he moved over her, she sighed her welcome and arched up to receive him. They were familiar lovers and clung to each other afterward, their kisses warm and loving.

"When I walked into the house, I thought I'd fall asleep on my feet," Jon told her. "I was that exhausted. Now I'm so excited I don't know if I *can* sleep."

"Me, too." Maryellen felt like giggling. "I'm dying to tell people. Mom phoned this evening and Rachel, too, and I didn't say a word." Her mother was a nervous wreck over the wedding reception; in fact, Maryellen had never seen her so unnerved by a social event. She'd thought of saying something about Cliff and Will Jefferson, but

hadn't. It all seemed too complicated, and she didn't feel she should involve herself or interfere.

"Well, you can tell them now," Jon said sleepily.

Maryellen nodded. As a matter of fact, she intended to let the whole world know.

Cuddling up with her husband, Maryellen murmured, "Rachel and I had a long talk."

Jon made a noncommittal sound, obviously drifting off.

"I'm afraid I'm going to lose her," she said.

"What do you mean?" Jon mumbled.

"She's been seeing this navy guy and he recently got transferred. She really misses him."

"That's nice."

It wasn't, but Maryellen didn't bother to explain, since Jon was more interested in sleeping. "You remember what it's like to be in love, don't you?" she couldn't resist teasing.

"Sure do."

Maryellen could tell he was smiling. "Lots of benefits come along with it." Maryellen kissed his jaw. "I think she might move to California."

"Who?"

"Rachel."

"Oh, yes, your friend..." His response was followed by a soft snore. For the next few minutes, she listened to Jon's deep, even breathing. He worked hard and was on his feet for a long, stressful shift. But that was about to change; soon his photography would bring in enough to meet their financial obligations.

Contented, Maryellen closed her eyes. She was almost asleep when Drake's hungry cry startled her. Her eyes flew open.

"Okay, okay," she whispered, tossing aside the covers and climbing out of bed. Although she'd begun her new role as Jon's manager, her job right now was that of a mother. Just to make sure she remembered that, Drake squalled again.

Twenty-Nine

The day of her reception had *finally* arrived. Preparing for it, trying to get all the details right, had made Grace more nervous than she'd been about either of her weddings. Her first to Dan Sherman, shortly after her high-school graduation, had been a large formal affair. Olivia Jefferson had been her maid of honor, and she'd had three bridesmaids. Her parents had invited a crowd of family and friends, some of whom she'd never even met.

Wearing a traditional white wedding dress had been hypocritical, since Grace was nearly four months pregnant with Maryellen at the time. Her mother, who'd wanted to keep the pregnancy quiet, had insisted, however. Grace had gone along with it, although she suspected that anyone looking at her would guess.

Still, she'd been a happy bride. She'd loved Dan, although in retrospect, she'd known virtually nothing about either love or life. The hard realities would hit soon enough. In an effort to support his wife and child, Dan had enlisted in the army and been sent to Vietnam. The young man who'd left her behind with their unborn child had

been forever changed in the jungles of Southeast Asia. The man she'd loved and married had never returned; a very different Dan Sherman had come home instead.

Her second wedding, of course, had been an elopement.

Their sudden marriage had upset everyone for one reason or another. Not surprisingly, perhaps, Olivia had been the most vocal. According to her, best friends should be informed of such plans, regardless of time or circumstances. Grace had come to regret not letting Olivia and her own family know until after the ceremony. Everyone now seemed convinced that Cliff and Grace needed to celebrate their marriage with family and friends in order to make it official—at least in their eyes. Pastor Flemming had agreed to perform a short ceremony, which would be followed by the reception.

"How do I look?" Cliff asked as he stepped into their bedroom. He was handsome in his tuxedo—and completely miserable. He held his head at an unnatural angle and scowled in her direction. There were only the two of them in the house, since his daughter, Lisa, and her family had already left for the church hall. She planned to help Maryellen and Kelly finish decorating.

"You look like you're going to a funeral," Grace told him truthfully.

That earned her a curt laugh. "I hate these things," he muttered, twisting the black bow tie.

"You don't need to wear it on my account," she assured him. "Actually, I'd rather you didn't."

"It came with the suit," Cliff muttered. "I didn't think one of my string ties would do."

"Why not?" She didn't want him to be uncomfortable; this day would be long enough as it was.

"Really? You mean it?"

"Yes, I do." Grace kissed his cheek.

Raising his eyebrows, he eyed her in the pale pink suit. "You wearing panty hose?"

"Truth?" Cliff knew her aversion to nylons, especially the control-top kind. "I cheated." She lifted the skirt to reveal her thigh-high stockings.

Grinning, Cliff reached for the corner of his bow tie and pulled. The black silk instantly unfolded. He walked into their shared closet, and when he reappeared, he looked like a different man, relaxed and at ease. The bowtie had been replaced with an elegant black string tie and opal clasp, the perfect complement to his formal attire. Now he resembled the man she'd married.

On the way to the church hall, Grace thought about mentioning a troubling conversation she'd recently had with Olivia. Her friend had suggested that Will Jefferson might have the audacity to show up uninvited.

Grace didn't want to believe that Will would crash their wedding reception, but she was afraid acknowledging it would only cause more trouble, so she kept the information to herself.

"Something's wrong with Olivia," she said abruptly as Cliff helped her into the car.

"Excuse me?" Cliff asked, giving her an odd look.

Grace hadn't intended to blurt it out. This feeling, this intuition, had hovered in her consciousness for the last couple of weeks, but Grace had tried to ignore it while she prepared for the reception.

At first she'd assumed that whatever it was had to do with Will. Now she wasn't so sure. Olivia and Grace hadn't met for aerobics class for the past two Wednesdays,

which was completely unlike Olivia. Grace would willingly have skipped the workout and gone straight for the coconut cream pie. Not Olivia. Her friend was a stickler about their exercise routine. If it hadn't been for Olivia, Grace would've dropped it years ago. The fact that Olivia had cancelled two weeks in a row told Grace something was going on.

She should've just asked.

This blasted reception was to blame. All her time and energy had gone into the arrangements for it.

"What's the problem with Olivia?" Cliff asked when he'd joined her in the front seat.

"I don't know," Grace muttered, "but I intend to find out." She wasn't leaving the reception until she did.

The private ceremony with Pastor Flemming took place at the church an hour before the reception, with immediate family and close friends in attendance. Maryellen and Kelly and their families were there, along with Lisa and hers. Olivia and Jack, Charlotte and Ben, Cal and a few other dear friends made up the rest of the gathering.

Grace studied Olivia, who served as her matron of honor, and couldn't see any obvious signs of distress. Jack, on the other hand, looked dreadful. The way he stayed close to Olivia's side was revealing, too.

"Tell me," Grace said as soon as the ceremony was completed and they had a moment alone. "What's wrong?"

Olivia's eyes welled with tears and she shook her head. "I will after all of this is over."

"No," Grace insisted, pushing her toward the church ladies' room and forcing her inside. "I'm your best friend. Tell me *now*."

"Well, you married Cliff without letting *me* know," Olivia reminded her, pressing her index fingers under each eye to forestall the tears.

"This is different."

"I'll tell you, I promise, but I'd rather wait until the reception's over."

Reluctantly Grace agreed. It must be bad since Olivia was almost in tears. Grace had no idea how she'd get through this afternoon without knowing. If time had allowed, she would've made Olivia tell her right then, but her guests had already started to arrive.

The church hall had been beautifully decorated, thanks to their daughters, who'd worked feverishly that morning. Soon it was overflowing with guests, all offering their best wishes. Cliff and Grace made sure they greeted everyone personally. Grace considered it the supreme compliment that so many people had chosen to share this special afternoon with her and Cliff.

They made the ceremonial first cut of the cake and fed each other a bite, to the applause and laughter of their guests.

The girls were cutting the cake and distributing slices when Grace noticed that Olivia, who stood at her side, had stiffened.

Sure enough, just as she'd feared, Will Jefferson hovered just inside the door to the church hall, near Cal and Vicki's table. Grace felt her heart constrict. This was exactly what she hadn't wanted, exactly what she'd prayed wouldn't happen.

Olivia frowned. "Let me take care of this," she whispered.

Grace put another slice of cake on a plate and, carrying it, went to search for her husband. Her stomach was in

knots. Under no circumstances did she want Cliff to think she'd invited Will to the reception.

Olivia wasn't the only one concerned about Will's presence. As soon as Charlotte saw her son, she hurried across the hall and stood directly in front of him, hands on her hips. Although Grace couldn't hear what was being said, Charlotte's body language clearly showed that she wasn't pleased.

Grace approached Cliff seconds after Charlotte had reached Will.

As she watched, standing beside her husband, Will nodded, looking across the room at Cliff.

"At the risk of stating the obvious, Will Jefferson's here," Grace said. "Before you ask, I didn't invite him."

Cliff slid his arm around her waist. "I know you didn't. I did."

"*You?*" She blinked in surprise.

"I ran into him at Maryellen's earlier in the week and the two of us had a chat. He apologized, and so did I."

Grace's mouth sagged open. "But...you didn't say anything."

Cliff rubbed his jaw. "Actually, I forgot." He shrugged. "You know what they say about keeping your friends close and your enemies closer. At any rate, he acted decent enough. You don't mind that I invited him, do you?"

It didn't matter whether she did or didn't. Will had shown up for the reception. At her husband's request...

"Come with me," Cliff said, taking her hand. Before they moved from the vicinity of the table, he grabbed the slice of cake she still held.

They held hands as they made their way to the table where Charlotte sat with Ben and now Will.

"Hello, Will," Cliff greeted him. He set the piece of wedding cake in front of him. "I'm glad you're here."

"I'm not," Charlotte inserted. "It's always been my understanding that only those invited to a party should attend. A lot has changed over the years, but I didn't realize manners had gone out the window with everything else."

"Like I explained, Mother, I *was* invited," Will said, glancing at Cliff with a wry expression on his face.

"That's right, Charlotte. I asked Will if he'd come today."

Charlotte looked taken aback. "You did?"

Lingering nearby, Olivia caught Grace's eye; she raised one shoulder, indicating she hadn't known anything about this.

"Welcome," Cliff said, extending his hand. "Grace and I are grateful you could join us. Stay as long as you like, and by all means have a piece of wedding cake."

Grace didn't speak. Fortunately, it wasn't necessary.

Two hours later, most of the guests had departed. The money tree for the animal shelter dipped under the weight of the attached bills. Grace sent her daughters home with their husbands and children, while Olivia and Jack stayed, helping with the final cleanup. Lisa and her husband took their restless little girl for a walk. April wanted to feed gulls by the waterfront, so Lisa gathered some scraps of bread in a cloth napkin.

While Grace collected the wedding cards on the table, Olivia unclipped the bills from the money tree and inserted them in an envelope. She and Cliff had requested donations for the shelter, a cause they both supported, in lieu of gifts.

Without Grace's prompting, Olivia released a shaky breath and announced, "My mammogram showed something…suspicious."

Grace froze.

"I went in for a second set of tests last week."

"The results?" she asked, instinctively fearing what her friend was about to tell her.

"I have an appointment Monday morning."

"Oh, my goodness, Olivia." Grace was devastated for Olivia and heartbroken that she'd felt compelled to keep this to herself.

"I couldn't tell you," Olivia whispered, as if reading her thoughts.

"I made it impossible, didn't I?" Guilt and self-contempt overwhelmed her. Caught up in her own life, in superficial concerns like a wedding reception, she hadn't been paying attention to Olivia.

"No… I didn't want to ruin your day."

Grace dropped the stack of cards and impulsively hugged her friend.

Olivia shuddered, clinging to her for a long moment before she stepped back.

"Do you want me to go to the doctor with you?" Grace asked.

Olivia shook her head. "Jack said he wanted to be there." She offered a brave smile. "He's been a wreck ever since I got the phone call."

"He loves you."

Olivia inhaled slowly. "Thank you for not telling me that everything's going to be all right. I don't think I could deal with platitudes just now. I'm frightened, and so is Jack. If anything, this scare has brought us closer together."

"You'll let me know right away?"

Olivia nodded. "Of course."

"What about Justine and her brother?"

"I haven't said anything to the children. I don't feel there's any need to worry them until I have all the facts."

Grace understood.

It was after ten by the time Grace and Cliff returned from dropping Lisa and her family at an airport hotel, since they were catching an early-morning flight to Maryland.

Cal was already back at the ranch and had seen to the horses. During the ride to Olalla, which felt far longer than usual, Grace's head spun with Olivia's news. It was all she could think about.

When they pulled into the yard, Cliff leaned over and kissed her, murmuring, "Glad to be home, Mrs. Harding?" She nodded, and not until they'd broken apart did she notice that Cal was standing outside the barn.

Cliff was out of the car right away, striding over to him, Grace trailing behind. If Cal was waiting for them, that meant some kind of problem.

"When I got to the house I picked up the mail," Cal said, extending an envelope to Grace. "I must've taken this by mistake. I wouldn't have opened it otherwise."

"Don't worry about it," she said, glancing down at the envelope, which bore the rental agency's logo.

"You might want to read it right away," he cautioned.

"Something wrong?" Cliff wanted to know.

"Yeah." Cal grimaced. "Apparently the check your renters gave them bounced."

"Again?" Cliff said. "Last month's was returned too."

Grace sighed. This was more bad news she'd rather not deal with. Letting those ne'er-do-wells rent her home had been a big mistake, and she had no one to blame but herself.

Thirty

Teri pored over a new cookbook on Sunday afternoon, searching for a recipe that would entice Bobby to eat. His appetite hadn't been good since he'd learned she was pregnant. Hers, on the other hand, couldn't have been better. Her morning—or rather, afternoon—sickness wasn't nearly as bad now; she only occasionally came down with a bout of queasiness. Bobby's appetite, however, had almost completely vanished.

Then, to complicate life even more, her husband had discovered the joys of televised marketing. If there was the slightest hint that a particular product might be appropriate for a baby, Bobby ordered it. They often received two and three shipments a day.

So far, Bobby had purchased three cribs, five bassinets and enough toys to fill a day care center. The last thing that was delivered, and it came in a huge truck, was an entire gym set. While she loved him for it, this had to stop.

"You're reading a cookbook," Bobby said as he wandered into the kitchen.

She nodded without looking up. She'd already put Post-

It notes on several of the pages, designating recipes she'd like to try. Although she hadn't made her final decision, she'd started a grocery list. "Some cookbooks are more entertaining than novels."

Bobby was supposed to chuckle or comment or *something.* He didn't.

"What's this?" he asked next, pointing to the sheet of paper on the table.

"That's a list of what I need to pick up at the grocery store."

"Send James," her husband ordered.

"I'd like to go." Teri braced herself for the discussion that would inevitably follow.

"That's not a good idea."

"Why?" Teri didn't want to bicker. In fact, she hated it when they argued. Bobby didn't understand that she was a social person and staying in the house, beautiful though it was, simply wasn't enough for her. She needed to see people, interact with others. All weekend she'd done nothing but watch TV shows and DVDs. Oh, and she'd reorganized her dresser drawers.

"I don't want you..." Bobby hesitated. Pulling out a chair, he sat down beside her. "I need to know you'll be safe. I'll come with you, okay?"

"Bobby, of *course* I'll be safe. And I know you hate going to the grocery store. This is Cedar Cove, not some huge, scary city, so nothing's going to happen to me. But if it makes you feel better, James can tag along." Although she doubted he'd be much protection. Bobby, however, seemed to think his driver possessed skills that rivaled those of Agent 007. Still, if it brought him peace of mind, she was willing to put up with James trailing behind her.

His gaze held hers and after a moment, he gave her a half smile. "Thank you."

"I'd like to invite Christie over. You don't mind, do you?"

"For you or for James?" he teased.

"For both of us. And I'll ask her to go to the store with me, too." She considered that a satisfactory compromise. James was clearly besotted with Christie, and Teri's sister…well, that had yet to be determined. Teri suspected her sister *was* attracted to him, only she wasn't sure she wanted to be.

"I thought I'd make spaghetti."

Bobby looked pleased. "The kind with clams?"

"Whatever version you like best," she said.

"Clams."

This was the first time in more than a week that Bobby had shown any interest in a meal, which was a relief. When she phoned, Christie seemed glad to hear from her and promptly accepted her dinner invitation.

"I'm going out grocery shopping. Want to come?" Teri asked.

"Why not," Christie said.

An hour later, when James eased the limo into the apartment parking lot, Christie was already waiting outside. She allowed James to open her car door.

"Good afternoon," he greeted her formally.

"James." She inclined her head in a regal nod.

This was progress, Teri mused. Christie didn't even sound sarcastic. It seemed to take her an inordinate amount of time to slip into the seat and when she did, she held a long-stemmed rose. The color of the flower matched the flush in her cheeks.

"I'm glad you're coming with me," Teri told her. She made a point of not remarking on the flower.

"I am, too."

Teri noticed that Christie met James's gaze in the rear-view mirror.

"James," Teri said, sliding closer to her sister. "Christie asked me an interesting question a little while ago. What do you do with your time when Bobby doesn't require a driver?"

He didn't answer immediately.

"You don't have to say if you'd rather not," Teri assured him. She didn't want to embarrass James.

"He *should* account for his time," Christie said. "He's being paid for all those hours, isn't he?"

James headed into traffic and, after another short pause, said, "I read."

This was news to Teri, but she supposed it made sense.

"What do you read?" Christie asked.

"Everything. Contemporary novels, classics, all kinds of non-fiction."

Teri was impressed by this and suspected her sister was, too.

When they got to the house, Christie helped Teri make dinner, amid much laughter and the occasional small confidence. Bobby came into the kitchen a few times to see what all the merriment was about; he even joined in once or twice.

Dinner was delicious—and fun—and although Teri had invited James, he'd declined. When she and Christie had put away the leftovers and finished with the dishes, the phone rang. Call display indicated that it was Rachel. As she picked up the receiver, Teri saw her sister slip outside, probably for a cigarette.

Now that she was only working part-time, Teri missed seeing her best friend as often as she had before.

"How's everything?" Teri asked, concerned because Rachel hadn't seemed herself lately.

"Oh, fine. Everything's great."

The bravado sounded false to Teri. She knew Rachel felt tense about the upcoming rally Nate had asked her to attend.

"And Bruce?" Teri pressed. She suspected that whatever was *really* bothering Rachel could be traced to her friendship with Bruce Peyton.

The question was met with silence. Then Rachel muttered, "Why are you asking me about Bruce?"

"Why are you so defensive?"

"I'm not defensive!"

Teri smiled to herself. "Yes, you are. In fact, anytime I mention his name, you clam right up. So what gives?"

"Nothing, absolutely nothing," Rachel insisted. Then, in a sudden reversal, she added, "I love Nate, you know. We'll be together this weekend."

Teri rolled her eyes. She'd heard enough about that stupid fund-raising rally to have memorized every detail. "I thought you and Bruce and Jolene were going to the Taco Shack tonight." Teri knew this because she'd called to ask Rachel to join them all for dinner. Rachel had to turn her down; Bruce, it seemed, was treating her and his daughter to reward Jolene for being elected class secretary.

"We *were* at the Taco Shack."

Either Teri was reading too much into it or something had happened. She hadn't expected to hear from Rachel so soon. Normally, Rachel couldn't shut up about Jolene;

she bragged about every achievement as if the twelve-year-old was her own daughter. Rachel's silence was highly unusual.

"And?" Teri prompted, convinced now that Rachel's odd behavior was somehow connected to Bruce.

"And…we had a very nice dinner," Rachel murmured. "And then something…happened after dinner."

Just as Teri had guessed. "You'd better tell me," she said matter-of-factly.

"It was a fluke. Neither of us intended this and now… now I'm afraid it's ruined everything." She gulped in a deep breath. "I don't know what to do and I think Bruce feels the same way and it's so *dumb* and—"

"Whoa," Teri said, stopping Rachel. "Start at the beginning."

Rachel took another deep breath. "Jolene was asked to spend the night with a friend and decided she'd rather do that. Bruce said okay, so the two of us went out to dinner by ourselves." There was a momentary silence. "That's no big deal, right?" she asked imploringly.

"Right."

"We drove there in separate cars," Rachel continued. "I had a few errands to run first."

"You had a good time? At dinner, I mean?"

Rachel paused. "We always do. Bruce and I get along fine." She laughed, but Teri thought it sounded more like a sob. "The staff at the Taco Shack knows us because we've been there so often and they have the impression we're married. It's kind of a joke, and Bruce and I play along."

"That's…sweet," Teri said, although she didn't think *sweet* was the best word.

Rachel ignored the comment. "I don't think I should have dinner with Bruce anymore."

"Why not? You have fun together. Nothing wrong with that."

"Nothing until tonight," Rachel said darkly.

Teri waited for Rachel to explain and a few seconds later, she did. "After dinner, we walked into the parking lot. You know how it gets dark early in the evenings now. Well, I was heading toward my car and obviously didn't watch where I was going because I stumbled."

"Did you fall?"

"No, Bruce caught me by the elbow and then…then—" she lowered her voice "—he kissed me."

"Okay, so he kissed you," Teri said. "Did you kiss him back?"

"Yes…"

"Okay, but you've kissed him before."

"I mean we *really* kissed," Rachel elaborated. "This wasn't any peck on the lips or friendly little kiss. This was kissing like I've never been kissed in my life. These were kisses I felt all the way down to my toenails."

"Kisses plural?"

"Yes."

"Oh-h."

"I think Bruce was as shocked as I was. He kept looking at me and I looked back at him and then he apologized and I apologized and told him I missed Nate and that's why I responded to him the way I did."

"Because you missed Nate?" Surely Rachel didn't actually believe that?

"Yes," she returned heatedly. "I need to move to San Diego like Nate wants…."

Teri resisted the urge to scream that leaving Cedar Cove would be a mistake. For some time now, Teri had sensed that Rachel's feelings for Bruce were more complex than either of them realized. The last person to discover this seemed to be Rachel.

"Those stupid kisses are an embarrassment to us both. He's sorry it happened, and so am I. Now I'm afraid everything's changed." She sounded miserable. "That's why I'm calling, Teri. I'm afraid it might never go back to the way it was between us and I don't know if I can stand that."

"Give it time," Teri said gently. "Bruce needs to think this over and so do you. You've both had a shock. You'll be seeing Nate soon, and then you'll figure out how you feel."

Rachel clearly wanted to believe it would be that easy. And for her friend's sake, Teri hoped it would.

When she hung up the phone, Teri went searching for her sister. She wasn't surprised to find Christie in the patio chair. James sat with her, and although the evening was cool, neither seemed to mind. The moon was full and the stars looked bright and cold in the cloudless sky. As soon as they saw Teri, James leaped to his feet.

"Is it okay if I join you?" she asked.

"Of course," Christie told her.

James pulled out her chair and Teri sat beside her sister. "James was just telling me about the book he's reading," Christie said.

He seemed ill-at-ease with her there and stood once again. "If you'll excuse me, ladies, I'll retire to my quarters."

"Yes, of course," Teri said.

"Goodbye, James."

He bowed his head. "Christie. Miss Teri."

As soon as James was out of earshot, Teri blurted out, "*Christie?*"

"I told him to drop the Miss nonsense."

Teri had asked him to do the same thing a dozen times, but he'd never paid any attention. He seemed willing to listen to her sister, though.

Thirty-One

Jack waited until Olivia had left the kitchen before he reached for the phone. Bob Beldon was his AA sponsor and if ever Jack had needed to talk, it was now. Good thing Bob was on speed dial, because the way his hand shook, Jack wasn't sure he could've punched in the right numbers.

Peggy answered, announcing the name of their bed-and-breakfast, Thyme and Tide.

"It's Jack."

Peggy instantly knew something was wrong. "Bob's in the other room," she said without asking for details. "I'll get him for you."

"Thanks."

Half a minute later, Bob was on the phone. "Hey, Jack. It's Bob."

Jack felt as if his tongue had swelled to twice its size.

"Jack, are you there?"

"Yeah," he finally managed.

"You weren't at the meeting tonight."

Jack leaned against the kitchen door. "I should've been. I need a meeting."

"Is there alcohol anywhere near you?"

Leave it to Bob to get straight to the point. "Not that I know of." Olivia might have a bottle of cooking sherry somewhere in the kitchen, but if she did, he wasn't aware of it.

"Good."

"Can you meet me?" Jack asked.

"Tell me when and where."

Jack closed his eyes. He was terrified to leave the house—it wasn't safe to go where there might be booze. Where he might pass a bar or a liquor store or even a grocery. Although he'd been dry for over fifteen years, he felt weak. Desperate. He *needed* a drink. He didn't think he could get through this ordeal with Olivia if he couldn't have one. The craving was like a knife twisting in his gut. One drink. The aching need refused to go away. One drink would make everything better. Ignoring the voices in his head was becoming more difficult. Too difficult. The whispers urged him toward oblivion with a promise he knew was a lie. A drink *wouldn't* make anything better.

Still, it was how he'd once smothered his pain, and he hungered for the oblivion, the escape. Fear of what might happen if he gave in was the only thing that held him back.

"Do you want me to come to you?" Bob must've read his thoughts.

"Please." Even getting out that one word was an effort.

"I'm on my way."

Jack knew then and there that he couldn't have found a better sponsor—and friend. He'd linked up with Bob years earlier while living in Spokane and working for the big regional paper, *The Review.* When Bob and Peggy

moved back to their hometown and opened Thyme and Tide, Jack had visited. He'd fallen in love with the town, the landscape and the slower pace.

Up to that point, Jack had pretty much screwed up his life with alcohol, a bad marriage and a mangled relationship with his only son. Eric had moved to Seattle, and it seemed that if Jack was ever going to reconcile with him, his chances would improve if he lived in the area. So he'd come to Cedar Cove, taken a job with the local paper and got himself a place to live.

"Jack?" Olivia's voice drifted out from the bedroom.

"In here," he said, trying to pull himself together. Olivia had enough to worry about without him. Dragging in a deep breath, he went down the hallway to the master bedroom, determined to hide his fears. "Do you need anything?" he asked.

She sat up in bed, looking pale and lovely. Jack resisted the urge to hold her in his arms, to protect her and love her. She was frightened. How could she not be? He was scared out of his wits, too. If he lost Olivia, he didn't think he'd survive.

"Did I hear you on the phone?" she asked.

Jack couldn't lie. He'd rather she not know he'd called his sponsor, but he wasn't going to lie about it. "Bob's coming by. I thought I'd talk to him for a few minutes. You don't mind, do you?"

"No, no, go ahead." She'd spent part of the evening with Grace and seemed fortified and optimistic afterward.

At the moment Jack could use a dose of that optimism. "I'll probably be a couple of hours," he said.

"Can I turn out the light, then?"

"By all means. You need to sleep."

Olivia gave him a tentative smile. "We'll get through this, Jack. I promise."

He should be the one reassuring her, and he hated himself for being so weak. "Of course we will."

Jack walked over to her bedside, bent down and kissed her, then switched off the lamp. Fearing she might overhear the conversation between him and Bob, he closed the bedroom door.

Halfway down the hallway, he stopped and leaned against the wall, covering his face with both hands, remembering. Remembering. Eric, his son, had leukemia as a kid. That was what had driven Jack to alcohol in the first place. That helplessness, that total dependence on others to care for his son, that inability to alleviate his suffering… Jack had barely made it then, and he wasn't sure he'd make it this time. Eric had gone into long-term remission, but Jack didn't know if he could watch someone else he loved endure all the pain and uncertainty. All the grief and fear.

He just couldn't do it. He just might have to.

Instead of using the doorbell, Bob knocked quietly at the front door. Jack hurried to let him in. When he saw his friend, it was all he could do not to break down. His weakness shamed and humiliated him.

"I've been repeating the Serenity Prayer for the last hour," Jack told him. "I think I'd be face-first in a bottle if I hadn't."

Bob nodded, and Jack was grateful that he understood. "You haven't had a drink?" Bob asked.

"By the grace of God, no." He was one sip away from a complete mental and physical breakdown. He couldn't explain why alcohol tempted him when he knew what it

did to him. Still, the pull was as powerful as an undertow, and Jack could feel himself being swept away with the need.

He was hanging on by a thread and that thread was Bob.

"Sit down and tell me what's happened." Bob led him to the sofa.

Jack slumped down, burying his face in his hands.

Bob pulled the ottoman closer and sat on it.

"Olivia went in for a routine mammogram," Jack began, his voice faltering slightly.

"Cancer?" Bob asked.

"We don't know yet. Not for sure. The Women's Clinic called her back for a second test, a more extensive one, and then for an ultrasound."

"You've seen the doctor?"

Jack nodded. "We went this morning. He has to do a biopsy."

Bob exhaled loudly. "You're afraid."

Jack nodded again. "I don't think I truly realized how much I love Olivia until this morning."

To his surprise, Bob smiled. "Olivia said almost those same words to me when you had your heart attack."

Now that their situations were, in effect, reversed, he could appreciate how hard it had been on his wife. The problem was, love opened you up to that kind of pain. He'd never expected to fall in love again when he moved to Cedar Cove. Even less had he expected to find someone who loved *him.*

He'd been attracted to Olivia right away. Sitting in her courtroom and watching her deny a divorce—that got his attention. Most family court judges were jaded by the

day-in-and-day-out bitterness of marriages gone bad. Not Olivia. She'd seen that the young couple was still in love and she'd intervened. Her compassion had stirred him. Her toughness had impressed him.

Jack knew that if Olivia hadn't denied that divorce, the couple would have gone their separate ways and carried around that pain for the rest of their lives. She'd forced them to deal with the grief of losing their child, forced them to resolve their differences.

Without knowing it, Jack had fallen in love with her that very morning. In fact, he'd written an entire column in the *Cedar Cove Chronicle* about her unusual stand. His attention had embarrassed her but she'd eventually forgiven him.

When they got married, Jack felt as though his life had begun again. He was crazy about her, although their relationship had never been easy. They were about as different as two people could get.

"Jack?"

Startled, Jack glanced up to see Bob staring at him. "You won't know for sure if it's cancer until they do the biopsy, right?"

His heart pounded against his ribs. "It's scheduled for this week."

"You want a drink now?"

"Yes," he said hoarsely. "A strong drink. Strong enough to take away this ache." Preferably hard alcohol, Scotch or brandy, something that would melt his teeth.

"A drink's going to help?" Bob asked.

They both knew the answer to that. "No. But that doesn't make me want one any less."

Bob cocked his eyebrow. "One?"

Jack didn't have to be told that one drink, even one sip, was a fantasy. For alcoholics like Bob and him, it never ended there. Jack had sat through enough meetings to know that. Lived it long enough to recognize the truth when he heard it. This was the lie so many alcoholics tried to believe: that they were strong enough to have one drink, just one, and then walk away. But that wasn't how it worked for people like him.

"You need a meeting to get your head on straight," Bob said. He stood up to take his wallet out of his hip pocket, then pulled out a small booklet and unfolded it. "There's one in Bremerton that starts in ten minutes. I'll drive."

Jack nodded. They'd be late but that didn't matter. A meeting was a meeting. He'd feel better after talking about this with other men and women who understood the addictive power of alcohol.

"Let me say goodbye to Olivia." Carefully opening the bedroom door a moment later, he paused, hesitant to wake her if she was asleep. Light spilled from the hallway into the bedroom.

"Jack?" Olivia rose up on one elbow. "Is everything all right?"

"It is now. Bob and I are going out for a while."

"Okay. I'll see you later."

"Will you be okay by yourself?" he asked. "I can call Grace if you want." She was the kind of friend to Olivia that Bob was to him. Any time of the day or night, Grace would be willing to help.

Olivia shook her head. "I'm fine."

Walking into the room, Jack sat on the edge of the bed and gathered Olivia in his arms. As they clung to each other, he felt her tremble.

"I need a meeting," he whispered.

"I know, Jack. Go." She stroked the back of his head, her fingers light against his hair.

It was the same way she touched him after they'd made love. The gesture brought emotion bubbling to the surface and Jack hid his face in her shoulder.

"Wake me when you get back," she whispered.

"Okay." He left her then, reluctantly.

Bob was waiting for him by the front door. Jack grabbed a fleece jacket from the hall closet and together they headed into the cold. A sporadic rain had begun, matching his mood, darkening an already dark sky. When they reached the address, they hurried into a church basement that smelled of stale coffee and damp coats. Jack was quickly immersed in the familiar and comforting routine of the meeting; it was exactly what he'd needed, he told himself an hour later.

During his first weeks of sobriety, he'd gone to thirty meetings in thirty days. He'd needed every one of those meetings. That was how he'd made it through the first month—one day at a time and on some days one minute at a time. Alcoholics Anonymous had given him a structure. And Bob had helped him at every step, listening, encouraging, cutting through the bull and self-pity. When his head was clear enough to listen, Bob reminded him that no one had poured the booze down his throat. No one had forced him to drink. He had to take responsibility for his own life, his own happiness.

By the time he let himself into the house, it was two o'clock. He, Bob and a couple of other people from the meeting had gone out for coffee afterward and they'd talked for another hour. Jack felt almost sane again.

He slipped off his jacket and hung it in the hall closet. Olivia had trained him well, he thought. Smiling, he started toward the bedroom. When he walked inside, he was surprised to see his wife sitting up in bed, a book lying open on her lap. She blinked at him, obviously a bit disoriented.

"Oh! I didn't hear you come in."

"I can tell." Moving to the side of the bed, he kissed her. He'd meant it to be light and easy, but the kiss quickly turned into something more, something urgent.

All at once, Olivia broke away from him. "Jack Griffin," she cried. "What's that I taste on you?"

"Ah…"

She ran her tongue over her bottom lip. "Cherry pie?"

He grinned. "Could be."

"Jack!"

"Hey, Miss Coconut-Cream-Pie-every-Wednesday-night. You've got no call to be criticizing me."

Her pretend outrage faded, and she set aside the book she'd been reading. "Do you feel better?"

"Much," he said.

"Me, too."

Jack knew he was ready for whatever the future held. He could—and would—be the man his wife deserved.

Thirty-Two

Rachel checked her watch, then peered out the living-room window again. Bruce was already five minutes late, and she wondered if he even remembered that he'd agreed to drive her to the airport today. She'd asked him weeks ago—long before he'd kissed her…before the less-than-subtle shift in their relationship. They hadn't talked since that night.

Normally she'd phone to remind him. She hadn't, mainly because she didn't know what to say. It was all so awkward. He obviously regretted those kisses as much as she did. Every time she thought about the way she'd responded to him, she got upset. They'd both been out of line, and her biggest fear was that this momentary slip might have ruined one of the most agreeable friendships of her life.

When Bruce's car pulled up to the curb, Rachel wasn't sure whether to be relieved or not. Reaching for her suitcase, she hurried outside, pausing only long enough to lock the door. According to the Pittsburgh forecast, which she'd looked up on the Internet, the weather there

was unseasonably cold for mid-October. She'd brought along her winter coat, slung over her arm because she certainly didn't need it in Cedar Cove right now. The Pacific Northwest enjoyed moderate temperatures, although it was uncomfortably cool at night.

Without a word of greeting, Bruce was out of the car. He took the suitcase from her hand and heaved it into the trunk. She noticed that his eyes avoided hers.

Rachel felt wretched. If they were going to remain friends, they needed to clear the air. She waited until she was inside the car and had fastened her seat belt.

"I really appreciate your doing this," she said, thinking that showing her gratitude was a good start.

"No problem." His response was clipped, as if he'd rather not talk to her at all. Driving into Seattle during the morning rush hour wasn't a negligible task; Bruce was doing her a huge favor. But he'd volunteered as soon as she'd mentioned it. He had his own business, so he could take the time off.

As they neared the freeway on-ramp she finally referred to that foolish kiss. "I guess maybe we should talk about what happened Friday night," she said, fiddling nervously with the strap of her handbag.

"What's there to talk about?" Bruce returned, focusing his attention on the road ahead.

"I want to be sure it hasn't damaged our friendship."

"It hasn't."

"I know you regret the whole thing. So do I," she continued.

He turned his head briefly, glancing in her direction. "I never said I regretted it."

"You apologized," she reminded him.

"That's not the same as regretting it."

Rachel frowned, a little confused. "Oh. I guess not." She didn't really see the difference, but that didn't matter. "Our friendship means a great deal to me."

"And me. You've been wonderful with Jolene."

"It's more than Jolene, though."

"Yes," he snapped. "It is."

A familiar ache came over Rachel. She loved Jolene, and she cared about Bruce. *More* than cared about him? Everything was suddenly too complicated. She grew quiet after his remark, and Bruce didn't seem inclined to speak, either.

When they arrived at Sea-Tac Airport, he stopped at the curb. The sidewalk in front of the terminal was swarming with people. Bruce left the engine running as he hopped out of the car and retrieved her suitcase from the trunk. He'd set it on the curb before Rachel had a chance to gather the rest of her things and climb out.

Apparently he couldn't get rid of her fast enough. They stood there awkwardly, facing each other in the midst of people coming and going, dropping off travelers, unloading bags. He seemed every bit as nervous as she was.

"Have a good flight," Bruce finally murmured.

"Thank you. I'm sure I will." Within hours, she'd be seeing Nate again and she should be feeling elated. Excited. Only she wasn't. She'd rather sort this out with Bruce. Or at least effect some kind of reconciliation before she left. She hated this unsettled feeling. Still, she'd tried, and he didn't seem interested. And Rachel didn't feel she could press any more than she already had.

It wasn't right to be flying off to visit Nate and his family while she was thinking about another man. This

would be an important week. The political fundraiser the next afternoon was critical to Nate's family, and Rachel was determined to do everything she could to become an asset to both Nate and his father.

Then, surprising her again, Bruce stepped closer and hugged her. This wasn't a token hug; he held her tight, as if he didn't want to let her go. After a moment, he dropped his arms. Shocked, and more confused than ever, Rachel moved toward her suitcase and without looking back, picked it up and walked into the terminal.

Nate had arranged his flight into Pittsburgh so that he'd arrive from San Diego thirty minutes ahead of her. When she came out of the jetway, he was at the gate waiting for her.

One glance at her handsome navy man, and Rachel gave a small cry of delight. She flew into his arms. It felt like forever since they'd been together, although it had only been a month.

"Dad sent a car for us," Nate said as he slipped an arm around her waist. He gazed down at her, his eyes full of warmth. "You look wonderful."

Rachel couldn't keep from blushing at his praise. "You, too."

"There's a dinner this evening that Mom suggested we attend. You don't mind, do you?"

Rachel *did* mind, but she couldn't protest, since Nate's family had paid for her airline ticket. She'd hoped she and Nate would have this evening to themselves. That obviously wouldn't be the case.

The driver found them in the baggage claim area, and soon they were on their way. As Nate relayed the itinerary for the next two days, it seemed unlikely that they'd

have more than a minute to themselves at any given time. The culminating event, the rally, was where Nate's father would announce that he'd be running for the senate.

"Stop," she said at one point. "My head is spinning. Are we required to attend *all* these functions?" In addition to the rally, there were a number of meals and cocktail parties, sometimes as many as three in a single afternoon. There were also visits to service clubs, senior citizens' organizations, schools and even a shopping mall, where they'd hand out flyers.

Nate seemed surprised that she'd asked. "Of course we're going to all of them. That's what you do during a political campaign. Trust me, I should know."

"Were you always this involved?"

"Except for the last few years, yes." He took her hand. "I should tell you that Dad and I've been talking."

Rachel didn't know if that was a good thing or not, although of his parents, she preferred his father. Nathaniel Olsen was a consummate politician and had a way of making everyone he met feel like his best friend. Still, as much as she hoped the congressman approved of her relationship with Nate, Rachel couldn't be sure.

Nate's mother, on the other hand, hadn't bothered to disguise her objections. This time Rachel was prepared for that. No matter what Patrice said or did, she refused to let the other woman upset her.

"Dad wants me to work for him when I get out of the navy," Nate said. He clearly thought she'd be pleased.

She wasn't; it was exactly what she'd always feared. When they'd first met, Nate claimed he had no political aspirations of his own. She was beginning to seriously doubt that. Nate loved campaigning, loved the challenge

and the excitement. He was used to privilege and to the advantages conferred by wealth and power. Wherever they went, as long as he was with his father, he was a guest of honor.

"I thought you hadn't made a decision about reenlisting in the navy?" They'd discussed this a number of times.

"I haven't," Nate was quick to tell her.

His flippant response gave her the distinct feeling that he actually had.

The driver delivered them to the Olsen residence outside the city. The huge, two-story house seemed more like a palace to Rachel; it was even grander than she'd expected. There were fifteen acres of beautifully landscaped grounds, and the house itself looked as if it belonged in a glossy architectural magazine.

"Come on," Nate said, taking her hand.

Rachel managed to close her mouth and gulp in a deep breath before Patrice Olsen, Nate's mother, came hurrying out the front door, arms wide. Nate released Rachel's hand long enough to hug his mother, lifting Patrice off the ground in his exuberance.

Inside the Olsen residence, everything seemed to be made of Italian marble or polished mahogany, and every piece of furniture looked like a priceless antique. Rachel was afraid to touch any surface for fear of smudging it, afraid to walk anywhere for fear of leaving footprints in the deep, soft carpeting.

She'd been escorted to a guest room that felt more like a hotel room, but far nicer than any she'd ever stayed at. Dinner was just an hour after their arrival so Rachel didn't have time to do more than admire her room, change her clothes and freshen her makeup before they had to leave.

The next morning, there was a breakfast at which Nate and Rachel were required to mingle. With Nate at her side, she found it wasn't as difficult as she'd assumed. Afterward he complimented her, and that went a long way toward soothing her nerves.

"You're doing really well," he assured her as they hurried from the breakfast to a factory and then a huge assisted-living complex. Naturally, the local press showed up everywhere. Rachel prayed no one would address any questions to her or ask about her role.

She marveled at both Nate and his father. At each stop, each occasion, she saw how effectively they spoke, how inspiring they were. The rally the next afternoon was the main event, followed by a formal dinner.

Saturday was another long day of appearances until finally they entered the auditorium where the rally would be held. Rachel sat with rapt attention through all the speeches and applauded at all the appropriate places. At the end of Nathaniel's speech, during which he declared his candidacy, she joined the crowd in giving him a standing ovation.

When the applause died down, the congressman brought Nate onto the stage and introduced him, telling his constituents how proud he was to have a son serving in the military. With tears in her eyes, Rachel clapped wildly.

To the sound of cheering, Nate stood next to his father and raised both arms. Then father and son embraced in what was truly a touching moment.

Patrice Olsen moved down one seat in order to sit beside Rachel.

"He looks good with his father, doesn't he?" she said, leaning close.

"Very good." Rachel smiled over at Nate's mother and continued applauding.

"Nathaniel has political ambitions for our son."

Rachel had already assumed as much. "I can see he'd do a wonderful job." After watching Nate with his father, it seemed inevitable that he'd follow in the older man's footsteps.

"Nate gets out of the navy in less than a year."

Rachel nodded. She and Nate had discussed that very subject shortly after she'd landed in Pittsburgh. Until that point, Rachel had been under the misconception that he hadn't decided whether or not to re-enlist. She'd guessed then that Nate wasn't going to.

"Dirk Hagerman is a friend of Nathaniel's. Dirk's retiring as a state representative, and they've been talking about getting him to endorse Nate as a candidate for his seat. Nate's military background and the fact that he went in as an enlisted man—it all bodes well. We have every belief that he could win his first time out."

Rachel's heart took a direct hit. "Is…is that what Nate wants?"

Patrice eyed her coolly. "Look at him up there with his father, Rachel. What do you think?"

Rachel couldn't deny it. Never had she seen Nate more in his element; like his father, he was a natural politician.

"He was born for this," Patrice said.

Rachel couldn't deny that, either. She half expected Patrice to point out her flaws, her inadequacies as the potential wife of a politician. Rachel bristled, waiting for some dig or slight, but to her surprise Nate's mother said nothing else. What Rachel discovered was that Patrice's

silence was more reproachful, more uncomfortable, than anything she might have said.

Rachel had been riddled with doubts before. She'd given this weekend everything she had. Nate had been with her almost every minute and while living in the public eye certainly wasn't her forte, it wasn't as bad as she'd thought.

Early on Sunday, Nate and Rachel left for the airport together. Both his parents hugged her farewell and repeatedly thanked her for being part of this important event.

Because their flights were going to different cities, she and Nate went their separate ways at the airport. Rachel's one regret was that they'd had practically no time alone.

Nate kissed her as they prepared to go to their departure gates. "You were terrific," he said, smiling down on her. "Absolutely terrific."

"So were you."

"I didn't realize how much I missed all of this," Nate confessed. "Being with the constituents who support our position is invigorating."

Rachel murmured her agreement.

They talked for a few more minutes and kissed again. By the time she made it to her gate, the flight had already started to board. Settling back with a couple of new magazines, Rachel took a deep breath and tried to relax.

After spending these days with Nate, she was more certain than ever that he'd enter politics. He hadn't told her of his decision, though, and now she understood why. He'd wanted to see how this visit went. It wasn't a comforting thought.

On her arrival in Seattle hours later, Rachel found Bruce and Jolene waiting for her in baggage claim. The second Jolene saw her she skipped over to Rachel's side.

"Rachel!" she cried as if they hadn't seen each other in years.

Rachel hugged her, twirling her around, although Jolene was almost too big for that now. Hard to believe she'd be in junior high next September.

"So," Bruce said, hands in his pockets. "How'd it go?"

"Really well."

He didn't seem happy to hear it. If anything, he looked irritated and out of sorts. Rachel wanted to confront him, ask what was wrong, but Jolene acted like a playful puppy, demanding attention as they walked toward the parking garage, making serious conversation impossible.

"So how was Lover Boy?" Bruce asked as he set her bag in the car trunk.

Rachel glared at him. "I wish you wouldn't call him that."

"Sorry," he muttered. "Sailor Man, then."

"He has a name, you know," she said sharply.

"All right, how's *Nate?*" Bruce opened the passenger door for her.

"Very well, thank you."

"Can we go out to eat?" Jolene asked, clambering into the backseat and searching for her seat belt. "I want to hear about the rally."

"No," Bruce said. "We're not going out to eat."

A little shocked by the vehemence of his response, Rachel turned around and looked at his daughter.

"He's been in a bad mood all day," the girl told her.

"I have not," Bruce barked. "Didn't you say you have homework to finish?"

"I do, but it's no big deal."

Rachel snapped her own seat belt into place. "We'll

go out another time, okay?" she suggested in an effort to keep the peace.

"Okay," Jolene said, easily mollified.

Judging by his dark, brooding expression, Bruce had no interest in spending time with Rachel. After those kisses, this was precisely what she'd been afraid of.

The drive back to Cedar Cove seemed to take twice as long as usual. Rachel managed to carry on a somewhat disjointed conversation with Jolene, mostly about sixth-grade gossip, who liked whom and so forth. Bruce ignored them both. When he pulled up in front of her house, he stomped out of the car to remove her suitcase from the trunk.

"See you soon," Rachel promised Jolene.

"Okay."

Bruce had already dropped her suitcase on the front step and started back toward the car, head down, his gaze averted.

"Thanks for the ride," she said.

"It was nothing," Bruce mumbled as he stepped past her. Her key was barely in the lock when he roared away.

Thirty-Three

Grace couldn't stop worrying about Olivia and the upcoming biopsy results.

Her friend minimized her fears, but Grace wasn't fooled. Olivia was afraid. Jack, too. The biopsy had been done and the lab required two days to do an analysis. This was the second day.

Just as she was about to go for lunch, the phone on her desk rang. "Grace Harding," she answered. "How can I help you?"

"Grace."

It was Olivia, and she didn't need to say another word. The tone of her voice said it all. *Cancer.* "Where are you?" she asked.

"At home. I didn't go the courthouse today." She paused. "My doctor called a few minutes ago."

"Listen, don't move, I'm on my way." Grace forgot about lunch. Her appetite had vanished the second she heard Olivia's voice. For two days she'd eaten practically nothing; all she could think about was her best friend and what she might be facing. "I'm leaving right now."

Grace arranged to take the rest of the day off, then rushed out the door, almost forgetting her coat and purse. She was outside before she'd even slipped her arms into the sleeves.

Thankfully, the drive down Lighthouse Road was just long enough to allow Grace to gather her thoughts. When she arrived, Olivia was standing on the porch waiting for her. Wearing only a sweater, she seemed thin and frail, buffeted by the cold autumn wind. Her arms were wrapped around her middle and her face was set in that determined expression Grace knew so well. It was the same look she'd worn the afternoon she announced that Stan, her ex-husband, had decided to move out. The look that said life was hard but you couldn't give up—that you had to be equal to the pain and the grief.

The sight of Olivia, her lifelong friend, standing alone brought stinging tears to Grace's eyes. Everything started to blur as she pulled the car to the side of the road and parked carelessly.

The wind whipped her coat around her as she got out. Dashing the tears from her cheeks, she didn't bother to hide the fact that she was crying. She rushed up the sidewalk and to the porch steps where Olivia stood. She stopped abruptly. They hugged, and the tears in her friend's eyes brought a sob to her own throat.

"Tell me…"

"It's cancer."

Grace tried not to cry. Crying wouldn't help Olivia. "How…how bad?" she asked.

"We don't know what stage it is yet. I have an appointment with the surgeon next week. We'll find out more then."

Grace swallowed in an effort to control her emotions. Fear sent a chill down her spine. Her friend, her dearest friend, had cancer.

"Grace," Olivia whispered. "I'm afraid."

Through the years, Grace had seen Olivia face every tragedy with grit and faith. When Jordan died it was Olivia who held the family together. A few months later, when Stan moved out, she'd dealt with that, too. Never once, through all the grief, had Olivia ever admitted she was afraid.

It took a diagnosis of cancer to do that.

"Let's have tea," Grace said and, with her arm around Olivia's waist, led her back into the house.

While Grace put the kettle on, Olivia sat at the kitchen table looking like a child, lost and lonely in her own home.

"Where's Jack?" Grace asked, wondering why he wasn't here when Olivia needed him so badly.

"He…he didn't take the news well," Olivia murmured. "I suggested he go and talk to Bob."

"He shouldn't have left you." Grace bit back her anger at Jack, knowing it was really anger at the unfairness of life.

"It's okay," Olivia said. "I told him you were coming."

"Well, I'm here now."

"Yes," Olivia whispered and a tear slipped down the side of her face.

"Does anyone else know?"

"Not yet."

Grace understood. Olivia needed to find her own balance, to consider her own future, before she told her mother or her children.

"I'll be right here," Grace promised.

The hint of a smile came to Olivia then. "I knew I could count on you." She stretched out her arm and they clasped hands.

Olivia had been with Grace when Dan disappeared, and later, too, when her husband's body was discovered and finally laid to rest. They were friends, would always be friends, no matter what the future held. For nearly all their lives, they'd shared their secrets, their hurts, their triumphs and joys.

"The part I have a hard time accepting," Olivia said after sipping her hot tea, "is that there's an invader inside my body. A disease that wants to steal my life away. I keep thinking about it." She placed one hand over her heart. "The enemy is *inside* me," she repeated. "In the past I've had to deal with forces outside me. What I'm confronting now is in *here.*" Her hand formed a fist and she closed her eyes.

Grace bit her lip.

"I wish I could explain it better," she said. "With everything else, I could close a door and retreat. Take a break from it, you know? I can't with cancer. There's no escaping my own body."

Grace merely nodded, having no comfort to offer except her presence.

She spent an hour with Olivia, and they drank two pots of tea before Jack returned. Whatever his problem had been earlier, apparently it was now resolved. He seemed confident and matter-of-fact, answering Grace's questions quickly and clearly.

Olivia went to lie down, and Grace was grateful for the opportunity to speak to him privately.

"Call me anytime, night or day," she said.

"I will," he promised.

"If you and Olivia need *anything,* call me."

He agreed. After a brief silence, he spoke again. "I don't mind telling you, I wasn't prepared for what this would do to me," he admitted. "I thought I was. You might remember that my son had cancer years ago, and I assumed I knew what it'd be like to hear that verdict a second time. I wasn't even close."

"Olivia's a strong woman."

Jack's eyes took on a resolute look. "Olivia needs a strong husband who'll stand at her side while she's going through this. I'm here and I intend to stay."

Grace left soon after, first hugging him goodbye. He thanked her over and over for coming to the house, for giving them her support, for being Olivia's friend.

When she got home, Grace immediately went looking for Cliff. She found him talking to Cal in the barn, but he broke off whatever he was saying as soon as he caught sight of her.

"I saw Olivia," she rushed to tell him, fresh tears filling her eyes.

Cliff put his arm around her shoulders and they walked slowly back to the house. Once inside, she turned to him. "It's cancer," she said starkly.

He nodded grimly. "What's the prognosis?"

"We won't know until she sees the surgeon, and that won't be until next week. We'll find out more then." Grace paused for a moment, her voice threatening to break. "She hasn't told Charlotte or her children."

Cliff urged her to sit down at the table and began preparing tea. Grace smiled, thanking him, and didn't say that one more cup of tea was probably the last thing she needed.

She saw the envelope with the returned rent check on

the table and sighed. Another concern to deal with, another problem to solve. It felt trivial compared to what Olivia was going through, but still…

Cliff glanced at the envelope, too. "Oh, I talked to Judy this afternoon."

Grace knew the rental agent couldn't be blamed. She herself had insisted Judy accept the Smiths as tenants despite their unsatisfactory references.

"Apparently, this isn't the first time these people have done this."

That didn't come as any surprise to Grace.

"Judy talked to another agent from the Bremerton area," Cliff continued. "She learned that this couple's made quite the habit of bilking their landlords."

"Could Judy tell you how long it would take to evict them?"

Cliff frowned. "People like this know how to work the system. She said it might take six months to get them out."

"Six months!" Grace cried. "That's ridiculous."

"I agree." He shrugged. "It's pretty hopeless. They'll exploit their rights as tenants and drag everything out until the bitter end."

"That's an outrage."

"For now there isn't anything we can do," Cliff said, "except file eviction papers and play this out."

She groaned, letting her head fall to the table.

He reached into a high cupboard and brought out a half-full bottle of bourbon. "There's one thing we *can* do—substitute strong drink for weak tea."

Despite herself, Grace smiled.

Thirty-Four

Teri could tell that something was bothering Rachel. The salon was humming with activity the way it always did on Fridays. But, busy or not, the two of them usually managed to arrange their schedules so they could have lunch together. At noon, Rachel claimed she simply wasn't hungry.

"What do you mean, you're not hungry?" Teri demanded. "Whatever's bothering you must be big. *Nothing* takes away your appetite."

Rachel didn't even smile.

In spite of Teri's efforts to get her to talk about her trip to Pittsburgh, Rachel had barely said a word. For that matter, she hadn't mentioned Jolene or Bruce, either, which was highly unusual.

If Teri had her guess, what distressed her friend was her ongoing confusion about Nate and Bruce. Nate hadn't made any secret of his intentions. And then there was Bruce.

Teri wanted to shake that man and tell him to take action, do something before he lost Rachel for good. If he

did, it would be his own stupid fault. As for Rachel… Teri didn't know what to think. She didn't doubt that Rachel loved Nate, but—in Teri's opinion—she loved Bruce more.

A few weeks ago, when Rachel phoned, rattled because Bruce had kissed her, she'd made it sound as though that was the first time it'd ever happened. News flash: Bruce had kissed her *long* before that night.

Although this last kiss—maybe there'd been more to it. Rachel had obviously been shocked. So, it appeared, was Bruce.

The only time she'd mentioned him was to tell Teri how angry he'd been when he picked her up from the airport. According to Rachel, he couldn't dump her on her doorstep quickly enough.

At four, Teri had a perm, and because she was too busy watching Rachel and worrying about her, she got behind schedule. When James showed up at five-fifteen to drive her home, she had another half-hour left.

"I'll wait," James, the soul of patience, assured her. He glanced nervously around the salon. "Perhaps it would be best if I waited in the car. By the way, you might bring your umbrella when you come out. It's really begun to storm."

Rachel had finished for the night. "I'll see everyone tomorrow," she said, raising her hand in farewell as she started toward the door.

"What are you doing this weekend?" Teri called out.

Rachel shrugged. "Nothing much. Right now I have to pick up my car at the garage on Harbor Street. I had the oil changed. Then I'm going home to soak in a hot bath."

"James can take you," Teri offered. No reason he

couldn't. All he'd be doing otherwise was sitting in the car—reading, no doubt. But it wouldn't take him long to drop Rachel off and by the time he came back, Teri figured she'd be ready.

"No, that's all right," Rachel said, shaking her head. "The exercise will do me good."

"But it's raining out! Why get wet when James is here twiddling his thumbs? He can easily drive you."

"It would be my pleasure, Miss Rachel," James told her in that polite way of his.

Rachel gave him a smile. "Thank you. Then I accept."

Teri walked out the door into the interior of the mall with her.

"I really appreciate this," Rachel said. "You're a good friend, Teri. The best I've got."

She sounded so depressed, it was all Teri could do not to throw both arms around her. "Hey, if you need to talk or anything, just give me a call."

Rachel smiled a little shakily. "Thank you, I will. Do *you* have plans for tonight?"

"Not really. Christie's coming over this evening and we're going to watch *Grease*." It was a musical they'd loved when they were kids. They knew all the songs and planned to sing along. They'd have popcorn and then later on, some ice cream, the expensive kind. It would be a girls' night in.

At the mention of her sister, James lowered his gaze. Their romance seemed to be at a standstill; something must've happened because Christie had insisted on driving over on her own.

"The weekend's open, though," Teri said.

"Okay. Let's get together. I'll phone you."

"Please do," Teri said, eager to help in any way she could. At the beginning of her relationship with Bobby, Rachel had been a wonderful confidante, discreet, sensible and encouraging. Teri wanted to do the same thing for her friend now. She looked over her shoulder and wished she had a few more minutes to talk. This was the first time all day that Rachel had opened up to her.

"I'll call you in the morning," Rachel said as she headed out the mall door to the parking lot.

Standing by the car, James had the umbrella ready. It was raining steadily now and almost dark.

Teri returned to the salon and finished Mrs. Dawson's perm and waited for James.

And waited.

Thirty minutes passed, and he still wasn't back. When she called Rachel's cell, she immediately got voice mail. James didn't answer his phone, either. She tried Rachel's house. Same thing.

Unsure of what else to do, Teri called her sister. "Do you mind swinging by the salon for me?"

"Where's James?" Christie immediately asked.

"I don't know. He was going to run Rachel to the garage to get her car, but he hasn't come back."

"Did you try his cell?"

"He isn't answering and neither is Rachel."

Christie hesitated. "That's a bit odd, isn't it?"

"Yes." More than odd. Definitely out of the ordinary—and even a little frightening. "Are you coming or not?" Teri asked. Otherwise she'd call one of the few cabs in town. Bobby was probably starting to worry.

"I'll be there in five minutes."

"Thank you," she said with a relieved sigh. Bobby

wanted her to quit her job, and incidents like this didn't help. She had no idea where James and Rachel had gone or why they weren't answering their cell phones. There had to be a perfectly logical explanation, she told herself; she wasn't going to stress over it.

Her sister drove up in her rattletrap of a car, the exhaust belching oil. Leaning across, she unlocked the passenger door and shoved it open. Teri leaped gratefully inside, damp from her short sprint to the car.

"Have you heard from James?" Christie asked before she'd said hello.

Teri hid a smile. "Not a word."

"I'll bet he's at your place now," Christie speculated. "He just forgot to come back for you."

Teri didn't believe that for a minute. James was a paragon of responsibility; he'd *never* shirk his duties. Despite her resolve not to worry, she was beginning to feel anxious.

Christie was unusually quiet on the ride home.

"Does he have the hots for her?" she blurted out as they approached the long driveway on Seaside Avenue.

"*What*?"

"You know."

"James for Rachel, you mean?"

"Who else do you think I'm talking about?" Christie asked irritably.

"No way." If James was interested in anyone, Teri suspected it was her very own sister.

As soon as they pulled in, the front door flew open and Bobby rushed out into the cold, drenching rain. He practically yanked her from the car. Then he was holding her. Hard. His fists dug into the small of Teri's back and his breathing was shallow and fast.

Something was drastically wrong. He'd been worried about her in the past, but he'd never done anything like this.

"Bobby! Bobby, what is it?"

By the time he let her go, they were both soaked to the skin, wet hair matted to their heads, rivulets of water running down their faces. He started babbling, the words frantic, incoherent.

Before he'd finished, the sheriff's vehicle rolled into the driveway, lights flashing. Troy Davis stepped out, and the four of them went into the house together.

"So everything's all right?" Troy said, looking at Teri. "*You're* all right?"

"Of course I am. Did my husband contact you?" Really, this was too much, even for Bobby. She was only an hour late.

"Kidnapped," Bobby said.

"What are you talking about?" Christie looked from one man to the other.

"He said he had you," Bobby said, his eyes wide with a mixture of shock and relief. "He didn't *say* it, exactly, but he implied it."

"Who?" Troy Davis asked sharply.

"Vladimir."

"James!" Christie shouted as understanding came. "They have James and Rachel."

Teri stared at her, then at Bobby. That was it—James and Rachel had been kidnapped. Whoever had taken them must've assumed they had Teri. If it was the two men who'd originally confronted her, they'd realize quickly enough that they had the wrong woman. The question was what they'd do once they became aware of their mistake. Terror froze her and she couldn't breathe.

The ringing of the phone cut into the room, freeing Teri from her sudden paralysis. Dragging in a deep breath, she lunged at the jangling phone. Caller ID told her it was Bruce Peyton.

She couldn't imagine why he'd called her unless he'd somehow heard…

"Bruce," Teri said, picking up the receiver. It took all her strength to speak normally.

"I'm sorry to bother you, Teri, but do you know where Rachel is?"

"Ah… Was she supposed to see Jolene tonight?"

His hesitation was brief. "No. I need to talk to her and I can't seem to find her. She usually has her cell phone but I haven't been able to get hold of her."

"Perhaps you should come to my house," Teri suggested. She couldn't very well tell him over the phone that Rachel had been abducted.

Again he paused. "Is everything okay?"

"Not…really. Could you stop by at your earliest convenience?" Then, thinking quickly, she added, "It'd probably be best if Jolene wasn't with you."

"This sounds serious," Bruce murmured, but without quizzing her further, he said he was on his way. When she'd replaced the receiver, she turned to the sheriff, intent on hearing exactly what had happened. Bobby, not surprisingly, was an emotional mess.

Before she could ask a single question, the phone rang again. Teri would've been content to let voice mail pick up when Christie suddenly screamed, "It's James!"

She would've grabbed it if not for Sheriff Davis. "Let me take this," he said.

Nodding shyly, Christie backed away, her mouth

covered with both hands. Teri noticed that her sister was trembling. At this point, she didn't know whom to comfort first, Bobby or Christie.

"Sheriff Davis," Troy announced. He listened for a minute, then said, "I'll send a patrol car for you. They'll be there in five minutes." He immediately ordered a patrol vehicle to the Dairy Queen off Highway 16, then requested an APB on Bobby's car. When he'd finished, he spoke to Teri, obviously considering her the most rational of the group. "It's James Wilbur and Rachel Pendergast. I'm having them brought into the station for questioning."

"You won't keep them long will you, Sheriff?" Christie asked.

"No, they've been through enough as it is." He frowned. "Apparently the two men in question pushed your friends out of the limo and made off with it. We'll be on the lookout."

He left soon afterward, telling them he'd be in touch soon, and Teri made a fresh pot of coffee. She was desperately in need of a heavy dose of caffeine laced with sugar, and she assumed the others were, too. The shock was just beginning to hit her; she couldn't seem to stop shaking.

They were sitting at the kitchen table, trying to make sense of what had taken place, when Bruce arrived. Teri answered the door.

"What's going on with Rachel?" he demanded as soon as he was inside the house. "Where is she, anyway?"

Teri released a pent-up breath. She wasn't sure how to explain that her best friend had been kidnapped, that the men who'd been after *her* had mistakenly grabbed Rachel. Apparently they'd decided to grab James, as well; they

must have overtaken him and stolen the car. Had they forced him to drive?

She glanced at her watch and tried to speak calmly. "My guess is that Rachel's talking Sheriff Davis's ear off right about now."

"Sheriff Davis? Why?"

"She was kidnapped."

"*Kidnapped!*" Bruce's eyes widened and his mouth sagged open as if he couldn't believe what she'd told him.

"Come with me," she said, leading him into the kitchen. Christie poured a cup of coffee and then spooned in sugar, stirring it briskly before she handed him the mug.

"What's going on?" he asked again, ignoring the coffee.

Bobby began to explain, but his version was confusing, and Christie's attempted corrections didn't help, and then Teri added her voice to the melee.

"Hey!" Bruce whistled loudly. "One at a time." He pointed at Bobby. "You first."

Bobby simply shook his head. "I can't. All I know is that Teri's safe. I'm sorry this happened to Rachel because of me."

"It isn't your fault," Teri said, reaching for her husband's hand. She chafed his cold fingers.

Finally Teri described the events of the night, insofar as she knew them.

"I'm going to the sheriff's," Bruce said. He got up immediately and tore out of the house.

"I am, too," Christie said, following Bruce.

"We'll wait here," Teri shouted after them. Sheriff Davis had said he'd call the house, which was a good

reason to stay. Besides, Teri doubted she and Bobby could contribute much to the investigation at the moment. The sheriff would have more questions for them later.

As soon as they were alone, Bobby stood and walked into the living room.

"Bobby!" Teri said, hurrying after him.

Then she was in his arms, and he was holding her and kissing her as if he never intended to stop. "I can't do this anymore," he whispered between kisses.

"Do what?"

"Risk losing you and our baby."

"Bobby, we can't let Vladimir blackmail you into giving up your title."

"I'll throw the match," he declared. "I don't care. Winning isn't important anymore. I won't put you at risk again."

"Bobby, please."

"No, Teri, the decision's already been made. I'm going to play Vladimir. That's what he wants. That's what this whole kidnapping was about. He wanted to force my hand. And he did."

Thirty-Five

Cold and shivering inside the sheriff's office, Rachel clutched the thin blanket a deputy had draped over her shoulders. James had been immediately transported to Harrison Hospital. Another deputy had talked to him briefly en route.

"I didn't really see anything," Rachel reiterated. "The men—there were two of them—swarmed the car when James drove into the service station. It was dark and rainy and everything happened really fast." Gathering the blanket more closely around her, she said, "They dragged me out of the car and blindfolded me, then threw me in the backseat."

The sheriff was taping her as she spoke. "At what point did they realize you weren't the person they wanted?" he asked.

Rachel couldn't be sure. All she remembered was that there'd been a flurry of raised, angry voices. "They weren't speaking English," she said. "Russian, maybe. That's what James told me later." She bit her lip, trying to recall any details that might help. "When they did speak English, they had quite heavy accents."

"Did you talk to them?" the sheriff asked next.

"No." Rachel doubted she could've uttered a single word. Terror had gripped her from the start. James was the one who'd put up a struggle.

"Is he okay?" she asked urgently. "James? Bobby Polgar's driver?"

"I haven't received an update yet," the sheriff told her.

"He tried to protect me," she said, feeling bad that she hadn't thought to ask about him sooner. Although she'd been blindfolded, she'd heard their captors hitting James, heard the thud of fists on bone, his grunts of pain. One of the kidnappers had been driving the car, the other riding shotgun. James had been bound and blindfolded, too, and shoved onto the floor in the back, at her feet. She'd been aware of the two men arguing, and then it had apparently been decided that she and James would be set free. Soon after that, they'd been pushed out, close to the freeway. She'd torn off her blindfold and helped release James from his bonds. He'd used his cell phone and called Bobby's house—the call Sheriff Davis had taken.

She'd lost her phone in the scuffle at the garage and, in retrospect, she was astonished that he still had his. She supposed it went to show that these kidnappers were amateurs—thugs and bumblers.

James had been so calm and professional, whereas she shook so badly that, despite his injuries, he'd had to support her as they stumbled to the restaurant. They weren't at the Dairy Queen more than two minutes when the patrol car pulled up. One of the deputies called the aid car for James; the other escorted Rachel to the station.

A commotion erupted outside the sheriff's office, and Rachel recognized Bruce's voice.

"Bruce." She jumped up from the chair and looked pleadingly at Sheriff Davis. "Can I speak to him? Please, I need to see him."

The sheriff nodded. "I'll be in touch tomorrow. Take it easy, now."

When she opened the door, she saw Bruce in the hallway, arguing with a deputy. "You don't understand," he was saying with barely controlled impatience. "I don't—"

"Bruce."

Their eyes locked, and without another word they were in each other's arms. His embrace was almost suffocating, but Rachel didn't care. She needed to be held and comforted and loved. She'd been so frightened, and that whole time, the one person she'd thought about was Bruce. Not Nate. *Bruce.* With a dirty rag covering her eyes, sprawled in the back of a speeding car, her life in danger—that was when she'd known beyond any doubt that she loved him.

Why hadn't she figured it out earlier? Nate was charming, she was fond of him, but he wasn't the man who'd moved into her mind and refused to leave. The man she thought about when she might have been on the way to her death.

Now she needed to tell both men her feelings....

"Are you hurt?" Bruce stepped back just far enough to study her. With gentle hands, he brushed the hair from her bruised forehead and gazed deeply into her eyes. Whatever he was searching for he must have found, because he drew her back into his embrace with a sigh of relief.

"Thank God you're all right," he whispered over and over again. "Thank God..."

In Bruce's arms, the trembling subsided, the bruises stopped hurting and she finally began to feel warm.

"Tell me what happened," he said, still holding her close.

She told him what she knew but the "why" of it remained a mystery.

"They were after Teri," she explained.

"Yes," he said. "They botched the kidnapping when they took you by mistake."

She'd worked out that this whole mess had to do with Bobby, but what the thugs had hoped to achieve she could only speculate. Right now, none of that mattered. Because Bruce was with her.

He continued to hold her, murmuring encouragement as they stood in that drafty hallway.

It suddenly occurred to Rachel to ask, "How come you're here?"

"I phoned Teri. You weren't answering your cell and I thought she might know where you were." She felt his shrug. "I wanted to talk to you about…something, but this isn't the time."

"What did Teri say?"

"She said I should come to her house, and that was when I found out you'd been kidnapped. I wasn't there more than a few minutes when James called and I heard you'd been set free. That's also when I learned you'd be at the sheriff's office, so I came straight here."

As if he'd just realized he was holding her—and shouldn't be—he abruptly dropped his arms.

All at once Rachel was cold again. She wanted Bruce to hold her. She *needed* him.

She took one small step toward him. "Please…"

He raised his arms, apparently to abide by her request, and then dropped them again. "I don't think that's a good idea."

"Why not?" she asked.

He frowned. "You know why not. How would Nate feel if he could see us like this?"

She knew exactly how Nate would feel. He'd be angry and upset. Jealous. "You're right," she began, "but—"

"I have to talk to you, Rachel. That's why I was looking for you this evening."

"Talk to me…about what?"

He shook his head. "This isn't the best time. We'll talk later."

She wanted to hear now. But if he wasn't ready to speak, she was. "I need *you,* Bruce, no one else. Not Nate. You."

"No," he countered sharply, as though afraid to believe her. "You need a warm body. If Nate was here instead of me, you'd want him. We'll talk about this tomorrow."

Her eyes pleaded with him for understanding. Her own feelings were clear now and although she recognized that she loved Bruce and wanted to be with him, she couldn't say any more. Not yet.

"Will you take me home?" she asked.

"I…" He hesitated.

"Please."

He nodded, but the look on his face was one of wariness.

After speaking to the sheriff again, Rachel hurried out to the car, where Bruce was waiting for her. He had the heater on, and the warm air welcomed her, enveloped her. She'd been terrified, her sense of security destroyed.

What she craved most—other than the comfort of those she loved—was to be surrounded by familiar things. She needed to be home.

The drive took place in almost total silence. When Bruce parked in front of the house, Rachel turned to him, hoping for some word, some gesture of reassurance. He kept the car running, letting her know he had no intention of going inside with her.

"I'll walk you to your door," he said curtly.

It was such an old-fashioned courtesy, and she was grateful for it. He took her house key from her trembling hands and unlocked the dead bolt and then, without looking at her, returned the key.

Before he could stop her, Rachel slipped her arms around his neck and raised her lips to his, showing how much she loved him, now and always.

He resisted, but not for long. His mouth opened to hers, his breath warm and moist. And for the first time since she'd been abducted, Rachel felt completely safe. Completely loved and cherished.

Bruce broke off the kiss before she was ready for it to end. "I'm glad you're…all right," he said, his voice husky.

"I am, too. Thank you for being here, thank you for bringing me home and thank you for that kiss," she whispered.

He stared down at the concrete step and nodded. Then he turned, stumbling in his haste to leave.

Christie wondered why the attendant behind the admissions desk in Harrison Hospital's ER was being such a grouch. All she knew was that she wouldn't let some old biddy keep her out. She was going to see James, whatever it took.

"You cannot go inside those doors and if you persist," the woman said, "I'll call security."

"Go right ahead." Christie figured she had a good two to three minutes to find James before the rent-a-cop located her and tossed her out. A lot could happen in those minutes.

But just as she made her way toward the swinging doors, James stepped out. His face was battered—one eye had swollen completely shut, his cheekbone was badly bruised and he had a split lip. His arm was bandaged and in a sling.

"James!" She breathed his name in a rush of near-panic.

For a moment, Christie thought she was going to be sick. To her horror, tears flooded her eyes. She wasn't the kind of person who wept easily, but she was weeping now.

"Oh, James…"

"Don't touch me," he said hoarsely when she came toward him. "I have two broken ribs and I'm afraid a hug would kill me."

She blinked rapidly in an effort to forestall the tears, not that it did any good. "Let me help you," she begged.

He seemed reluctant to have her touch him. "Be careful."

"Yes, yes, of course." Slipping her arm around his waist, she led him outside. At least the rain had stopped. They walked, step by unhurried step, to where she'd parked her car. "Did the doctor give you a prescription?"

"Yes, it's in my pocket. For pain. What I need most, they told me, is rest."

"And chicken soup," she added. It was all she could

think of. "I'll get the prescription filled and buy you a can of soup."

She half expected him to argue. His acceptance of her being there told her how much pain he was in.

Although he didn't complain, the walk to the parking lot obviously left him in agony. He looked pale and drained by the time she got the passenger door open and helped him inside. Then she dashed around the front of the car and slid into the driver's seat.

"I would've taken a taxi home," he murmured.

"I'm here." She put her key in the ignition, then glanced at him. "I should call Bobby and Teri," she said, "but I don't have a cell."

"I spoke to them a few minutes ago," James informed her. "From a pay phone near the ER."

She nodded.

"He told me the police have already recovered the limousine. It was abandoned by the railway tracks."

She shifted the car into gear, watching as even the slightest movement made him grimace in pain. "I'll drive very slowly."

Halfway back to the house, she started to cry again, the tears slipping soundlessly down her cheeks. She was shocked that seeing him like this had such an emotional impact on her. She told herself a dozen times a day that she found him a nuisance, but she knew that wasn't how she really felt. She was falling for this guy. Falling hard.

As soon as she pulled up to the house, Bobby and Teri hurried out to see James.

"He's badly hurt," Christie said in a stern voice. "Keep your distance. His ribs are broken."

"Oh, James." Teri began to cry, too. "James, stay at our

place, okay? Those stairs to your apartment are too much. We have a downstairs guest room and—"

"No," he insisted. "No. I can manage."

Christie knew his stoicism and his need for privacy would keep him from accepting Teri's suggestion, and she understood that, but it was hard to watch him suffer.

"I'm going to make Vladimir pay for this," Bobby said through gritted teeth. His fists were clenched at his sides.

Christie's hand was on James's arm as she turned to look at Bobby. "If you need any help with that, let me know." She spoke fiercely and she meant every word.

"Is there anything I can do?" Teri asked.

Christie took the prescription out of her purse. "Get this filled and pick up four cans of chicken noodle soup." She'd seen a grocery store flyer that advertised four for three dollars; having grown up poor, she automatically noticed a bargain.

"I'll go with you," Bobby said, following Teri.

"I'll take you to your rooms," Christie said, again clasping James's elbow and gently steering him toward the outside staircase that led to his quarters above the garage.

"I'll be fine now. Thank you," he said when they'd reached the bottom of the stairs.

"Forget it." Christie wasn't taking no for an answer, and he must've realized that because he capitulated without an argument. Bad enough, she figured, that he'd been so stubborn, refusing to stay at Teri's house. They took the stairs slowly and each one made him wince. When they finally got to the landing, Christie had her arm around his waist and he was leaning against her. The door was unlocked and, as she'd suspected, his quarters were im-

maculate. He pointed in the direction of the bedroom and she supported him as he hobbled toward it.

His bed was made with military precision and even when he sat down the blanket didn't wrinkle.

"I'll be fine now," he said again, more firmly this time.

"I…" Christie was reluctant to leave.

"I don't need your help anymore."

"Do you mean that?" she asked, trying to disguise the pain his comment had inflicted.

He wouldn't meet her gaze. "You said I'm a stuffed shirt."

"So? You are."

"You don't want anything to do with me," he reminded her. "You said that…the last time I drove you home…"

"I did?" She couldn't even remember, although they'd argued about what she'd called his "hovering" and "overprotectiveness."

"You asked—yet again—that I not drive you anymore."

She didn't see that as any big deal. "I'm capable of driving myself, you know."

He didn't miss a beat. "And I'm capable of looking after myself."

"Fine," she said, hands on her hips. "We're both capable people. Now climb into bed and I'll tuck you in."

"Then you'll go?"

She hesitated. "Yes."

"Good." He averted his head as he mumbled, "Please leave the room."

Furious—and not sure why—she stomped out of the room and slammed the door. Then she stood on the other side of the door and waited. Twice, when she heard him stifle a groan, she nearly burst in, but she knew he

wouldn't appreciate the intrusion. Fine, she'd see that he was safely in bed and then she'd take off. If he didn't want her around, she wasn't going to make a pest of herself.

After two or three minutes of silence, she asked, "Can I come in now?"

"If you insist."

"I do." She turned the knob and cautiously opened the door, to find him dressed in pajamas. He'd apparently taken off the sling around his arm, then put it back on, all by himself. That must've hurt. So he was a stuffed shirt *and* a glutton for punishment.

She peeled back the sheets and plumped up the pillows and finally assisted him into bed. He lowered himself onto the mattress with his teeth clenched and eyes tightly closed. Christie bit her lip, resisting the urge to cry out.

"Is there anything else I can do?" she asked once he was settled.

"Leave me alone."

"Okay." But instead she leaned down and pressed her lips to his forehead. "Good night, James." When he frowned, she whispered, "Don't worry, I'm going now." What she didn't say aloud was *I'll be back.* He'd discover that soon enough.

Then she left his apartment and bounced down the outside stairs. Thirty minutes later she returned from her trip to the all-night grocery. Teri came out to meet her.

"He's sleeping."

"Good."

"Bobby and I got the medication and the soup. I gave him the first capsule with a glass of water but he didn't want anything to eat." She walked with Christie to the bottom of the stairs that led to his apartment. "Apparently he put up a